D0323545

THE
COLLECTOR

Also available by Anne Mette Hancock

The Corpse Flower

THE COLLECTOR

A NOVEL

ANNE METTE HANCOCK

NEW YORK

This is a work of fiction. All of the names, characters, organizations, places, and events portrayed in this novel are either products of the author's imagination or are used fictitiously. Any resemblance to real or actual events, locales, or persons, living or dead, is entirely coincidental.

Copyright © 2022 by Anne Mette Hancock
By Arrangement with Nordin Agency ApS, Copenhagen

All rights reserved.

Published in the United States by Crooked Lane Books, an imprint of The Quick Brown Fox & Company LLC.

Crooked Lane Books and its logo are trademarks of The Quick Brown Fox & Company LLC.

Library of Congress Catalog-in-Publication data available upon request.

ISBN (hardcover): 978-1-63910-117-7
ISBN (ebook): 978-1-63910-118-4

Cover design by Melanie Sun
Translation by Tara Chace
Thank you to The Danish Arts Foundation for translation funding

Danish Arts
Foundation

Printed in the United States.

www.crookedlanebooks.com

Crooked Lane Books
34 West 27th St., 10th Floor
New York, NY 10001

First Edition: November 2022

10 9 8 7 6 5 4 3 2 1

To Vega and Castor
You were written in the stars.

CHAPTER

1

THE MAN MOVED quickly, sliding past the bushes and the bare trees. The February wind seemed to come from all sides at once, feeling like thousands of little needles hitting his cheeks. He pulled at the strings on his hood so that it tightened around his face and he looked around.

There were no joggers or dog walkers out today on the grounds of Kastellet, the old seventeenth-century Citadel. The temperature had been like a buoy in the water for days, bobbing steadily up and down around the freezing point, and the strong wind made it feel like the harshest winter in decades. Copenhagen seemed deserted in the cold, like a ghost town.

The man stopped and listened.

Nothing.

No sirens to break the controlled rumble of the city, no flashing blue lights out there in the twilight.

He walked up to the top of the fortress's old earthwork rampart and looked over at the entrance to the grounds by the parking lot at Café Toldboden and Maersk's headquarters. He wrinkled his brows when he saw that the parking lot was empty, then looked at his watch.

Where the hell are they?

The man pulled a cigarette out of a pack in his inside pocket and squatted down in the lee of one of the cannons. He tried to light his lighter, but his hands were yellow from the cold and felt dead. He extended and bent his fingers a couple of times to get the circulation going and noticed the blood spot, a small, coagulated half-moon of purplish black substance under the tip of the fingernail on his index finger.

He made a half-hearted attempt to scrape out the congealed substance, then gave up and got his lighter lit. As soon as the fire caught, he thrust his hands back into his pockets and held the cigarette squeezed tightly between his lips as he paced back and forth on the rampart, impatiently eyeing the parking lot.

Come on, damn it!

He didn't like waiting. It always made him feel restless and gave him a twitchy feeling in his gut. He preferred to keep busy, constantly in motion. Silence meant time for reflection and made his thoughts wander back to a smoke so thick that he had to feel his way past the dead, mangled bodies, back to the blood running out of his eyes, down his cheeks, and to the silence, the deafening silence that followed the blast, when those who were able crawled out of the dusty darkness and gathered in front of the destroyed building.

Paralyzed. In shock.

If only he could shake those images, release them like a bouquet of helium balloons and watch them float away, dancing in the sky until they were out of sight.

The man looked down at the café again and spotted the silvery gray Audi pull up in front of the building and stop. The engine was on, its exhaust warm and steamy in the cold. A single blink of the high beams told him that the coast was clear.

Finally!

He started walking down toward the car, but halfway down the earthwork, he spotted something that made him slow his pace. He scrunched up his eyes and focused on the pedestrian bridge over the moat that surrounded the Citadel.

Then he came to a complete stop.

There was a figure standing in the middle of the bridge, almost camouflaged by the twilight, a hooded person wearing an orange backpack.

It was the strange, bent-over posture of the figure that had made him slow down. But it was the child the person was holding that had made him stop.

A boy he estimated to be eight or nine years old hung limply over the side of the bridge while the person with the backpack held the fabric on the shoulders of the boy's down jacket. The person was yelling, but the wind snatched up the words, punching holes in them, so he couldn't hear what was being said.

He looked over at the car again and saw yet another insistent blink of the headlights. He needed to hurry now, but . . .

He looked down at the bridge again.

Then the figure let go of the boy.

2

THE CLINIC ENTRANCE was through the back side of an ivy-covered building that leaned curiously against the wall around Frederik VIII's palace. From the window of the waiting room, Heloise Kaldan could see the top of the Marble Church's frost-stained dome and the guards in the palace square, who were parading back and forth in front of Amalienborg Palace like loose-limbed sleepwalkers in a snow globe.

She reached for a fashion magazine and swung one foot back and forth nervously as she browsed through it. Adrenaline tingled at the ends of her nerves, and her eyes roved absentmindedly over the fashion reports and articles about skin care regimens. Shallowness and the glorification of teenage anorexia, wrapped up in pastel colors.

Who the hell reads this garbage?

She tossed the magazine aside and looked around the waiting room.

The whole room looked like something right out of some Californian interior design magazine. It was decorated in white and cognac-colored hues, punctuated only by succulents in oversized clay pots. The walls were adorned with posters and lithographs of all shapes and sizes, hung so closely together that you could just barely glimpse the asphalt-colored wall behind them. The floor was covered with a cream-colored Berber rug, which tied the room together in one final stylish touch. The whole thing was so delightful that you'd almost be able to forget why you were there.

Almost . . .

There were two other patients in the waiting room: a gaunt, elderly man and a young girl with milk-white skin and big silvery gray eyes. Heloise estimated her age to be no more than eighteen and hoped that the girl had come to the clinic for some purpose other than her own.

A tall, blond man in white canvas pants and a mint-green T-shirt stuck his head into the room and the girl across from Heloise immediately sat up straighter in her chair. She inhaled oddly through her nose, moistened her lips, and tried to make them seem fuller by half-opening her mouth into a pout. The expression left her looking like she had just detected some objectionable odor in the room.

Selfie face, Heloise thought. One of the era's oddest inventions.

The man in the doorway swept a lock of hair out of his eyes with a toss of his head and then nodded to Heloise.

"Heloise?"

She stood up.

She just had to get it over with now.

* * *

The doctor showed her into the exam room with a motion of his arm. He read her records on the computer screen and then looked at Heloise.

"So, Heloise . . . You're pregnant?"

He mispronounced her name. The hard "H" made her name sound harsh, like an effort. Heloise had corrected him at every appointment for the last four years. This time she let it go. Instead she said, "Yes, so it would appear."

"Have you ever been pregnant before?"

She shook her head and showed him the test, which she had brought in her purse. There were two red lines inside the plastic window in the middle of the stick. One was very clear, the other a misty watercolor, weak like the beginning of a rainbow that you could see best by not looking at it directly.

The doctor looked at the test and nodded.

"Yes, it looks positive. And am I to understand that this doesn't suit you well?"

"It wasn't part of my plan, no."

He nodded and sat down behind his white-lacquered desk.

"No, well, that happens, I guess."

Heloise sat down on the other side of the desk and set her purse on the old parquet flooring. The floor was like the rest of the building, strangely bowed and crackled like an old soup tureen, and made the chair rock under her.

The doctor smiled warmly to emphasize that she could speak openly. Dimples bored into his cheeks, like fingers in soft clay, and his blue eyes looked boldly into Heloise's. It had taken her a couple of years to discover that his magnetic charisma and forward eye contact were not reserved only for her. He was not flirting. He was just genuinely interested in her health. Plus, the gleam of his blue-green eyes was competing with the wreath of polished white gold that ran around his left ring finger.

"According to the information you provided when you called this morning, you're about five weeks along. Is that correct?"

Heloise looked down and nodded. That was what the calculator said on the due date website she had found online.

"That's good," he said. "The thing is, a medical abortion is only possible during the first seven weeks of a pregnancy. From eight to twelve weeks, the only option is a clinical termination of the pregnancy."

Heloise glanced up again. "Which would involve hospitalization?"

"Yes. It's a quick procedure, but nonetheless it's always preferable to avoid anesthesia. So instead you'll get this . . ."

He handed Heloise a single pill from a package that said Mifegyne in green letters.

"You'll take this once we've confirmed your due date, and that will effectively terminate your pregnancy."

He turned his chair halfway around and typed a few lines into the computer in front of him.

"I'll also write you a prescription for fifty milligrams of Diclon, which is a muscle relaxant, and a medication called Cytotec."

Heloise's heart began beating in a strangely irregular rhythm as he spoke.

That will effectively terminate your pregnancy . . .

What the hell was she doing? How had she ended up here?

"It shouldn't take more than a few hours, and for the most part it's pretty undramatic," the doctor continued. "But it's still best if you set aside a whole day for it and have someone around while it's going on. Are you seeing someone right now who can look after you?"

Heloise shook her head. "Yes and no. It's . . . complicated."

The doctor pursed his lips and nodded in understanding.

"This kind of thing generally is. It's a tough situation for most people."

Heloise looked down at the pill in her hand and thought about Martin.

She knew he would be excited about the idea of a baby, happy and far too hopeful, and it would force their relationship into the next phase. He would insist on taking a Neil Armstrong–sized step forward, whereas she would want to take three steps back.

Heloise preferred things the way they were. Or to be more precise, the way they had been. Their relationship was fun and comfortable and—most of all—still fairly casual. But now, from one day to the next, it felt as if there was a ticking time bomb between them. The countdown had begun with those two lines on the pregnancy test, and Heloise could see red digital numbers blinking like a doomsday clock in her mind's eye. It was going to explode whether she cut the red or the blue wire, she knew that.

She might as well get it over with.

The doctor studied Heloise intently, as if he were trying to decode her inexpressive body language.

"If you're having any doubts, it's no problem to wait—"

"I'm not having any doubts."

"Okay, well then why don't we just see how far along you are?"

He pointed toward the exam table with his chin and put on a pair of steel-colored acetate glasses. The lenses looked curiously small on his square face.

"A home pregnancy test like that can be a little off, so we'll just confirm that you're on the right side of the eight-week mark."

Heloise took a deep breath and took off her leather jacket.

*   *   *

The silence in the room was broken only by the ticking of the clock above the table and by the doctor's calm breathing.

Heloise was holding her breath.

She lay with her face turned away from the monitor, away from the scanning images she was afraid she would never be able to erase from her mind again if she caught so much as a glimpse of them. She had tried all week to avoid imagining what was in there, but she had slept fitfully at night, tossing and turning, her sheets wet from sweat, seeing little arms and legs in her dreams. Fingers and toes. A head covered in brown curls.

But no face.

Each time there had been only a featureless circle at the top of the neck. A concave surface, without any further form or color, like a baby with a dinner plate where the face should have been.

What did that mean?

That she didn't want to pass on Martin's genes? That she was terrified by the thought of passing on her own?

She couldn't stop speculating about whether there were hereditary variants of evil, whether a rottenness could hide in a person's blood, like a sleeping cell, that could skip a generation or two. In any case, that was not an experiment she wanted to conduct.

"All right, Heloise," the doctor said. "As it turns out, the test was accurate."

Heloise reluctantly looked up.

"Here's your bladder and your stomach." The doctor pointed at the screen in front of him, where a vague black and white shape filled the screen. "And there, that's your uterus. Do you see?"

Heloise tilted her head and stared blankly at the splotch in front of her. It could have been an ultrasound scan of anything: a human brain, a cow's stomach, Jupiter! She wouldn't have been able to tell the difference.

He drew a circle on the screen with his finger around a little peanut-shaped spot.

"There. You see? It looks like you're right around five weeks—give or take a day or two."

Heloise nodded and looked away.

"Are you okay?" he asked, turning off the monitor. "Your mind is made up?"

"Yes." She raised herself up a little on her elbows. "But there's actually something else I'd like to ask you about. I've been having this uncomfortable trembly feeling for a while now."

The doctor pulled off his latex glove with a talcum-powdery snap and nodded for her to continue.

"Can you try to describe it in a little more detail?"

"I don't know how to explain it. It's just something that feels . . . *off*. A weird fog around me, as I'm looking at the world through a glass dome, and my head is teeming with thoughts. It's gone on for a long time now, I think. Several months, long before this." She nodded at her belly.

The doctor removed his glasses from his nose with a pincer grip and cleaned them on his T-shirt as he studied Heloise.

"You said a trembly feeling? Do you mean a type of uneasiness?"

"Yes."

"Pressure in your chest? Palpitations?"

She nodded.

"What are you doing professionally these days, Heloise?" Still that harsh H sound. "You're a journalist, aren't you?"

"Yes."

"So, does your job keep you fairly busy?"

"Well, I suppose so."

"Do you bring work home with you?"

"Doesn't everyone these days?" Heloise said with a shrug.

He crossed his arms and bit his lower lip as he regarded her. "It sounds like you might be under some pressure. Have you been through a particularly stressful period recently?"

Heloise noticed a tingling in her temples as the memories bubbled up inside her like foul-smelling methane gas in a swamp: Hands tightening around her throat. Children with closed eyes. The engraving on her father's headstone . . .

Memories that had left Heloise's heart blue-black with cold.

A particularly stressful period?

"You could say that," she said, sitting up.

"They sound stress-related, your symptoms," the doctor said. "But I'd like to get you tested for hypothyroidism, so why don't we just take a blood test to be on the safe side—"

They were interrupted by two quick knocks on the door. Without waiting, the elderly receptionist stuck her made-up face into the room.

"I'm sorry to bother you, Jens, but there's a call for you." She pointed to the phone on a light Wegner table at the other end of the room. "It's from the school's office. They say it's important."

The doctor furrowed his brow, and a vertical line appeared above the bridge of his nose.

"I'm sorry," he said, turning to Heloise and smiling, mildly embarrassed. "Do you mind if I just . . ."

"No, of course not," Heloise said, waving his question away.

He closed the frosted glass sliding door that divided the room, and Heloise could hear him walking rapidly over to the phone.

She looked down at the pill she was still holding in her hand. It had grown damp from her sweat and some of the color had come off onto the palm of her hand, filling her lifeline with a white powdery mass. She set the pill down on a small stainless-steel tray and half listened as the doctor answered the call behind the sliding glass door.

"Hello? Yes, it's me. Why, yes, he should be. What time is it, did you say? Well then, he got out twenty minutes ago and he's probably on his way downstairs. He has certainly been known to take his own sweet time at that kind of thing . . . Well, maybe he went straight to the playground with Patrick from the rec center. I know that they were going to get together today. Have you checked there?"

Heloise got up and put on her pants and her leather jacket.

"No, he's not," the doctor continued. "No, he wasn't picked up. I'm positive about that because my wife is supposed to pick him up today and she's still at work and . . . Yes, but I can't . . . Okay. Yes, okay. I'm on my way now!"

Heloise heard him hang up and dial a number on the phone.

"Hi, it's Dad. Where are you? Give me a call when you get this message!"

And then another call.

"It's me. Did you pick up Lukas? . . . They just called from the rec center, and he hasn't shown up there after school."

Heloise could hear the increasing panic take hold of his voice and squeeze. She turned to look at the framed photo on the windowsill. The doctor looked younger in the picture than he did now, but Heloise could recognize his kind eyes and pronounced jaw line. He had his arm around a pretty woman with dirty blond hair, who was wearing a yellow sun dress with spaghetti straps over tan skin, and standing between them was a child who looked to be about three or four years old, excitedly waving an Italian flag.

"I'm heading over there now," came the voice from behind the sliding door. "Yes, but let's just take it easy. He's gotta be there somewhere."

The fear churning in his voice emphasized to Heloise that she never wanted to live like that, in fear. The responsibility a child would entail. The vulnerability that would impinge on her life.

Better to feel nothing.

She picked up the pill from the metal tray, folded it into a paper towel and stuck it into her pocket.

Then she slung her purse over her shoulder and left the clinic.

3

T HE WAIL OF the smoke alarm yanked detective Erik Schäfer out of the reverie he had fallen into at the kitchen sink.

He smacked the alarm with a fist the size of a pomelo and turned off the toaster. The disappointing scent of cold plastic welcomed him when he opened the fridge, and he stared at the half-empty shelves, unimpressed.

There was nothing in there besides a container of butter, a jar of marmalade, and a liter of whole milk that he and Connie had bought at 7-Eleven after they had landed at Copenhagen Airport last night.

He set the items out on the kitchen table and pulled his vibrating phone out of his back pocket. It was Lisa Augustin, his partner from the Violent Crimes Unit, calling.

"Yup. Hello?"

"Hi, it's me." Augustin's voice sounded chipper and far too loud.

Schäfer made a face and pulled the phone a little away from his ear.

"Good morning," he muttered.

"Well, 'good afternoon' you mean. Jet-lagged?"

Schäfer grumbled noncommittally in response.

"How was your trip?"

"The trip was good," he said, carefully extracting the charred bread from the toaster. "I was this close to not coming home again."

He scraped the worst of the charring off the bread with a knife. The dark particles lingered in the air like volcanic dust and then silently drifted down onto the counter. It reminded him of the black sand beaches on Saint Lucia in the Caribbean, where he and Connie had spent the last five weeks in their vacation shack at Jalousie Beach. A ramshackle house painted a pale pink with white shutters and palm trees, yellow oleander, and mango trees in the backyard.

He missed it already.

They had been going to the island, where Connie had been born and raised, for the twenty-nine years they had known each other, and Schäfer was starting to prefer life there to his everyday life here in Copenhagen. Even so, there was always something that made him board the plane again to head back to Denmark. He told Connie every time that it wasn't the job that drew him back, and then she smiled at him as if to say, yeah right. She loved him enough to let him spin the truth as he saw fit.

Lisa Augustin didn't.

"Bullshit," she said and laughed. "You missed me. Admit it!"

Schäfer ignored her comment.

"What do you want?" he asked.

"I just wanna know if you're on your way?"

"I'm leaving in ten," he said and took a bite of his toast. "See you at HQ."

"No, that's why I'm calling. I'm not at headquarters."

"Where are you?"

"I'm on my way to the Nyholm School."

"The Nyholm School?" Schäfer woke up. "What's going on there?"

"There's a kid missing."

He closed his eyes tight. First day back and one of *those* cases?

"All right," he said. "What do we know?"

"Not much yet, but as I understand it, the case involves a ten-year-old named Lukas Bjerre. He disappeared from the rec center that runs the school's aftercare program at about two o'clock."

Schäfer looked at the clock over the stove. It said 3:33 PM.

"Who's with you?"

"No one. That's why I'm calling."

"What about Bro and Bertelsen? Where are they?"

"They're investigating a death on Amerikakaj. And Clausen broke his collar bone, so I've been flying solo the last few days."

"I'm on my way," Schäfer said.

He hung up and took one sip of the coffee Connie had made for him before she had left for the store. It was lukewarm now.

He put his gun holster on over his shoulders in one quick motion and found his winter jacket.

On his way to the front hall, he glanced out at the patio in front of his little red brick house in Copenhagen's pleasant Valby neighborhood. A sparrow landed on the birdhouse Connie had just decorated with little balls of birdfeed wrapped in light green mesh and was pecking at one of the fatty clumps of seeds.

Schäfer's eyes scanned the tired winter lawn and stopped at the plastic yard furniture stacked in the corner of the yard, covered in dust and shriveled, rust-brown leaves. It was getting dark again already and he thought of the sun that was no doubt shining on a beautiful morning in Saint Lucia.

He shook his head as he stepped out into the cold.

"What the hell are we doing here?" he muttered, slamming the front door closed behind him.

4

HELOISE KALDAN AIMED the gun at the man at the big double desk in the middle of the room.

He sat as if in a trance, his eyes glued to the screen in front of him, hammering out a drum solo on the edge of the desk with his two stiff index fingers while the music poured out of the cell phone on the desk in front of him.

One hard strike on the hi-hat, as his left foot worked the pedal of an invisible bass drum.

Welcome to the jungle. We've got fun and games.

Heloise looked at the dark brown curls that covered his broad forehead and the white, freshly ironed shirt that was a little too tight around his muscular upper arms and chest.

She smiled at the sight.

Such a gifted man, she thought. So smart, so talented, and so extraordinarily vain.

She leaned farther in the doorway, silently, slowly, and put her finger on the trigger.

"Bøttger?"

"Hmm?"

Journalist Mogens Bøttger looked up from his computer the second the foam bullet hit his chest. An animal-like sound came out of his mouth, and he propelled himself backward in his office chair.

"What the hell?!"

He looked angrily up at Heloise, who was weeping with laughter, both hands on her knees. With the pill tucked safely in her pocket she felt light, almost cheerful. The day had started out so gloomily, and now it felt like she had an escape route. She could wipe the slate clean and start over.

Like dodging a bullet!

"You should have seen yourself," she exclaimed, laughing.

"Kaldan, you . . . jerk!" Mogens complained and grabbed the right side of his chest. "That freaking hurt!"

"Oh, please!" Heloise blew the imaginary smoke off the muzzle of the fluorescent-green Nerf gun. "It's a toy. How painful could it possibly be?"

"All right, give it here then!"

Mogens got up. At six foot eight, he towered over her. He tried to wrest the gun out of her hand.

"You'll see how it feels!"

Heloise tossed the plastic gun away, toward the far end of the room, where it landed on an old, beat-up Chesterfield couch.

"Okay, okay, you win!" she said, holding both hands up in surrender.

Mogens reluctantly let go of her and sat back down in his desk chair, his facial expression childishly aggrieved.

"You look like one of the old men from *The Muppet Show* when you laugh, Kaldan. You know that?"

He made a goofy face and raised, then lowered his shoulders in a carefree caricature gesture, mimicking her silent laughter with a silly smile so big you could stuff a slice of watermelon in.

"That's you, Kaldan! An old, laughing buffoon."

Heloise smiled and sat down at her desk across from him.

He nodded toward the couch.

"Where'd you get the murder weapon from anyways?"

"It's Kaj's."

Mogens's eyebrow bent into a skeptical arch over his left eye.

"I'm sorry, what?" He turned down his music. "Did you say it's Kaj's?"

His surprise was well justified.

Kaj Clevin was an older gentleman with age spots who worked as a food critic for *Demokratisk Dagblad*. He was known for being a self-righteous snob who nursed a latent hatred of anything that might appeal to the proletariat, and his restaurant reviews were always narrowly targeted at the fraction of readers who shared his enthusiasm for what Heloise described as gastro-masturbation.

"What in the world would Kaj be doing with a neon-colored Nerf gun?" Mogens asked.

"He brought his grandson to work last week," Heloise said with a shrug. "The kid must have forgotten it here."

Mogens's eyes widened.

"That ugly little monster with the underbite who was running around making a fuss in here the other day?"

"Mm-hmm."

"That was Kaj's grandson?"

Heloise nodded.

"Ugh," he said, wrinkling his nose.

"I'm pretty sure you're not allowed to say *ugh* about a kid."

"Oh, I don't give a shit. He looked like an orc!" Mogens jutted out his lower jaw, his eyes focused on some point in the distance. Then he turned his brown eyes to Heloise again and turned his palms upward. "Am I right?"

Heloise shrugged and started pulling notepads and work papers out of her black leather shoulder bag.

"I'm right," Mogens said. "But to be fair to the young orc, there are exceptionally few kids who are actually charming. When I drop Fernanda off at day care in the mornings, they're all sitting there with snot pouring out of their noses . . . absolutely beyond disgusting. Plus, they smell bad!"

"Don't hold back, Bøttger. Come on, tell me what you *really* think." Heloise smiled. She took out her phone and opened an email she had received from Morten Munk in the research department with the subject line *Veterans vs. Background Population: Suicide Rate.*

"If I can't share this kind of thing with you, Kaldan, then who? You're the only person I know who hasn't been brainwashed. You remember my sister, right?"

"What about her?"

"She used to be such great company. She always had something exciting to contribute to the conversation, an interesting perspective. But then she met Niels, *Nordea-Niels* as they call him because of his job at the bank. And then they had kids, one of each—and okay, they're very cute, they are. But now they've moved to Holte, where they bought a one-story house and an electric lawnmower with all the bells and whistles in terms of attachments and special features."

"So what?"

"So now she's just mind-numbingly boring."

"But is she happy?"

"Of course she's *happy*! But it really doesn't suit her." Heloise suppressed a laugh.

"Well, then it's a good thing that having a kid didn't change *you*." She eyed him sarcastically.

Mogens responded with an annoyed shake of his head.

"Of course you *change*, otherwise you'd be made of stone. But I have preserved my cynicism, and that is a darned important attribute in a person." He emphasized his point with an insistent index finger.

"If you say so, Captain Haddock."

"It's true! Plus, it's one of the reasons I like you so much, Kaldan. You're one of the most cynical people I know."

"Aw, that's almost too kind of you."

Mogens bowed his head in respect, as if he had just knighted her.

"Never change!" he urged.

"Don't worry," Heloise said wryly. "There's no risk of that."

She read the email from Morten Munk regarding what they had learned about suicide among veterans. Then she called Gerda, her best friend. It was her third try today. Gerda usually called her right back, and it rarely took more than an hour before she at least texted.

Today an unusual radio silence had prevailed.

"Hi, it's me again. Please call me," Heloise said after the beep. "I need your help with the article I told you about the other day."

She ended the call just as the investigative team's editor, Karen Aagaard, poked her head through the doorway.

"Where the hell is everyone?"

Heloise turned in her seat and looked toward the door. Then she smiled.

"Oh, hi! I thought you were out sick today."

"I'm not sick. What's going on? Where is everyone?" Karen peered critically at Heloise over the rim of her horn-rimmed frames and nodded over at the empty desks in the room. She was usually the department's breezy motherly presence, but today she was giving off a surprisingly toxic vibe.

"I don't know," Heloise said, raising an eyebrow in surprise. Then she shrugged. "Out, I guess?"

"Editorial meeting. Now!" Karen barked.

Without another word, she turned on her heel, and you could hear her royal blue stilettos clicking, making a grouchy *tsk-tsk-tsk* sound all the way down the hallway to the meeting room.

Heloise and Mogens looked at each other.

Heloise shrugged and stood up.

"Are you coming?"

CHAPTER

5

ERIK SCHÄFER SWITCHED off the siren as he passed the
National Gallery. Word of the boy's disappearance
would spread soon enough, like lice at a Girl Scout camp,
and the school's parents would work themselves up into a
foaming frenzy. There was no reason to accelerate the
process.

He reached the school and parked his black, scratched-
up Opel Astra half up on the sidewalk next to a statue of
King Christian IV. His majesty peered at the school, which
sat looking like a gigantic Monopoly hotel on a narrow strip
between Østerport Station and the Royal Navy's mustard-
colored barracks.

The Nyholm School was to schools what the Marble
Church was to churches, Schäfer thought. Not a dull avant-
garde chapel with an organ whose pipes looked like the cylinders on an oil rig, but a place with a soul, with . . . *spirit*.
He didn't give a rat's ass as to how many international
awards the current era's young star architects won or how
many parades were held in their honor. They could build
however many sustainable ski slopes, like the roof of

CopenHill power plant, or however many eco-blah-blah buildings they wanted; Schäfer couldn't stand all the glass constructions that had been popping up all over the city of late.

Sometimes he thought he must be the only person in all of Denmark who hadn't been "drinking from the chamber pot," a colloquial way of saying you'd lost your mind. Other times he figured he was starting to get old. Maybe both.

He scanned the schoolyard, where a crowd had now gathered in the twilight. Mothers and fathers stood in clusters, keeping their children on a tight leash, and even from far away he could decode their facial expressions. His efforts had been for naught. The lice were already starting to itch.

Schäfer spotted his partner of the last four years, Sergeant Lisa Augustin, as he passed the play court where a lanky, acne-ridden teenager was shooting hoops. Augustin stood with two uniformed officers, talking to a couple that—judging from their long, easy-to-read faces—Schäfer took to be the missing boy's parents.

Aside from his height, the father resembled a young Robert Redford, Schäfer thought. Golden-blond hair, a pronounced nose, and a jaw that gave him an Old Hollywood sort of look. The woman at his side was also attractive but drowned out a bit in the crowd of mothers in the schoolyard—women who, like her, were wearing sensible shoes and coats that were appropriate for the weather. She looked practical and down to earth, a diametric opposite to Mr. Hollywood, but the look in her eyes stood out, Schäfer thought—a look of unmitigated horror.

Schäfer made eye contact with Lisa Augustin, and their reunion after five weeks apart was marked by a single nod.

She walked over to meet him, and when they reached each other, Schäfer asked, "Has he turned up?"

Augustin shook her head. Her blond hair was pulled into a tight knot on the back of her head.

"No, and it's worse than I thought."

"What do you mean?"

"The boy wasn't in school today at all. No one knows where the hell he is."

"What does that mean? When was he last seen?"

"This morning, here in the schoolyard. Witnesses saw him walk through that door there just before eight."

She pointed to an old oak door behind them, one of the school's two entrances off the schoolyard.

"But he didn't show up in his classroom on the third floor when the first bell rang, so no one has seen him for . . ."—she looked at the TAG Heuer men's watch that was strapped tightly around her sinewy wrist—". . . for almost eight hours."

"Eight hours?!" Schäfer repeated, the blood starting to tingle in his temples. "Why the hell didn't the school react sooner?"

He looked around for a teacher or school employee, and his eyes fell on a middle-aged man leaning against the big climbing structure on the school's playground. He was wearing a suit of armor made of spray-painted plastic, and the hilt of a foam sword stuck out under his one arm.

"His classroom teacher assumed the boy was out sick," Augustin said. "Apparently there's no procedure to check on absences during the day. That doesn't happen until school gets out and they take attendance at aftercare." She pointed with her thumb over her shoulder. "The Labyrinth—that's what the aftercare program is called—is located here on the ground floor. Parents are supposed to notify them online if a child is sick, and if there's an absence they weren't notified about, then the teachers call and make sure the children were picked up or were out sick."

"And?"

"And when the boy didn't show up, they called the parents, who basically went into a coma, and now here we are."

Augustin handed Schäfer a photo.

"This picture was taken at the beginning of the school year, but they say he has the same haircut and that he hasn't changed much since August."

The picture showed a boy with blond hair and thin lips, who looked curious, as if the flash had gone off right when he was asking a question. His blue eyes were wide and wary, his skin fair without seeming pale. He was a good-looking kid, Schäfer could tell. With those fine features and long, tangled eyelashes, he was pretty in a way that was usually reserved for girls.

"So that's him," Schäfer mumbled. He tucked the picture into the inside pocket of his bomber jacket and gazed up at the school building. "There must be hundreds of places in there to hide—attic, bathrooms, gym, storage rooms in the basement . . . We'll need to search the whole thing. You said he went in here?"

Schäfer walked over and put his hand on the door handle, and it occurred to him that a school with old bones like this came with some inconvenient features. He had to put his full body weight into it to pull the oak door open.

Inside the entrance Augustin pointed to a large, two-lane, half-turn staircase, which ran along one side of the entrance hall.

"He usually goes up the stairs here to get to his classroom, but the back entrance to the school is right there. So he could basically have gone straight out there when he arrived this morning." She nodded over at a door on the opposite side of the hall.

"You think he cut school?"

"It's possible," Augustin said, flinging up her hands.

Schäfer walked over and pushed open the door and immediately found himself out behind the school.

He looked around.

The Hotel Østerport was in front of him, a hideous, prison-like block of concrete. He walked to the left along the hotel until he came to an overgrown slope behind a chain link fence. The fence had been clipped open in several places, so gaping holes allowed free access to the slope, which led down to the train tracks behind the hotel. Østerport Station was located a little farther down the tracks.

Schäfer stepped through one of the holes and studied the area on the other side of the fence.

Could the boy have come through here? Could he have hopped onto a train or walked over into Østre Anlæg Park, which sat like a jungle on the other side of the transit station's graffiti-painted walls?

Every train line in the city stopped at Østerport. There were departures headed for every corner of the world, and in eight hours the boy could have made it to Berlin, to Stockholm, or somewhere else entirely. They were too late getting started.

Way too late.

Schäfer's thoughts were drowned out by a commuter rail S train, which pulled into the station, its squealing brakes ripping through the clear, frosty air. He walked back to Augustin with a finger in one ear.

"We need to search the whole school," he said. "We need to obtain any surveillance footage from the hotel and down at the station and interview people in the area about whether they saw the boy during the day. Does he have a cell phone?"

"Yes."

"Get it pinged right away so we can see if it's on or off and where it was last used. The witnesses you've already spoken to will need to be formally questioned." He pointed ahead of him. "Østre Anlæg Park is over there on the other side of the tracks. So we'll need to pick that apart, too."

"That's a big area."

"Yup, so we'd better hop to it!"

Augustin held her phone up to her ear and asked, "How many people should I ask Carstensen for?"

Per Carstensen was the commissioner, and he had been uncharacteristically generous with his people lately. After the government's decision to have the military take over a range of policing roles, the Investigative Unit had had enough manpower available for most of their duties. It was like a waterfront mansion for newly rich rappers from Copenhagen's west side: an unaccustomed luxury, which everyone in the unit was afraid of losing again. But it was only a matter of time before they were bombed back to the Stone Age.

"We need to get a whole major circus set up," Schäfer said. "And tell them to bring the dogs. We need to find that kid now!"

Augustin nodded.

"Eight hours . . . ," Schäfer said.

He and Augustin exchanged a look, and he could tell from the lines in her face that they were thinking the same thing.

"It's getting dark now, and the temperature has dropped below freezing," he said. "This is a total shit show."

6

"WELL?"

Editor Karen Aagaard looked around the conference room. She was like a prison guard doing cell inspections—ready to search the contents, flip up mattresses, and investigate hollowed-out deodorant containers in pursuit of illegal drugs, weapons—anything that might result in a whipping in the courtyard and a trip to solitary.

"What are you working on?" Aagaard glanced at Mogens, who began with his standard arrogance.

"I'm working on a story that has Cavling Prize written all over it," he said.

Aagaard snorted.

"Let's just hear what you've got before we start engraving your name on the little brass nameplate."

"I have three sources who say that all the crime statistics released by the last government were significantly manipulated."

"Manipulated? In what way?"

"They were incomplete, to say the least. Important numbers that went before the judge were left out. When they realized how overrepresented immigrants were, they decided *not* to include them in the overall statistics. They were simply scared of the outcry it would have caused if the truth came out. So they intentionally left immigrants out of the cumulative statistics, which artificially lowered the percentage of criminals from other ethnic backgrounds—just like they did in Sweden. The results were completely airbrushed."

"Who decided to do that?"

Mogens shrugged.

"It was indubitably done at the ministerial level, but the national police commissioner must have been involved in some form or another."

"And what would the purpose of this have been?"

"Politics!" Mogens flung up his arms to emphasize the obvious. "As long as the majority of the population believe that the horror stories are nationalistic propaganda, then Mr. and Mrs. Middle of the Road will stay calm. They intentionally misled Danes to make the immigration situation appear less critical than it is."

"What kind of sources do you have?" Karen asked.

"Two officers from Station City and one from Central Station. They say the fact that the numbers were skewed is common knowledge among the police. They're also sick and tired of dealing with immigrant gangs and bullshit, so they want the actual numbers daylighted."

"Are any of them willing to go on record?"

Mogens shook his head.

"No one dares to say squat. But I have the actual numbers here."

He took a little black notebook and swung it in front of Aagaard like a pendulum.

"So the story will compare the published statistics with the actual numbers and then question why this kind of monkeying around with the numbers was orchestrated. The turd lies on the red side of the fence, politically speaking, so someone over there has some explaining to do, as does the national police commissioner."

"Okay." Aagaard nodded. Her stance had softened a little. "I don't think this is going to win you any awards, but fine. Have at it!"

"Kaldan?" she said, turning to look at Heloise. "What've you got?"

"I'm gathering material for a story on post-traumatic stress syndrome in veterans with the working title 'The War's Delayed Victims,'" she said. "In the last month alone, three veterans with PTSD have committed suicide. That's a pronounced increase compared with the same month over the last ten years."

Karen Aagaard's mouth dropped down her face.

Heloise hesitantly regarded her editor. Aagaard's dark hair was pulled tightly back into a ponytail, and her pearl stud earrings were in their customary place as well. But something looked . . . off. Then it hit her that Aagaard wasn't wearing any makeup. Heloise couldn't remember ever having seen her editor without it. Her winter-pale skin and tired eyes surrounded by eyelashes so pale they seemed transparent made Karen Aagaard look like a corpse that had bled to death. To put it mildly, it wasn't a flattering look.

Heloise blinked away those thoughts and held up her cell phone. She pointed to a text exchange she had had with Gerda earlier in the week.

"I have a friend who works for the military. Her name's Gerda Bendix. She's a trauma psychologist and of course she can't say anything about personnel matters, but I know that one of the individuals who died was a client of hers. So she might be able to help shed some light on the challenges soldiers face when they come home from war."

Heloise pulled a sheet of paper out of her bag—a graph of military suicides since 2001—and pushed it across the mahogany table to Aagaard.

"When they deploy, the vast majority are really young men, who don't have the slightest idea what awaits them when they get there. And now there's been a fourth."

"A fourth what?" Mogens asked.

"Suicide. As recently as yesterday, they found the body of a young female soldier, who—"

Karen Aagaard stood up.

Heloise looked at her in surprise. Mogens's mouth opened in silent amazement.

"I have to run," Aagaard said and started packing up her papers. "I totally forgot that I have a . . . We'll have to talk about this another time, right?" She took a couple of steps backward, turned around to face the door, and left the room.

"What the hell?" Mogens said to no one in particular. Then he looked over at Heloise. "She's acting really weird today."

Heloise shrugged, still surprised.

"Mikkelsen said this morning that she was out sick, but then she showed up after all . . . I hope nothing serious is wrong with her."

"With Karen? No way! She's so ridiculously healthy that it makes you want to slap her. The woman has no vices at all, it's infuriating. She's probably just—" Mogens's eyebrows shot up as he put two and two together. "Huh, it's probably because of the business with Peter."

"Her son?" Heloise asked. "What's going on with him?"

"He's going to be deployed again. I was with Karen yesterday when he called and told her. She went pretty pale then, now that I think about it . . ."

"I didn't think he was still in the military," Heloise said, her brow furrowed.

Aagaard's son had been in the military for years, but for the last year he had been working as a shift manager for a credit and loan company, and Aagaard had been happy that his days of waging war were over.

"He resigned from BRF, because he wanted to ship out again," Mogens said.

"And here I am talking about soldiers committing suicide." Heloise sighed and ran a hand through her hair. "Poor Karen."

She glanced down at her phone, which was vibrating in her hand. Gerda's number lit up the display.

"Ah, there you are," she said into the phone. "I've tried calling you a few times, but maybe you've—"

"The school is crawling with police!" Gerda blurted out. Her voice sounded unusually loud, as if she were trying to talk over music.

Heloise felt a wave of cold sweat wash over her body. In a hundredth of a second images of various worst-case scenarios flashed through her mind.

A terrorist attack, a school shooting, a teacher unzipping his pants . . .

"Is Lulu okay?" Heloise asked. She was already on her feet.

"Yes. I'm sorry, I should have led with that. She's with me," Gerda said. "But one of the boys from the school is missing. I saw him being dropped off this morning and now he's gone. No one has any idea where he's been all day. I think he's been abducted!"

7

"WHO HAVE YOU talked to?" Schäfer asked, looking at Lisa Augustin when they were back in the schoolyard.

"Jens and Anne Sofie Bjerre," she said, pointing to the parents.

They were arguing with a couple of uniformed officers and a woman who looked like a comic strip line drawing, so paper thin that she seemed two-dimensional.

"That woman they're talking to runs the aftercare program. I also spoke with that woman over there." Augustin pointed to a tall, dark-haired gazelle of a woman who was standing in the middle of the schoolyard with a cell phone in one hand and a child in the other.

"And with that teacher over there."

She nodded toward a young, androgynous figure who looked like they might be Asian. The person had long black hair that had been gathered up into a fountain on top of their head, makeup around the eyes, and a distinctly masculine build. Schäfer was having a hard time deciding if it was a man or a woman.

"A Kevin something-or-other," Augustin said.

A man, then. I'll be damned, Schäfer thought, scanning the rest of the schoolyard.

"What about Mr. Game of Thrones over there?" He nodded with his chin toward the role player, who was still standing by the jungle gym sobbing.

"His name is Patrick . . ." Augustin glanced down at her notes. "Jørgensen, teacher's aide. He and Lukas were working on a project on the playground; something involving a sword fight. They were supposed to have a duel today."

Schäfer raised one eyebrow. He was equally jealous and suspicious of adults who were *that* in touch with their inner child and their tear ducts. There was quite simply something unnatural about grown men who ran around wearing dress-up clothes and playing make-believe. And crying.

He looked back over at the gazelle. She was talking to one of the other parents, whose back was turned to Schäfer. He could tell from her breath—which emerged visibly from her mouth in tense, steamy bursts in the cold air—that she was upset. There was something about her face that rang a bell somewhere inside him, a memory he couldn't put an image or words to.

"Who's the supermodel?" he asked as the wails of emergency response vehicles materialized in the distance.

"Here name's Gerda," Augustin answered without consulting her notes. "Gerda Bendix."

Schäfer knew why the name had already stuck. The woman was almost provocatively beautiful, and if there was one thing Lisa Augustin was particularly fond of, it was beautiful women.

"She's the mother of one of the girls at the school and, as far as we know, the last person to have seen the boy."

"Bendix?" Schäfer repeated, scratching under his chin so the stubble made a surprising amount of noise. "Where do I know that name from?"

The woman Gerda Bendix was talking to turned toward Schäfer and a feeling of cheerful astonishment instantly spread through his chest. He had been wrong. It wasn't another parent from the school. It was Heloise Kaldan, the journalist.

Kaldan spotted him just then, and her face lit up in a smile. She started walking over to him immediately.

"Hi, Schäfer," she said once they stood face to face. "Welcome home."

He smiled warmly. "Heloise."

They hadn't seen each other for a few months, and under normal circumstance he would have given her a hug, maybe even lifted her up and shaken her a little in excitement. But this wasn't a normal circumstance.

"Well, you sure got here fast," he commented instead, a bit warily.

It wasn't unusual for the press to show up so early in an investigation, but usually only the tabloid rats—the blood-thirsty, obnoxious ones—came sniffing around at stage one. *Demokratisk Dagblad* and other serious media rarely covered personal stories until they had some sort of relevance to the public, and even then the coverage was mostly refreshingly concrete and respectful.

Schäfer had only been on-site at the school for a couple of minutes and Heloise Kaldan was already there, ready to ask questions. That was unusual. And not entirely unproblematic.

"I'm not actually here for work," Heloise reassured him, as if she could smell his skepticism. "Well, I guess I should say I'm never *not* at work, but the newspaper didn't send me."

"Oh?" Schäfer raised an eyebrow.

"You remember my friend Gerda . . ." She nodded behind her.

Yes, of course. That's where Schäfer knew the woman from. They had met each other one time at the National Hospital the previous year when Heloise had been a patient. But he had been too preoccupied with the case he was investigating to pay any real attention to her.

"Although since I'm here anyway, I'd really like to hear a little more about what's going on," Heloise said. "What can you tell me? Do you think he was abducted, or did he run off? What do you think?"

Schäfer regarded her hesitantly as he considered his options.

Here we go again, he thought.

There were a handful of people he had tried to coexist with when things were at rock bottom. People he had clawed for until his fingernails bled. Schäfer felt bound to them in a way that would last his whole life. He knew that. That's how he felt about the men from his unit, the people he had been stationed with during the Gulf War, as well as medical examiner John Oppermann, with whom he had stood in mass graves in Kosovo. He felt the same gloomy shared understanding with his old police partner, Peter Rye, and now also with Kaldan.

There was a mutual understanding between them, a covenant that not even Connie could understand. He always shared his experiences with his wife, though, without leaving out any details or thoughts. He needed her care, needed her to listen to what he shared. But she would never be able to understand what the daily shadow of death did to him, for the simple reason that, thank God, she had never experienced it herself.

These days it was standard procedure at police headquarters to cry your heart out to the police psychologists after you'd worked on a particularly gruesome murder case or horrific accident. The younger police officers were willing to allow academics with manicured fingernails and neatly pressed slacks to psychoanalyze them, but Schäfer refused. He couldn't imagine anything hollower than showing the scars in your heart to someone who had never been the first one to walk through a doorway with a loaded Heckler & Koch in their hand, someone who hadn't inhaled the stench of death and didn't know how it made you want to gargle bleach and scrape your mucus membranes with a spoon.

Was he supposed to sit there and talk about the dark sides of his job with someone whose frame of reference consisted of PowerPoint slides about the self-reinforcing cycle of anxiety and cognitive self-help tools?

Schäfer didn't give two shits about that kind of thing.

But Heloise Kaldan had tried staring into the depths herself, and it was there—at the edge of the abyss—where Schäfer had met her last year when a wanted murderer had started sending her letters, letters that had forced her to face her own reality and say a final goodbye to her father. Her father's death had made it clear to Heloise that the world was fundamentally a crummy place, and that realization had settled over her like a cold, impenetrable membrane. She had become cynical, and Schäfer recognized something of himself in her. But there was one thing that would always remain a wedge between them: her job.

Could he trust Heloise in a life-or-death situation?

Absolutely.

When it came to work?

That was another matter.

Schäfer cleared his throat.

"We need to get a better handle on the situation before we go public with anything."

"Of course. I can certainly understand that." Heloise nodded. "But I'm assuming that means that our dinner plans for tomorrow night are canceled?" She smiled fleetingly.

"Well, we'll see about that," he said. "Connie's really looking forward to seeing you, so . . ."

Heloise looked back over at Gerda Bendix, who was now squatting in front of her daughter and soothingly tucking the girl's dark hair behind her ears.

Heloise lowered her voice.

"I'm not asking about the case only for, uh, professional reasons. I'm a bit curious, because I was with the boy's father when he got the message."

Schäfer squinted, his head shooting back.

"You were?"

Heloise nodded.

Schäfer raised both eyebrows in hesitant wonder. "But . . . what about Martin? Aren't you two . . ."

They were interrupted by the sound of raised voices. Schäfer turned toward the ruckus and saw that Lukas Bjerre's father had grabbed one of the young officers by the collar.

"Well, *do* something!" Jens Bjerre yelled. "You're just standing here and . . . and . . . *talking*?!"

Lisa Augustin grabbed Jens Bjerre calmly around the neck.

"Calm down," she said unflappably. "You're going to need to calm down. Do you understand?"

"Well then, *do* something!" He turned to Augustin and pressed his palms together as if in prayer. His wife stood next to him, her mouth open and trembling, the expression on her face stiffened in infantile helplessness.

"*Find him!*" Jens Bjerre's voice rang out in the winter darkness. "*Find my son!*"

"WATCH YOUR HEAD."

Schäfer raised one of the candy-striped police tapes blocking the main entrance to Nyholm School and made a sweeping gesture with his arm: *After you!*

Anne Sofie Bjerre ducked and entered.

She was a thin woman, Schäfer noted. Her dirty blonde hair hung loose and framed a face that was pretty without being over the top. Schäfer knew from Augustin that she was a teacher at a private school not far from where he and Connie lived and that she taught German and English. He also knew that she and Jens Bjerre had been together for fourteen years, married for twelve, and that Lukas was their only child.

"It's this way," he said, overtaking Anne Sofie in one single long stride.

"Where are we going?" she asked wanly. She had her arms around herself. "Where's my husband?"

"He's talking to my colleague. If you could please have a seat here, then she'll come join you in a moment." Schäfer pointed to a chair in the classroom.

Anne Sofie reached out and grabbed his rough fist with both hands. Her skin felt cold against his.

"Promise me that you'll find Lukas."

Schäfer met her penetrating, slightly swimmy gaze. He could smell alcohol on her breath.

"We have our best people out there," he said, and it was true. Over the course of the last hour, the Nyholm School and the surrounding streets had been flooded with a veritable tidal wave of police personnel. Detectives from the Violent Crimes Unit, canine units, and crime scene investigators were examining the basement storage rooms, dumpsters and trash cans, and the many small apartments and yards of the navy's old, uninsulated barrack rowhouses, many of which were vacant year-round. They had looked up all the registered sex offenders in the neighborhood and were already knocking on their doors. Lukas Bjerre's description and photo had been sent out to the patrol cars and police precincts throughout the entire country, and they were working on obtaining video and still images from the surveillance cameras in the area. But so far they hadn't found a single trace of the boy.

"Promise me you'll find him," Anne Sofie repeated.

Schäfer smiled noncommittally and put a hand on her shoulder.

"If you'll have a seat here, my colleague will be in to see you in a moment. Okay? Wait here."

She reluctantly walked into the room. Then she turned to face the door again.

"Schäfer? Is that your name?"

He nodded.

"How many of these types of cases have you had, cases involving missing children?"

"A lot."

"And how many of the children were found?"

Schäfer hesitated for a moment.

"Most of them."

He left Anne Sofie Bjerre and walked to a room three doors farther down the hall. The Nyholm School's entire ground floor had been temporarily converted into impromptu interrogation rooms, where detectives were questioning witnesses and family members about the case.

"Okay, let's go through this one more time," Schäfer said and pushed a glass of water over to Jens Bjerre. "It's important that we get as many details as possible, even things that might not seem important at the moment—people you encountered on the way, Lukas's emotional state, that sort of thing."

Jens nodded.

He still had his navy-blue trench coat on, with its wool collar flipped up, and he looked oddly large, sitting there in the small, matchbox-sized student chair. His knees were almost at the same height as his shoulders. He sat with his eyes closed and his face in his hands. What had seemed like abject panic out in the schoolyard had now given way to a pleading willingness to negotiate.

"We said goodbye by the Christmas tree," he whispered. His voice sounded frail like a child's. Scared.

"The Christmas tree?"

"Yes, that's . . . that's what Lukas calls it." He opened his bloodshot eyes and pointed out at an enormous climbing structure with metal branches and garlands of twisted rope. "I stood there until Lukas got to the door, and then he went in without looking back."

Jens stared blankly straight ahead, remembering the moment, and smiled a joyless smile, which immediately faded.

Schäfer leaned further forward in the chair. "Without looking back, you say?"

"Yes, he . . . he didn't turn around when he got to the door. He usually does. Sometimes he runs all the way back for one more hug, but this morning he just went in . . . without looking . . . back." Jens took short, shallow breaths between the words, fighting back tears.

"And you thought that something was wrong since he just went in, or what?"

"No." He shook his head. "He was in a good mood on the way to school and his just going in felt almost like a little . . . *victory*. It stung a little—it always does, right, every time they move on to the next stage—but I was also proud of him. Proud that he had gotten to be so . . . so *big*." Jens looked into Schäfer's eyes. "Do you have kids?"

Schäfer shook his head, and Jens's shoulders drooped.

Schäfer had had this experience before, relatives who needed someone who understood them, someone who grasped the severity of the situation. They were afraid that a childless detective would not try as hard, would be less dedicated in the search for their beloved children, that he wouldn't be able to understand just how scared and frustrated they were.

Maybe they were right about that last part, Schäfer thought. But not about the first part.

"Sometimes you wish time would stand still," Jens said. It almost seemed like he was talking to himself. "That they would stay little. But they do need to learn to manage on their own, so you try to let go. Just a little, so they can learn to . . ." He paused. He looked as if he was fixated on a thought, the idea of a horror scenario. He squeezed his eyes shut tight and emitted a brief, pained moan. "Oh God . . . Where is he?"

"What did you do after that?" Schäfer asked. "After dropping Lukas off?"

Jens took a deep breath and wiped his nose with the tissue he had been holding in his hand for the duration of the questioning. It was beginning to fall apart at the edges from the moisture.

"I went to work."

"Did you walk, drive—what?"

"I walked. I work just around the corner from here."

"Did you run into anyone on the way? Anyone who can confirm your story?"

"Confirm my story?" he asked, his eyes opening wide. Then he squeezed them shut again in disbelief.

Schäfer met his silent protest with open arms and a shrug to defuse the situation.

"Look," Schäfer said, "my job is to find Lukas, and I do that best by determining as quickly as possible which streets and alleyways I can rule out. Do you understand?"

The balloon deflated again. Jens lowered his head and nodded.

"Good," Schäfer said. "This isn't a personal attack on you. We just need to know as many details as possible about your and Lukas's movements this morning."

Jens nodded again and wiped a tear away. "Just help us, please," he said.

"That's what we're working on. So—did you talk to anyone after you dropped Lukas off this morning?"

"I . . ." He shook his head slightly, struggling to recall. "I talked briefly with Toke's mom."

"Toke? Who's he?"

"One of the boys in Lukas's class."

"You talked to his mom?"

He nodded. "Mona, I think that's her name. Or Rosa or something like that."

"You ran into her in the schoolyard?"

"No, out in front of the bike rack by the intersection. She was standing out there smoking with a couple of other people. She asked if Lukas was coming to Toke's birthday party next week . . . I don't remember what else she said. I wasn't really paying attention."

"And who were the other people with her?"

"I don't know. A couple of dads. They weren't parents from Lukas's class. One of them was pretty fashion forward—with a cravat and pointy-toed shoes. I often see him at school in the mornings, but I don't know his name."

Schäfer looked up from his notebook. "And then what?"

Jens shrugged. "Then I went to work."

"I understand that you're a doctor?"

"Yes."

"Do you work in a hospital or a private practice or what?"

"I share a practice with another doctor here in the city. His name's Pelle Laursen."

"And where is it located, your office?"

"On Amaliegade, by the palace."

"All right," Schäfer said. "So you went straight to work?"

Jens nodded again.

"Alone?"

"No, I was with an acquaintance, a guy I know whose name is Mads Florentz."

Schäfer wrote the name down on the notepad in front of him. "Who's he?"

"He's a consultant. He works in the same building where my medical practice is located. He has a daughter in first grade here at the school, and we've played squash together a few times, so . . ." Jens pressed his fingers to his temples as he spoke. "We go to work together in the mornings when we run into each other out by the stoplight."

"What time did you arrive at your office this morning?"

"About eight o'clock, quarter past eight, thereabouts."

"Was there anyone there when you arrived?"

He nodded. "My secretary. Marie."

"Last name?"

"Kammersgaard."

Schäfer wrote down the name. "And what did your day look like today? Patients the whole day or what?"

Jens nodded. "I saw my first patient at eight thirty and then they kept coming until school got out."

"When did you become aware that Lukas was missing?" Schäfer asked.

"When school got out."

"Was anyone with you when they called?"

"A patient."

"Heloise Kaldan?"

Jens looked up, puzzled. "How do you . . . ? I can't . . . you know, because of doctor–patient confidentiality, I can't . . ."

"Okay, fine." Schäfer changed gears. "Are you and your wife having any marital problems?"

"Wait . . . Why are you asking about my patient? Do you think she has something to do with Lukas's disappearance?" Jens sat up straighter. "Her? The journalist?"

"No."

"But how can you be sure? She . . . she showed up today wanting an abortion, but when I came back out after talking to the school, she was gone!"

Schäfer noted the words without writing them down.

"Kaldan is not a suspect." Schäfer smiled briefly. "But is there anyone that might have it in for you or your wife? Maybe someone you owe money to?"

Jens leaned back in the small chair again. He shook his head.

"Neighbors who have complained about you, that kind of thing?"

"There's an elderly woman who lives in the apartment above us, who complains about every conceivable thing all the time. Eva. But she's eighty-something. She's harmless."

"And you live in Nyhavn?"

He nodded. "On Heibergsgade. On the other side of the canal behind Charlottenborg Palace."

"What about Lukas? Has he had any sort of problems at school, teachers he was afraid of or didn't like?"

"No, no, there hasn't been anything like that." He shook his head adamantly. "Of course, he likes some of them more than others, but in general he likes the teachers there—especially Kevin."

"And there hasn't been anything strange going on there?"

"In what sense do you mean?"

Schäfer shrugged. "I'm old school, you know. From back when teachers wore form-fitting shoes and cardigan sweaters, and this Kevin, for example . . . Well, I noticed he was wearing makeup."

Jens shrugged. "So?"

Schäfer held the eye contact for a few seconds but received no further response.

"Fair enough," he said and crossed something out on his notepad. "So no problems with the teachers." He glanced up again and caught something or other in the look in Jens's eyes. "What?"

"Patrick," Jens said.

"The role-playing guy?" Schäfer pointed with his thumb out toward the schoolyard. "What about him?"

Jens shook his head. "I'm sure it's nothing."

"But?" Schäfer made a rolling gesture with his hand to get him to elaborate.

"Well, they fight together, him and Lukas, fencing. Lukas sometimes comes home with little scratches from their fights, and . . ." Jens held his hands over his eyes and then immediately moved them away again. "No, I don't know. I'm just trying to find something that . . . Lukas loves Patrick, but I don't know him that well and now that you ask, well . . ."

"We'll talk to him," Schäfer nodded. "Has Lukas been involved in any fights of any kind? Conflicts with any of the other kids?"

"No, Lukas isn't the sort to make trouble. It's important that you understand that Lukas is an . . . an *exceptional* child." Jens scooted forward in his seat, closer to Schäfer. "He's highly gifted. I know everyone thinks that about their own children, but Lukas is special. Academically he is way ahead of the other kids in his class. He might be a little behind in terms of social things, but he's not a trouble-maker. When the others make a fuss, he recedes. Toke is the troublemaker in that class."

"Toke? In what way?"

"He's completely out of control. He's physically aggres-sive with the other kids and the teachers. Lukas doesn't like him, so he makes a point of keeping his distance from him. He's done that since kindergarten."

"Is there anyone else that Lukas has seemed to have res-ervations about?"

Jens shook his head. "At least not that he's mentioned. And I think we would have been able to tell if that were the case."

"What about outside of school? Anyone he might have met on his own in the neighborhood?"

"He walks home from school by himself on Tuesdays and Thursdays because my wife works late those days, but he hasn't said anything about—" Jens paused and blinked a couple of times. Then he looked up, his eyes wide as the sky.

"What?" Schäfer asked vigilantly.

"One time Fie mentioned something about a man Lukas had told her about—"

"Fie?"

"Anne Sofie, my wife."

"What man?"

"Something about someone who had given the boys some fruit. A man who had reached over the fence on the playground with some fruit . . . the Apple Man!" Jens sat up again. "Fie said Lukas called him the Apple Man."

"The Apple Man," Schäfer and wrote the words down on his notepad. "And where did you say Lukas has seen this . . . Apple Man?"

CHAPTER

9

T HE FRUIT GLISTENED under the gleam of the flickering
fluorescent tubes on the ceiling, so it looked like it had
been dipped in a crystal-clear glaze. The skin of the apple
Finn had placed on top of the pyramid-shaped pile was
completely flawless. There wasn't a single brown spot or
scratch in the lime-green membrane that was stretched tight
over the juicy fruit flesh inside.

He took a step back, admiring his work of art. There
wasn't much left to do now. Most of the day's boxes had
been emptied. The lemons, avocados, kiwis, and now also
the apples were neatly stacked like cheerleaders in perfect
formations. Balanced on each other's shoulders, they
stretched thirstily up toward the sprinkler system on the
ceiling, which rewarded them every thirty seconds with a
refreshing drizzle.

It was perfect, quite simply perfect.

The door into Føtex Food slid open behind Finn, and
he could sense the child's presence in the store before he
even turned around.

He turned his head and surveyed the child with his eyes.

It was a small boy with big, ice-blue eyes and dark brown hair, wearing an Angry Birds pompom hat. His mittens dangled from strings, hanging out of the sleeves of his down jacket, one farther down than the other, practically touching the dirty terrazzo floor.

Finn smiled at the sight.

The boy walked purposefully over to the refrigerated dairy section and stood on his tiptoes to reach the yogurt drink. He grabbed a bottle of the raspberry flavor and then shuffled around the rest of the store with his hat sitting a little too high on his small head.

Finn eagerly reached for the apple on the top of the pile and was about to approach the boy, when a sharp voice sounded behind him.

"Finn?"

He turned his head in fear.

Anja with the eyelashes stood behind him. The chubby girl who worked the cash register on Mondays. They were glued on, the eyelashes. He could see that. And they weren't put on all that well. Sometimes there was a whole bouquet of long, black brushes on her cheeks. Thick acrylic tufts that had fallen off without her having noticed it. They stuck to her greasy foundation, looking like little black footprints that had run down her meaty face. An attempt to flee, heading down toward her manly chin dimple.

Finn found her repulsive, gross. And she always thought she got to decide everything.

He reluctantly looked her in the eyes. "Yes?"

"If you go on break now, then Malik will have time to fit in a smoke break afterward, okay?"

Finn turned his face away from her. He looked around for the kid. "Yes, but I just need to . . ."

"No, *now*, Finn! You need to go take your break. I get off at five and that's when I'm leaving." She tapped a sharp, gel-polished fingernail on the face of her cheap wristwatch.

"I still need to empty the box of mangoes, so if I could just . . ."

"No!" She pulled the apple out of his hand and set it down hard on top of the pyramid, causing the fruits on the bottom to slip out and ruin the pile's perfect shape. "You'll have to do that afterward. Get going!"

"Excuse me . . ."

An old man wearing a camel hair jacket and a tartan flat cap asked with a polite hand gesture if he could get past in the narrow aisle.

The girl with the eyelashes flashed him a rehearsed smile and stepped aside. Then she looked at Finn, snapped her fingers in a bossy way, and pointed to the staff room before she returned to the cash register.

"Excuse me, where do you keep the plastic bags?" the old man in the flat cap asked.

Without looking at the man, Finn pointed over to the rack with the bags next to the zucchini. He looked around for the boy but couldn't see him anymore. He must have left again. To Finn, the disappointment felt like a hard jab into unprepared abs.

"Ah, yes. There they are." The man nodded. He pulled a bag off the roll and shook it once to open it. Then he reached a bony hand out and took the perfect apple from the top of the pile.

10

THE STORY RAN on a loop feed on the TV 2 News at six-minute intervals. The young anchorwoman's face took on concerned furrows, while her older male colleague informed viewers about the case.

"The Copenhagen Police are searching for ten-year-old Lukas Bjerre. The boy disappeared today from Nyholm School in Copenhagen, and the police are now asking for assistance from anyone who might have information on the case."

A photo of Lukas and a silhouette of a boy's body filled the screen and then, with gloomy authority, the anchorwoman's voice relayed:

"Police describe Lukas as small for his age. He is four feet six inches tall, with blue eyes and blond hair. He was last seen at the Nyholm School at eight o'clock this morning wearing a dark-blue down jacket, black snow pants, and an orange-colored backpack." A computer-generated sketch of the jacket and backpack appeared. "The down jacket Lukas Bjerre was wearing has artwork stitched on the back depicting Canadian pop star Justin Bieber, and the boy's orange school bag is LEGO Ninjago brand with a Storm-trooper reflector dangling from it, like the one pictured here."

The male anchor nodded somberly and added:

"The police request that anyone who might have seen Lukas during the day or has any other information about the case please contact the Copenhagen Police by dialing 114. Once again, the number is one hundred . . . fourteen."

The stylized pause in the middle of the phone number marked that the story was over for now. The newscasters packed up their sad expressions and sashayed onward into their program.

"And now, the weather forecast. What do you say, Michael Sjøll? Any chance that we'll be seeing slightly warmer weather?"

"No, Poul, unfortunately there's no sign of that. The next few days are expected to bring temperatures as low as twenty degrees as well as plenty of snow."

"Who does he look like, this weather guy?" Heloise asked, getting up sleepily from the sofa as Gerda came into the living room.

Gerda cocked her head and studied him for a moment.

"The man in the yellow hat from *Curious George*, maybe?" she said, flopping down onto the soft sofa cushions.

Heloise smiled.

She went out into Gerda's kitchen and got a bottle of chardonnay from the fridge. She didn't ask for permission, and she didn't need to, either. Gerda was family. Sure, not by blood but in every way that mattered. She took two stemmed wineglasses from the cupboard over the sink. Then she returned to the living room and crawled under

Gerda's soft plaid blanket. Gerda was absorbed in the clip, which had started over again from the beginning.

"Man, this is just awful." Gerda put her hands up to her cheeks and shook her head. "We should still be out there looking for him. It feels wrong to just sit here."

Many of the parents who had been at the Nyholm School when the police arrived had immediately set out searching for Lukas, both inside the school building and in the neighborhood. They had activated phone trees, assigned streets to different groups of volunteers, eager, like people with donation buckets collecting for the Red Cross.

Heloise, Lulu, and Gerda had searched on and around Bredgade and in the restaurants and bodegas in Nyhavn. No one they talked to had seen the boy. Eventually Lulu's lips had started turning blue and they had decided to go home. But there were still tons of volunteers walking around out there, and the flashing blue police lights were making their silent way around the neighborhood for the fifth hour in a row now.

Heloise poured the wine and handed Gerda one of the glasses. Gerda took it without taking her eyes off the screen, and Heloise observed her for a moment. It hit her that Gerda had lost weight. Her collar bone was more clearly pronounced than usual in the neckline of her T-shirt, and her arms looked thin, sinewy.

"Say, have you not been eating lately?" Heloise asked.

"What do you mean?"

"You've lost weight."

"You think so?" Gerda looked down at her arms. Then she shrugged. "Maybe a little. It's because Christian is off traveling so much these days. So meals end up being whatever's easy, something Lulu will want to eat, and after three days of spaghetti and meatballs I just lose my appetite."

"Where is he this time?"

"Denver."

"Denver?" Heloise wrinkled her forehead. "Isn't that one of those places where people wear cowboy hats and leather chaps?"

"No, maybe you're thinking of Dallas. Denver's in Colorado."

Heloise was used to hearing about Christian's trips, and they were almost always to the same small handful of cities: Hong Kong, New York, Shanghai, Paris . . . fashion centers. She'd never heard Denver come up before, not in connection with Christian's job.

"His firm acquired a company over there, so now Denver's on the list too. As if we didn't have enough destinations." Gerda gave Heloise a sleepy look. "How about Martin? Where is he tonight?"

"At Bryggen. Almost as exotic as Denver."

"Is he spending the night at your place later?"

"No, I'm not really up for it today." Heloise got up and looked out the window. On the other side of Olfert Fischers Gade, one floor higher than Gerda's, she could see her own living room window and balcony. The green windbreak had come loose on one side and hung, flapping in the wind so that it banged each time it hit the metal bars in the railing. It had woken her up several times in the last few nights, and she reminded herself that she needed to fix it before she went to bed.

She thought about the pill and contemplated when to take it. The doctor had said that she should set aside a whole day for it, but he had also said that she had plenty of time. Still a few weeks before it became critical. Maybe get the PTSD article out the door first and then take one day off next week?

"What aren't you up for?" Gerda asked. "Martin?"

Heloise blinked her thoughts away. She sat down on the windowsill and rubbed her eyes so the black mascara rubbed off onto her fingertips.

"Mm-hmm," she nodded.

Gerda furrowed her brow. "Why not? Are things not okay?"

"No, they are, but . . . He keeps talking about the future." Heloise put air quotes around the word.

"So what?"

"The *future*," she repeated, as if the very use of the word were equivalent to putting her in checkmate. "I think he's somehow decided that I'm the kind of person you start a family with."

"And that's a problem?"

"Uh, yeah. That's a problem! The only family I'm interested in being part of is yours. You, Christian, and Lulu make sense. The rest of the world?" She shook her head. "Not so much."

The previous weekend, Martin Duvall, whom Heloise had been dating for the last year and a half, had invited her to a rented summer home up in Rørvig. Up until then, she had believed that he understood who she was and that he accepted her this way: Broken. And thus different. But in Rørvig he had taken every opportunity to draw dreams in the sand and toss out future plans like you cast a fishing line.

This is the kind of place one can imagine growing old in, right? Here by the water! Somewhere where you could enjoy your old age. Teach your grandkids to fly a kite. Grill fish on the beach. That kind of thing.

Heloise had stared at him in speechless terror, paralyzed by the thought of this peach-colored old age in the distant future that Martin seemed to be picturing, like some montage from a German chocolate commercial.

What do you say, Helo? You and me, old and gray. Right here!

He had taken a deep breath, inhaling the fresh, frosty scent of wet moss, pine forest, and the ocean. Then he had looked at her through lenses that were completely fogged up from contentment and smiled.

You make me happy, you know that, right?

Heloise had evaded all his questions with a noncommittal smile and well-choreographed dodges. She lied about work calls she needed to answer so she could get away from the house, out into the orchard by herself. She had taken long walks in the woods and had been better able to imagine a life of solitude in one of the battered old cabins she had seen deep in the woods than see herself as part of a nuclear family in a top-of-the-line architect-designed summer home.

Happy?

What Martin called being happy was nothing more than a mirage to Heloise. An electric current that might hum through a person's body without warning, giving you a feeling of well-being. Deceitful impulses in the brain, whose purpose was to obfuscate the feeling of meaninglessness that had become the foundational condition of her life.

"Mommy?"

Lulu called out from her bedroom at the other end of the apartment for the eighth time since she had been put to bed. Gerda had been back and forth ad absurdum and had brought her a glass of water and fluffed her pillows until she was bug-eyed with weariness. Her head lolled backward now to rest on the back of the sofa as she responded, the patience in her voice strained.

"Yeeeees?"

"I think I heard something," Lulu called. "Could you just come check the back door again?"

"Everything is closed and locked, honey. It's just me and Heloise, and it's time for you to go to sleep now."

"Are you sure?"

"Yes, I'm sure."

"No one can get in here?"

"No one can get in here!"

"Okay . . . goodnight."

"Goodnight, sweetie."

Gerda looked exhaustedly over at Heloise. She raised both eyebrows and then mimed wringing her own neck. Then she raised her wineglass in a silent toast with Heloise.

Heloise caught herself swallowing twice before she removed the glass from her mouth. For a split second she contemplated whether she should be drinking alcohol at all and then instantly decided to have another glass.

"Goodniiiiiight!" Lulu called out again.

"Good*night*, Lulu! Settle down now!" Gerda looked at Heloise and whispered, "Oh my *God* already . . . Go to sleep, little girl!"

"No wonder she's having trouble falling asleep, what with everything that happened today."

"That's not why." Gerda shook her head. "At least that's not the *only* reason. She's been like this for weeks now. I don't know where it came from. She's just suddenly so afraid of everything."

"Are they friends, she and Lukas?"

"No, he's a good bit older than her, but he's in her friendship class."

"What's that?"

"When they start in kindergarten, they get paired with a class a couple of grades ahead of them, so the youngest kids get to know some of the bigger kids. That way they have someone to go to on the playground if they need help. It's a really nice setup, and Lulu's class has been paired with class 3X. They've had classes together once a month for a year and a half. But I don't think Lukas made all that much of an impression on her. Right now she's mostly into a fifth-grade boy named Tristan who plays basketball."

"So Lukas isn't the boy you told me about recently? The one who was acting up and ruining class for the other kids?"

"No, that's Toke. He's in Lukas's class too. It's the same fuss every time, and the staff say they can't do anything about it. They've set up this screen now in the classroom that separates him from the rest of the students so he can't see them. It's totally nuts."

"A screen?" Heloise raised an eyebrow. "What do you mean?"

"I mean a big old screen! Like in an old locker room. I guess the idea is that it's supposed to keep the peace during class time, but as soon as recess comes along, boom, he's hitting the other kids, pushing them down the stairs, kicking them . . ." Gerda shook her head. "Welcome to public school in Denmark in the twenty-first century, where the buzz words are *inclusion* and *conflict resolution*."

"But a screen doesn't help anyone."

"Oh, you don't say."

"I mean, not Toke and not the other kids in the class."

"Right again."

"Does he seriously push the other kids down the stairs?"

Gerda nodded and reached for the wine bottle. "He put Lulu in a chokehold last year."

"You're joking."

"No, really. He's a little shit, but his parents are the real mess. They've simply ruined that boy. Lukas, on the other hand . . ." Gerda pointed at the TV and sighed. "He's always so sweet when you see him. And polite. That's so rare with kids that age, that they're polite. Oh, this whole thing is so awful. Jens and Fie must be scared to death."

Heloise nodded and then lapsed into thought about what that would feel like, the ultimate fear and powerlessness. She couldn't imagine anything worse.

Gerda looked at her out of the corner of her eye. "I thought I heard you tell your police pal that you were with Jens today?"

Heloise looked up. "Huh?"

"Were you at the doctor's today?"

Heloise confirmed it with a nod.

"What for?"

Heloise shrugged. "Oh, nothing, really. I've just been feeling a little weird lately. I have this uneasiness in my chest and thought that it might be stress or something like that."

"Stress?"

"Yeah, you know . . . My job, my dad's death, and so on. That could all sort of pile up and come out in a sort of stress reaction, right?"

"Yeah, but you could have just talked to me about that."

"Well, yeah, of course I could . . ." Heloise smiled disarmingly. She wasn't used to lying to Gerda, and the words tasted bitter in her mouth. "But Dr. Bjerre suggested that I should get my metabolism checked instead. He said that an anxious feeling like that could be related to my thyroid."

"Hmm," Gerda said and studied Heloise. "Did you do that, then?"

"Do what?"

"Get your thyroid tested?"

"No, because then the school called and . . ." Heloise pointed to the TV screen. "Then I just hurried out."

Gerda looked over at the TV again and sighed heavily. "Surely they'll find the boy soon, right? I don't know if I can take any more horrors today. The idea is for this kind of thing to stop when I leave the barracks. School is usually the place where life makes sense, but now . . ." She leaned her head back and closed her eyes.

"Hard day at work?" Heloise asked.

"Mm."

"I tried calling you a couple of times."

Gerda opened her eyes again and got up. "Yeah, I saw, but I was crazy busy."

"At the barracks?"

She ran a hand through her long, dark hair. "No, I was at National Hospital most of the day."

"At the hospital?" Heloise leaned forward on the window ledge. "Why?"

"Because one of my clients is an inpatient over there right now. He is seriously messed up."

"What's wrong with him?"

"He's been struggling with PTSD for a long time, but they keep deploying him over and over again. He just came home from a special assignment yesterday and apparently fell asleep on the sofa in his living room late last night."

Gerda leaned in the doorway and stuck her hands in the pockets of her faded jeans.

"Then he woke up sometime in the middle of the night, jet-lagged and disoriented in the dark, and saw that little red diode light on the TV. And he instinctively thought it was the laser sight from a sniper rifle being pointed at him."

Heloise's eyebrows shot up. "Whoa!"

"Yes, a lot of soldiers have thoughts like that," Gerda nodded. "They're ever vigilant, always ready for battle. So this soldier, he sees something he recognizes and he follows through, based on his automatic reflex. The problem is just that when you do that, two plus two doesn't always equal four. So before he even had a chance to think about it, he ran and jumped through a window in his apartment."

Heloise covered her mouth with her hand. "Please tell me he lived on the ground floor!"

"Third floor."

"No way!"

"Yeah," Gerda nodded. "Luckily he landed in the grass, but he broke both femurs and has a deep gash in his right forearm from the window glass. And we're talking about a man who's been in war zones I don't know how many times. He's been shot at. He's killed people. He's seen several of his buddies blown to smithereens, but he himself had never suffered so much as a scratch during a deployment. He's a real tough guy. And now suddenly one day he gets so scared of his TV that he jumps from the third floor. His TV! I'm telling you, PTSD sucks."

"That's why I want to write about it," Heloise nodded. "About war trauma and delayed reactions. Do you think he'd be interested in being part of my article?"

Gerda smiled. "And talk about his drop roll? Hardly."

"What about you? Would you be willing to be part of it?"

"I can't tell you these things on the record. You know that."

"No, but you could give me a big picture view of PTSD as an expert source."

Gerda shrugged in agreement. "I think a couple of my other clients might like to talk to you. Or some of their family members. It's something that affects the entire family, this stuff."

"Would it be okay if I stopped by the barracks one of these days?"

Gerda yawned and looked at her watch. Then she nodded. "Sure. But now I've got to go to bed. I'm beat. Do you want to sleep on the sofa or are you going home?"

"I'm going to go now." Heloise got up and pointed the remote at the TV to turn off the news.

"Wait," Gerda said. "Look!"

Heloise looked at the strip of yellow text rolling across the bottom of the screen:

BREAKING NEWS: Development in the case of missing student Lukas Bjerre. Police have blocked off Kronprinsessegade.

11

T HE LID WAS partway open, making the garbage can look like a short, fat man stuck in mid-yawn.

Schäfer leaned in over the plastic edge and pointed his flashlight down into the trash. The sweet stench of household waste hit him like a knee to the groin and kicked his jet-lag nausea up a notch.

"Was it down here?" he asked the colleague who had reported the discovery in the little alley.

"Yes. The dogs alerted us as we came out of Østre Anlæg Park around seven PM and started walking down Rigensgade." The officer pointed toward the road that ran parallel to Kronprinsessegade. "It didn't take them long to find their way here."

"Have you been through the whole can? And all the trash cans here?"

The man nodded. "There's only trash left. The team from NKC is about to open the bag."

Schäfer glanced over at the group of crime scene investigators from NKC, Denmark's National Forensic Center, standing by an unmarked police SUV at the mouth of the alley. The back of the car was open and the bottom of the trunk was covered with a thick, white tarp. A black trash bag sat on top of that. It was lit by projector lamps that had been set up.

Schäfer stepped away from the row of bins and started walking back over to the flashing blue lights. He walked past the frozen yards alongside Nybodergården Nursing Home, which abutted the little lane. In the windows he could see dimly lit living rooms furnished with plush furniture and droopy balloon curtains; picture frames containing hand-tinted photos of men in uniform and children with water-combed hair. A lonesome elderly person sat in each apartment, separated from the other residents by plaster walls covered in wallpaper, and Schäfer imagined the silence in there. He remembered it from the final years of his mother's life in an equivalent catacomb of nicotine-colored degeneration. A silence that was broken only by the solitary ticking of the pendulum clock and sporadic rattling moans here and there throughout the property.

The sound of prolonged death.

Schäfer's eyes fell on a small, shriveled woman, sitting in an armchair in one of the living rooms. Her milk-white hair stuck up from her scalp in random tufts, and her lower jaw looked as if it were resting on her chest. As he passed the window he saw that the woman was staring blankly, lost in her own thoughts, fossilized, with no view other than a row of stinky garbage cans.

Schäfer thought again of the Caribbean and Saint Lucia and the life of a retiree that one day awaited him over there and sped up.

"What have we got?" he asked as he reached the NKC team.

They stood clustered around the trunk. The bag that was sitting there had holes in it, partially from rats that had gnawed through the plastic in a couple of places, partially from the scalpel, which had just sliced open the rest of the bag.

"We're going to examine it now," said a female investigator that Schäfer didn't know and then stuck a latex-gloved hand into the bag. When she pulled her hand back out, there was something on her fingertips that in the projector light looked like blood.

Schäfer instinctively tensed his stomach muscles to prepare himself for the kidney punch it would be if the next thing to come out of the bag was part of a ten-year-old's body.

Dead children were always bad. Murdered children were worse.

The investigator cut the bag open a little more and carefully pulled a sticky, light gray clump out of it.

Schäfer scrunched up his eyes.

"What are we looking at here?" he asked, his pulse throbbing in his ears.

"It's some kind of fabric," the investigator said. She smoothed out the bundle. It had begun to stiffen around the edges and resisted a little. "A . . . sweatshirt. Adult size. Something from the trash spilled on it, something sticky of some kind, that maybe leaked into the holes in the bag, but try to see these red flecks here . . ." She pointed to a few stains on the front of the sweatshirt. "I can't say for sure until we've had it analyzed, but it looks like blood."

"It's blood," Schäfer affirmed. The sweet, metallic smell was unmistakable. That must be what the dogs had tracked.

"Do we have the boy's DNA?" the investigator asked.

"We have his toothbrush and a hairbrush." Schäfer nodded. "Is there anything else hiding down there?"

The woman inspected the bag and shook her head.

"All right," Schäfer said. "Drive it over to the lab. You know what needs to happen, right?" He glanced at her through his eyebrows.

"This isn't my first day on the job," she said and smiled.

Schäfer started running down the list anyway. "We need to check the bag for fingerprints, and we need to know: What kind of trash bag is this? Is it from a roll of bags? What else is on the sweatshirt aside from blood? Fibers, hairs, etc. We need to get a DNA test done and fast. Tell the Forensic Genetics folks to park everything else and focus on this. You got that?"

She nodded.

"Good," Schäfer said. "Get going!"

He walked back to his car and got into the driver's seat. As he turned the key, he cast one last look back at the nursing home and saw that the old woman had gotten up. She was standing at the window, small and frail as a ceramic garden gnome, looking forlornly at him.

Schäfer waved once. Then he backed out of the alley and headed for police headquarters.

* * *

Schäfer tossed a sugar cube into his instant coffee and looked around for something to stir it with. There were no spoons on the tray, so he pulled a ballpoint pen out of his inside pocket and stirred the coffee a couple of times with that and then threw it on the table in front of him.

He looked at his colleagues seated around the large, oval conference table at police headquarters. The ones who had been there all evening and the ones who had not come in until midnight.

"Listen up, people," he said, leaning in over the table. "It's eight minutes after midnight, and we're having a quick briefing on the search for Lukas Bjerre. What do we know right now? Augustin?"

Lisa Augustin stood up and walked over to a large bulletin board that was hung with photos, a map of the city, a timeline, and witness statements. She pointed to the area around Frederiksstaden and Østerbro.

"We know that the missing individual was brought to school this morning by his father. They left the family home, an apartment on Heibergsgade on the boring side of Nyhavn, at around seven twenty-five AM to bike to school." She pointed to the address on the map. "Behind their building, where the family normally locks its Christiania cargo bike, they found that someone had sawed through the railing and their cargo bike was gone."

"Coincidence?" Detective Nils Petter Bertelsen asked. He sat with his tanned arms crossed, listening to the case details with concentration. Schäfer did not attribute the glow under Bertelsen's graying beard to a few weeks spent under Caribbean skies. With the exception of the deep, white grooves that radiated out from his eyes like the lines that come off the sun in a child's drawing, he maintained a year-round solarium tan. Schäfer teased him every chance he got.

"According to the family, this is the third cargo bike they've had stolen, so we don't see any immediate connection between its theft and the boy's disappearance," Augustin said. "But because of the theft, the missing boy and his father walked to school. Jens isn't one hundred percent sure of the exact drop-off time, but he said that the crossing guard was still directing the morning traffic at the crosswalk in front of the school when they went by. Therefore we know that it couldn't have been later than seven fifty when they reached this point." Lisa Augustin drew a red X on the map with a felt-tip pen. "We have witnesses who place the boy here in the schoolyard, but no one that saw him anywhere else in the school."

"Which witnesses are we talking about?" Bertelsen asked.

"We have a statement from a military psychologist, Gerda Bendix. As far as we know, she's the last person to have seen Lukas."

"What time was that?"

"She saw him walk into the school building as she was on her way out after dropping off her daughter. It was a couple of minutes past eight at that point, and after that we've got *zilch*. None of the employees at the hotel behind the school or the shops at Østerport Station remember having seen the boy during the day."

"What about the parents? Are they suspects?"

"They were both at work all day. Solid alibis."

"And that soldier woman. Has she been cleared too?"

"She's not a soldier. She's a military psychologist, and yes, she has also been cleared. All of the involved parties have been thoroughly checked out."

"Have there been any recent sex crimes in the area or any other factors along those lines that you've considered?"

"The usual assholes are out there—a couple of registered pedophiles in the neighborhood over by the Rosenborg Castle Gardens. We've been to their places and there's nothing to go after there," Augustin said.

Schäfer pitched in: "The boy told his parents about a man who had recently tried to make contact with the kids at the rec center by passing them apples over the bushes from out on Øster Voldgade. They call him the Apple Man."

"Like in the song?" Bertelsen asked.

Schäfer nodded. "Yup. So mention that name to everyone you talk to in the neighborhood. Ask people if they know the individual in question. Maybe other kids have talked about him. Someone must know who he is." He turned to Michael Voss, the information technology coordinator from Computer Forensic Investigations. "What do we know about the boy's cell phone? Anything new?"

Voss shook his bald head. "We pinged his cell phone and it's turned off. The last cell tower that picked up a signal from the phone is located here . . ." He walked over to the map of the greater Copenhagen area and put a finger in the middle of a heart-shaped splotch.

"When was that?" Schäfer asked.

"Sunday at 5:54 PM. In other words: A long time before he disappeared."

"What else?"

"We're working on reviewing the video materials from the surveillance cameras at Østerport Station to see if we can spot the boy boarding a train. But there is a ton of footage from four different platforms. It's going to take all night, maybe longer," Voss said.

"What about having a psychologist profile a possible perpetrator?" Bertelsen asked. "Do we have any plans to do that?"

"Yes," Schäfer nodded. "We've assigned that to Joakim Kjærgaard."

"What about Michala Friis? Can't we bring her in?"

Schäfer shook his head. "My impression is that Ms. Friis is too busy at the moment saving lives in the financial world to help us. And by 'saving lives' I mean 'making money.' So we'll have to make do with whatever Kjærgaard can come up with."

Schäfer grabbed hold of the edge of the big conference table to stabilize his delayed feeling of jet-lag nausea, which had reared its head over the course of the evening.

"All right," he said. "Bertelsen, you take over tonight, and this will be a pure relay, friends. If someone needs a rest, pass the torch on before you sit down. We have a lot of officers out on the streets right now, but they need all the help they can get, so get going, people. We need to find that boy!"

Nils Petter Bertelsen nodded and signaled for his partner at the end of the table to get up.

Bertelsen was an experienced detective, and Schäfer had known him since the police academy. Over the last four years, they had both picked up far younger wingmen from the deputy superintendent. Schäfer was content to have been teamed up with Lisa Augustin, while Bertelsen had been stuck with the obnoxious young Lars Bro. A classic millennial, a typical newbie who walked with his feet angled in a ten and two o'clock position. Schäfer did not envy Bertelsen at all.

"We'll meet back here again in six hours," he said and got up.

* * *

There was no moon in the sky when Schäfer pulled up in front of his little red brick house in Valby. Apart from the porch light shining above the front door, and a faint glow from the kitchen, the house was dark.

Schäfer tried not to make any noise as he let himself in. He set his file folder on the kitchen table and hung his jacket up on the back of one of the chairs. Then he opened the fridge and smiled in gratitude at the sight of the shelves, which were now packed like Tetris blocks, full of fresh fruit and vegetables, fat-marbled steaks, cold cuts, and chilled cans of beer.

Hallelujah!

He pulled a Carlsberg Classic out of the plastic six-pack holder and pulled up on the tab. Then he sat down at the table and opened the folder. Lukas's face smiled at him from the top of the pile.

How could the boy just disappear from the face of the earth without having run into a single teacher at the school, without having made a blip on a single radar?

Schäfer had torn the story apart at the seams. The father's alibi was solid, and so was the mother's for that matter. But there was something about Anne Sofie Bjerre that had left Schäfer with a funny feeling.

She was a private school teacher, and she smelled unmistakably like alcohol, but not like someone who had been to the annual Christmas party and had an ordinary hangover. This was the very faint, licorice-like fog of someone who drinks straight out of the bottle—a smell you can only identify if you've grown up with it. And Schäfer had.

He looked at the time and exhaled heavily. It was already 2:08 AM.

Four hours, he thought. That wasn't enough sleep, but it was all he was going to get.

He drank a long sip of the beer. Then he pushed the half-empty can across the table away from him, closed the case file, and headed for the bedroom.

He got into bed with all his clothes on and leaned into Connie's sleep-warmed body. Her skin was soft and beautiful, black against the white sheets.

Schäfer closed his eyes, and the bed immediately started to rock very gently, like a dinghy on a lake.

Damned jet lag.

He sat up, rearranged his position, straightened out his pillow, lay back, and started the process over again.

The third time, Connie opened her eyes a crack.

"What's wrong, babe?"

"Nothing." Schäfer leaned closer and kissed her. "Just go back to sleep."

He took a deep breath and slowly exhaled. He tried to shake off the aftermath of the air travel, even though he knew that was an impossible task.

Four hours in a seaplane the size of a slipper. Twelve in a Dreamliner in a row right by the bathrooms. It would take a few days before the ground underneath him was still again.

He closed his eyes and forced himself to think about palm trees and tropical humidity, to picture endless days of sunshine and sand between his toes as he sank further and further down into the mattress. But when he finally fell asleep, he saw only one thing in his dreams.

Lukas's face.

12

I T SNOWED OVERNIGHT.

It had not been the snowstorm the meteorologists had forewarned of, but there had been a fine, white cotton blanket over all of Copenhagen when Kevin Shinji woke up around five o'clock to check and see if there was any news on the case. Now it was seven thirty, and the morning traffic had gradually transformed Esplanaden into an ice rink of brownish gunk. He could just make out the grass through the freshly made tracks on the Citadel's sledding hills, but it was still there, the snow.

"Should we go outside, Kalaha? Into the snow?"

Kevin looked over at the caramel-brown cocker spaniel who stood eagerly beneath the brass hook where his leash hung. He scratched the dog behind the ear and broke into a song.

"Do you want to build a snowman? Come on, let's go and play!"

The dog wagged his tail and danced so his little claws scrabbled loudly against the herringbone parquet flooring.

"Well, come on then!" Kevin said patting his thighs.
"Come on!"

He clicked the hook to the collar and left the leash lying
on the floor while he put on his coat and tied the laces on
his Sorel boots, which were so heavy that it was an effort for
him to lift his feet. Then he took the cherry gloss from the
dresser and dabbed some pomade onto his puckered lips
while he continued humming the Disney song. He sucked
in his cheeks, raised one made-up eyebrow, and regarded
himself in the front hall mirror.

"How do I look?" he asked the dog, who was sitting
with its back to him, trying to push its nose into the gap
between the door and the frame, eager to get outside.

Kevin picked up the leash from the floor and undid the
chain on the door.

Down on the street they had to wait for an unmarked
police car that zoomed past with a light flashing in the
windshield, and once again Kevin felt incredibly sad.
According to the morning news, the police still hadn't
found Lukas, and Kevin couldn't help feeling a little guilty.
If he had reacted right away when he had discovered that
Lukas was gone, maybe the police would have had a better
chance of finding him. Every minute counted in a case like
this, he knew that, and maybe he had wasted enough of
them in the staff restroom that it would have made a difference. He hadn't been paying attention as he sat there scrolling through Facebook, and before he knew it, twenty
minutes had passed from when he had marked the boy
absent until he had called the parents.

What if he had called right away? Would that have
made a difference?

He crossed the street and let Kalaha off the leash in
Churchill Park, where the dog ran in circles chasing some
imaginary prey. The dog continued contentedly up to the

bunker in the middle of the lawn, sniffing tree trunks and dirty, foul-smelling things in the grass, and then caught up with Kevin, who had crossed the bridge to the Citadel and was heading up the gravel path by King's Gate.

"Come on, pups, let's get this over with so we can go home again. It's way too cold out here today."

Kevin clicked the leash back onto the dog's collar. He wiped his running eyes, pulled his jacket tighter at the neck, and headed toward the windmill. They would have to make do with a quick walk today, he decided. Instead of their usual walk down to the marina, he would just turn around by the windmill.

Kevin sped up and felt Kalaha resisting. He gave the leash a loving tug, but the dog wouldn't budge. He looked back and discovered that its attention was focused on a point down by the foot of the embankment.

He followed the dog's gaze and stiffened.

There, a boy and a girl were standing on the recently frozen surface of the moat and throwing snowballs at each other. Kevin knew that the ice was too thin to be able to move around safely on it. It was covered in snow and might look like it was frozen solid at the water's edge, but from Kevin's position on the top of the bank, he could see that in the middle, not far from where the children were, there was a dark circle of slushy brash ice.

"No, no, no! What are they thinking?" he mumbled without taking his eyes off the children. Then he yelled. "Hey, you can't go out there. Can you come back off the ice?!"

The kids, whom Kevin estimated to be around ten to twelve, didn't hear his warning. Instead, the boy pulled the girl farther out onto the ice and tickled her so she squealed in delight and flailed her arms around, not hitting anything. She twisted free of the boy's grasp and squatted down, where she scraped up enough snow in her slightly oversized mittens to make a snowball. She got up and took a couple of steps farther out toward the dark patch as she hunted for ammunition.

"*Hey!*" Kevin called again, this time louder, putting a hand on his hip. "The ice is too thin. Come back to shore!"

Still no reaction.

Unmoved, the girl threw the snowball at the boy, who ducked and laughed.

Kevin shook his head, annoyed. "Ugh, I can't believe this!"

He started moving down the slope and looked back over his shoulder.

"Stay!" he ordered the dog, who politely sat down in the snow, only to then immediately lift his rear end back up again off the cold ground.

Kevin took a couple of cautious steps but halfway down the combination of the slope and his heavy boots forced him into a run. He lost his balance, fell, and slid the rest of the way, so the snow flew up into his face and got up underneath his jacket.

He stood up and smoothed out his clothes, embarrassed. Then he rapidly strode over to the edge of the moat.

"*You two!*" he yelled, stomping furiously. His shame at having fallen came out as hysterical rage.

The kids looked up in fear.

"Come back here! It's dangerous out there!"

The kids exchanged skeptical looks and the girl started moving back toward the shore, but the boy wasn't going to let anyone order him around.

He held his head high and said, "You're not the boss of us!"

"I'm a grownup, so I decide," Kevin said. "And I say you can't be out there."

"But we're just playing," the girl said, trying to smooth things over.

"Yes, sweetie, but it's not safe out there." Kevin bent down toward her. "If you fall in, you could drown, because the water is very, very cold. You understand that, don't you?"

The girl nodded and looked down at her green lined rubber boots.

"Um, hello? There's *ice* on the water, you know," the boy yelled, signaling with a patronizing look that he didn't acknowledge Kevin's authority.

Kevin stood back up to his full height and walked right up to the water's edge.

"Yes, that may well be, but a big, fat boy like you, you're risking your life out there. The ice is way too thin."

Kevin made a show of scraping his heavy boot over the ice, removing the thin layer of snow like a windshield wiper.

"See for yourself!" He pointed triumphantly down in front of him, so the boy could see that he was right. "And it is super dangerous to . . ."

Kevin stopped mid-sentence and squinted. He hesitantly bent over and tried to focus on the thing that had caught his attention under the ice.

It was dangerously thin, the ice layer, just as he had said, and he could see little air bubbles underneath. But there was also something else down there . . .

"What is it?" the boy asked, sensing that something was up. Curious, he came a couple of steps closer to Kevin.

Kevin didn't respond.

What the heck was that down there?

He squatted down and reached out with his hand to sweep the last of the snowflakes off the surface. He leaned closer to the ice, trying to decode the pattern he could see down in the dark water.

Then his eyes widened.

For a brief instant he was completely immobile. His body screamed one big, silent scream, as he stared at the face under the ice.

The snow crept in under his collar and the edge of his pants when he fell over backward, scooting himself away from the water's edge with his feet.

"*Back!*" he screamed at the kids. "*Get back!*"

This time the boy obeyed without asking questions. He walked over to the girl in quick, stiff strides and took her by the hand.

Kevin turned over onto all fours and crawled away from the shoreline. He stood up and fumbled for his phone in his pocket. A paralyzing fear grabbed him around the neck and squeezed while he waited for the call to go through.

"Police? I need help!" he sobbed almost soundlessly into the phone. "I found him. I found Lukas."

13

IT FELT LIKE a lightning strike every time the shovel hit the ground. The bolt of pain branched into an explosive zigzag from Finn's right elbow up to his clenched jaws. The frozen dirt was hard as a rock wall, and after an hour the hole still wasn't big enough.

Finn was running out of strength.

He pulled his knife out of its leather sheath in his old scouting belt and started hacking at the ground with wild, vicious motions. One last big desperate push to loosen the dirt, but it was still going too slowly.

He got up and, his energy drained, walked into the barn behind the main building and found a rusty garden mattock in the tool shed. Then he walked back to the hole, made sure that no one was watching him, and continued hacking away at it.

The tears and snot raced each other in the biting morning wind, and after yet another hour he had at long last managed to make a nice, small burial chamber.

Finn sank down on his knees in front of the hole and panted in short, winded gasps. He had seen on the news that the police were involved in the case, and now he was scared.

How could he have been so stupid? Why couldn't he just have left it alone? He knew it was wrong, but . . .

He started slapping himself on the face.

You're so dumb, dumb, dumb.

Eventually he stopped hitting himself and just sat there rocking back and forth, crying. A little because of the cold and exhaustion, but mostly because it was so unfair, the whole thing. He was never allowed to do anything fun.

"*Finn?*" The voice blared from the courtyard in front of the farm, hoarse and terrifying. "Finn, where are you? Come here!"

Finn jumped to his feet and wiped his hands on his pants. He ran around the building and found his mother, who was standing in the middle of the courtyard looking for him. He instinctively lowered his head when he saw her.

"What are you doing out here, you fool?" she said, putting her hands on her hips.

"Nothing," Finn said. He slowed down as he approached her. "I just couldn't sleep anymore."

"Come over here," she ordered, waving him over to her. "And pick up the pace."

Finn reluctantly approached her. He watched her as he walked. Her red apron fit tightly and was tied surprisingly high up on her torso, all the way up by her armpits, as if her waist began right underneath her large breasts. Her cheeks hung heavily on her face, grayish and wrinkled.

She looked old, Finn thought, old and deformed, and he hated everything about her.

"Do you have any idea what you look like?" She studied him angrily from head to toe. "You're filthy! Your face and your clothes. What in the world have you been doing?"

She spat on the corner of her apron and reached out to wipe the dirt off Finn's cheek.

Finn instinctively pulled his head back.

Her eyes flared wide in anger, and she grabbed his chin with a cold hand. "What are you thinking?" She took a firmer hold, mashing Finn's cheeks together so he got a faint taste of blood. "You just click your heels together when I say something, you understand?" She leaned closer to him and scrunched up her eyes. "Or maybe you think you should have some say here in this house?"

Finn managed to shake his head.

"That's right," she nodded. "You have no say. None! 'Cause you're stupid, Finn, an idiot. Do you understand?"

Finn nodded.

"And you look like a filthy foreigner with all that dirt on your face. Into the shower with you," she commanded and pushed him into the main house as she went. "You'd better make it quick, Finn. You need to leave in half an hour if you're going to be on time."

"Yes, Mother," Finn said.

He scowled over at the barn as he walked. Now he wouldn't have time to finish before he had to go to work.

It would have to wait until later.

CHAPTER

14

"WHY ARE YOU drinking that shit?"

"Excuse me?"

"Milk." Lisa Augustin nodded at the carton, sitting on the desk next to Schäfer. "Why are you drinking that?"

He shrugged. "It's good for the bones?"

"It's a hormone drink for baby cows."

"What is your point?"

"Seriously? It's full of bacteria. And fat. It's disgusting."

Schäfer's eyes fell on Augustin's sandwich, where pale slices of ham poked out between the lettuce.

"With all due respect, I don't take dietary advice from someone who is willingly stuffing a slaughterhouse scrapfest sandwich into their gullet."

"I'll have you know that this is organic ham from Normandy." Augustin lifted the top piece of bread like a magician who wanted to reveal the secret behind a card trick.

"It's meat waste," Schäfer said dryly.

She waved his comment away. "Ugh, whatever."

"Just finish eating. Morning meeting starts in five minutes."

The phone on the big double desk rang, and they both reached for it. Augustin got there first and flashed Schäfer a gloating smile.

"Too slow."

She turned halfway around in her desk chair and answered the call with her back to Schäfer.

He immediately reached for the milk carton and quickly poured a dash of hormone drink into her soy latte.

Augustin hung up and said, "Meeting's canceled!"

Schäfer looked up. "Why? What's going on?"

"The boy's been found."

Schäfer got to his feet and put on his bomber jacket in one quick, fluid motion.

"Where?"

Augustin took a quick drink from her coffee.

"In the moat at the Citadel."

* * *

The divers were all wearing identical black wetsuits, and their faces were hidden behind black face masks. Still, it was clear which ones were from the Frogman Corps and which ones were from the Greater Copenhagen Fire Department. The latter group included both men and women of varying sizes and builds, while the frogmen were all the same sex and had the same silhouette: shoulders that were as wide as highways, calves as big as Christmas hams, and necks you could split firewood on. They looked like steroid machines, robots from a futuristic movie, whenever they popped up at the surface of the water. Mechanical, experienced, impossible to shake.

A jet ski–sized ice breaker had created a long swimming lane the whole way around the fortress's star-shaped moat, where the divers periodically stuck up their heads, like the dorsal fins of a pack of sharks.

On the muddy bottom they had found a couple of rusty bicycles, a moped, a baby car seat, bottles, glasses, shoes, keys, sunglasses, and other junk.

But no body.

"He's not here," one of the frogmen said. "We would have found him if he was. If he was tossed into the moat, he would either have sunk to the bottom if he was tied to something that could pull him down—an iron chain or something like that—or he would be floating on the surface, just beneath the ice."

"Couldn't he have drifted out to sea?" Augustin asked, nodding toward Øresund on the far side of the Citadel.

The frogman shook his head so that water droplets flew in all directions.

"The water inside the moat is pretty much still," he explained. "There's no current that could make anything the size of a human being float around in here, and even if there was, we would have found him in the grating at the outlet to the harbor. Unless you're the size of a sardine, you can't get out of here. It's closed off the whole way around, like an aquarium." He did a 360-degree helicopter swing with his muscular arm.

Schäfer nodded. "Okay, but we need to be absolutely certain, so you've got to go back down. Check and double-check. Go over the bottom with a fine-tooth comb. We can't overlook anything."

Lukas Bjerre's jacket, which had been found under the ice, had been picked up by the forensic techs and driven out for evidence analysis by the NKC.

Schäfer turned toward the entrance to the Citadel, where he could see the teacher from Nyholm School through the windows of a police car. He walked over and opened the car door.

"Could you come out here for a sec?"

The man staggered out of the car with a little dog in his arms. His smeared mascara and the golden thermal blanket he had around his shoulders made him look like a young Asian Liberace wearing a Las Vegas show cape.

"I understand you're the one who found the jacket," Schäfer said.

"Yes," the man nodded. "I was down by the water, and then I spotted the blond hair under the ice. And the eyes. Lukas always wears that Justin Bieber jacket, so I thought that . . ." He paused and bit his trembling bottom lip.

Over the teacher's shoulder, Schäfer could see the growing group of people who had flocked to the opposite side of the police tape at the entrance to the Citadel. They were all attentively watching the divers in the water. All except for one, a man wearing a red cap, glasses with yellow-tinted lenses, and dressed in something Schäfer would describe as a pilot's suit. The man was staring, strangely engrossed, in the opposite direction toward a point somewhere to Schäfer's right.

Schäfer turned his head that way but didn't see anything other than the many policemen wandering like weevils in a line formation up and down the snow-covered embankment.

"Have you found Lukas?" the teacher asked. A black tear slid down his cheek. "Is he dead?"

Schäfer was about to answer when he heard a loud yell from one of the investigators.

Schäfer started running over toward the sound.

"What is it?" he called out. "What have we got?"

"There's something over here."

The investigator led Schäfer over to some bushes and pointed to a laurel bush. The evergreen leaves acted as hundreds of little cocktail umbrellas, protecting a small cave in the ground right by the trunk.

Schäfer reached out and pulled the branches aside. It looked as if the things had just been tossed in there. As if someone had turned the bag upside down and shaken out the contents.

"We have a pencil case, schoolbooks, a lunch box," the crime scene investigator said. He pulled out a hardcover math book and read the name on the name plate: "It says 'Lukas, Class 3X.'"

The crime scene investigator grabbed the sausage-shaped black leather pencil case. The case was stretched taut around the angular contents, looking like a black snake that had swallowed a shoebox.

He unzipped it and looked inside.

"Bingo!" he said and held the pencil case out to Schäfer.

There was an iPhone inside, one of the larger ones. A 6 Plus or 7 Plus, Schäfer estimated. He took out his own phone and called Michael Voss from the Computer Forensic Investigations section.

"Voss, drop what you're working on," he said. "We found the boy's phone, and I'm going to have it brought to you right away."

Schäfer hung up and looked back over at the crowd behind the barricade. More people had gathered, and even from this distance he recognized several reporters from the tabloids, their eyes agleam with anticipation at the prospect of death porn.

Damned rats, Schäfer thought.

His eyes scanned the other faces in the crowd. There were women and children. Tourists who looked like they had just arrived on the latest cruise ship. Old men with their hands clasped behind their backs.

They were all watching the show on the other side of the police barricade, curious to see what would happen next.

Schäfer scanned the faces yet again, looking for what had given him the strange knot in his stomach before, a hunch.

The man in the pilot's suit was gone.

15

THE WHEELS SLID out from under Heloise, and she gave up on biking any farther on the icy road. It had started snowing again. Fluffy flakes fell heavily from the sky in vertical columns, like anemone flower heads on a string. She pushed her bike the last few hundred yards down Ryvangs Allé and looked over at Svanemøllen Barracks on the other side of the train tracks.

Even though she could see uniformed soldiers on the grounds, the place didn't have much in common with West Point. It was more like a LEGO version of a military base; the roofs of the tower's parapets looked like a harmless lower jaw of baby teeth surrounded by rust-red brickwork gums.

It wasn't exactly something that screamed superior force, not something that seemed particularly menacing. The sight reminded Heloise that the Danish military's disarmament since World War II was one of the most frightening realities of all time. If the Russians come, we're screwed, she thought.

She parked her bike in front of the barracks' trauma center and took the stairs up one floor in just a few long strides. She had texted Gerda that morning that she would drop by around ten o'clock but hadn't received a response. Heloise hoped to catch her between appointments, so they could grab a quick cup of coffee and have a chat.

She unwound the scarf from around her neck as she reached Gerda's floor and was just about to push open the glass door to the therapy department when she felt a familiar rumble in her pocket. She recognized the number on her cell phone as one belonging to *Demokratisk Dagblad* and answered it, a little out of breath.

"Kaldan speaking."

"This is Karen."

"Hi, Karen. I'm glad you called," Heloise said, unzipping her leather jacket. "I just arrived at Svanemøllen Barracks, and I want to find out if we can set aside space for an interview with a veteran who . . ."

"No, drop that story," Karen Aagaard said.

Heloise contemplated for a second how to word her response. It was understandably a personal tragedy for Karen that her son had to go to war, but the paper had always selected its stories based on five news criteria: timeliness, relevance, conflict, identification, and sensation. They couldn't suddenly start taking an editor's private family circumstances into consideration, Heloise thought.

"Look, Karen, I understand that you don't want to read about soldiers with PTSD right now," Heloise began. "But I think that . . ."

"That doesn't have anything to do with it," Aagaard interrupted. "Mikkelsen and I are sitting here talking about the boy who disappeared, and we just realized that your friend is the lead detective on the case, that guy, Erik Schäfer."

"So what?" Heloise already knew what was coming when the editor-in-chief got involved. Sensation, check! Increased newspaper sales, check!

"That means that you have access to an important source for this case," Aagaard said. "Find out what's going on—whether there's anything the press doesn't know about yet. So far we've assigned the newsroom to cover the story, but if it suddenly blows up—if the boy is found dead—then we need as many details nailed down as possible."

Through the glass door to the hallway, Heloise saw Gerda's office door open. Heloise saw her shake hands with a young man dressed in camo. The man saluted Gerda and then continued down the hall and out of view.

"I'm *friends* with Schäfer," Heloise responded. "But that doesn't mean that he tells me about the cases he's working on."

"Then you need to get him to open up."

"How?"

"You're a woman. Think of something."

Heloise's eyebrows shot up. "You're kidding, right?"

"Relax. I didn't say you should take your clothes off. I said, think of something. Use your imagination! It's your job to dig up the stories, Heloise, and we want this story."

"Like I said, I'm already at the barracks, so when I'm done here, I'll stop by . . ."

Heloise didn't have time to say any more before she realized that Karen Aagaard had already hung up. She put away her phone and was about to walk in when she saw a man she didn't know with dark hair come out of an office and approach Gerda, who was standing in the hallway smiling at him.

There was something about his facial expression that gave Heloise pause. She put a hand on the door handle, but was hesitant to go in.

The man reached Gerda. She spoke to him, and his face lit up in a flirtatious smile.

Something felt wrong.

The man peered up and down the deserted hallway and then leaned in toward Gerda. His cheek grazed hers, but she didn't pull her head back. Instead, she closed her eyes and her smile widened. The man whispered something and allowed a far-too-familiar hand to slide from Gerda's neck down to the small of her back, where it lingered for a second. Then he walked away down the hallway, and Gerda disappeared back into her office.

Heloise stood still as acidic saliva filled her mouth.

Then she pushed open the glass door with an indignant shove.

16

"WHAT THE HELL are you doing?"

Heloise had opened the door to Gerda's office without knocking. She stood in the doorway now, thoughtfully eyeing her friend, the girl she had known since kindergarten, the woman who, over the years, had become her closest family, her *only* family.

Gerda looked up in surprise and smiled. "Oh, hi! You're here?"

Then the echo of Heloise's question reached her ears, and she furrowed her dark brows.

"What am I *doing*? What do you mean?"

Heloise's face stiffened in indignation. "You know what I mean."

Gerda quickly averted her gaze. Then her eyes met Heloise's again.

"I'm not quite following . . ."

Heloise crossed her arms in front of her chest and cocked her head slightly.

"Um, that guy you were just talking to . . ." She nodded to the hallway. "Who's he?"

"Who's *who*?" Gerda flung up her hands. "I've talked to a lot of clients today."

Heloise scrunched up her eyes. "Do you think I'm an idiot? That guy you were just rubbing up against. Who's he?"

"Kareem?" Gerda pointed to the office next to hers. "He's just a colleague. He's a trauma psychologist. We work together."

"I *saw* you. I know you, Gerda. I know your body language. You're screwing him."

Heloise could tell from the way the color of Gerda's eyes changed that she knew she'd been caught.

Gerda didn't say anything. She walked over and sat on the windowsill with her back to Heloise.

"What are you thinking?" Heloise said. "What about Christian?"

"Yes, what *about* Christian?" Gerda asked. She was staring out at a squad of young soldiers who ran by the building while a sergeant kept time by bellowing a bawdy sailor's song. Then she turned to Heloise. Her easygoing façade had vanished; her smile was now stiff and standoffish. She nodded defiantly. "Where did *he* go? I'll tell you: He's in fucking Denver. And next week, he's in Tokyo. And then no doubt he'll stop by Melbourne and Aspen and wherever else. If we're lucky, he'll be home for a couple of days around Easter."

Heloise shook her head in disapproval. "And he trusts you while he's away."

Gerda laughed a short, joyless laugh. "How would you know? You always see only what you want to see."

"*I* trusted you."

"You *trusted* me? Past tense? I've never betrayed your trust, Heloise, and this . . ." She put a hand over her heart and waved the other one around. "With all due respect, this doesn't concern you."

"Oh, but it does," Heloise insisted. "The fact that apparently you're the type of person who might decide to cheat on the people who are closest to you *does* concern me. When you pretend to be one thing and then lead a secret life behind Christian's back—behind *my* back—then it does concern me. And if there's one thing I won't accept, it's—"

"Don't project that nonsense onto me." Instead of raising her voice, Gerda's had dropped down into a low, almost guttural tone. "Those are *your* issues, Heloise. That's about you and your past, not about me."

"Perhaps." Heloise nodded. "But I need the people I surround myself with to be who they say they are. I can't live with secrets. You're married, Gerda. Act like it, damn it!"

"My nuclear family was not created for your sake. Do you understand how messed up it is, that you would expect that of me?"

"What the hell is that supposed to mean?"

"That means that you've made up your mind that the whole world is shit and that Christian, Lulu, and I are the only things that make any sense. But I can't live up to that ideal, Heloise. I can't be the only thing in the world that makes any sense to you. I don't *want* to be the only thing in the world that makes sense to you. I love you, but do you have any idea how much responsibility you're piling onto my shoulders?"

"You need to tell Christian the truth," Heloise repeated stubbornly. "He trusts you."

"HE'S NEVER HOME!"

Gerda had stood up. There were fine, white lines of rage around her nostrils. Her gaze was fixed, her eyes dry as rockwool.

"He made a choice not to be here with us, don't you see? Every time he boards yet another airplane, he's choosing something other than Lulu and me. And it's very possible that he has not yet realized that that kind of thing has consequences, but it does, and he's going to find that out. But it will be when *I* feel like telling him—not you. So don't you come here and play cop with me and demand that my life be an open book. You don't share everything with me, either."

"I never lie to you."

"Oh yeah?" Gerda crossed her arms. "What was it that you said you went to the doctor about yesterday? Stress, wasn't that what you said?"

Heloise blinked a couple of times. Then she turned around and left the room.

"Okay, so the rules only apply to me, is that it?" Gerda called after her. "You're a hypocrite, Heloise."

17

"WE'VE TAKEN THE phone apart."

Michael Voss plunked a four-finger-thick stack of papers onto the desk in front of Schäfer and Augustin. Beads of sweat trickled out on his bald egg, like little transparent flower buds.

"That was fast," Schäfer said, impressed, making himself comfortable in his chair in front of the stack.

Voss and his colleagues from the Computer Forensic Investigations section had been busy investigating Lukas's cell phone since it had been found at the Citadel two hours earlier.

Voss now pointed at the stack of papers in front of him.

"We extracted all the contents from the phone, and this is a summary of all the boy's incoming and outgoing calls and texts over the last four months. His Google search history, photos and documents, social media profiles, streaming and search histories from Netflix, HBO, YouTube—you name it."

"That seems pretty hefty," Augustin remarked. "How can there be so many pages?"

"We're talking about a kid from the online generation, so there's page after page of searches and downloads. They don't do much other than stare at their cell phones."

Augustin pulled the stack of papers closer. She started flipping through, slowly, her eyes meticulously scanning the pages.

"Warcraft . . . war games . . . wizard power," she rattled off. "Searches for role-playing gear, war games, samurai swords . . . Did you find anything conspicuous?" she asked, without looking up from the papers.

"We still haven't gone through most of it yet. Like I said, we've been moving quickly, but so far the most interesting thing I've seen is the boy's Instagram account."

"His Instagram account?" Augustin raised a judging eyebrow and looked up at Voss. "The boy's ten years old. Why does he have an Instagram account?"

"There's absolutely nothing unusual about that. What *is* a little atypical for someone Lukas's age is how topic-specific his posts are."

"Topic-specific?" Schäfer asked. "What do you mean by that?"

"There's a lot of Insta types out there," Voss explained. "Most people upload photos of a lot of different topics to their profile: sunsets, birthdays, vacations, Halloween costumes, nature—a mix of everyday life. But there's also a lot of Instagrammers who keep their profiles to one consistent topic. There are foodies who only share pictures of lumpfish caviar and that kind of thing. Then there are cake ladies, soccer bros, selfie girls, car nerds, fashionistas, and so on."

"And?" Schäfer spun his index finger around in impatient circled to get him to speed up his explanation. "What does this have to do with our victim?"

"Lukas Bjerre's Instagram profile is dedicated to . . ." Voss paused for effect and then point to his cheeks. "*Faces!*"

"I'm sorry?"

"Faces! More specifically to a phenomenon called pareidolia."

Schäfer raised one eyebrow. "Parabolia?"

"No, this doesn't have anything to do with parabolic antennae. It's called par-ei-do-lia," Voss enunciated.

"What the hell is that?"

"It's a psychological phenomenon in which random patterns are interpreted as faces."

Schäfer and Augustin looked at each other blankly.

"I'm sorry?" Schäfer asked running a tired hand over his eyes. "Patterns as faces?"

"Yes. So, you see a thing that doesn't have anything to do with a face, but for some reason or other, your eye decodes it as if it did."

Voss pulled a folder out of his bag and took out some photos, which he pushed across the desk.

"Look at this! No doubt you're familiar with the stories about how some old lady in Colombia saw the Virgin Mary in an oil slick and believed it was a personal greeting from the powers that be. And a woman from Missouri identified Donald Trump's face in a butter container. People claim to see the devil in a building's façade, that kind of thing."

Schäfer gathered up the photos.

He was aware of the stories, and even though the photo of the tub of butter clearly contained just random ripples in the churned cream, the first thing he thought of was indeed Trump's fish mouth and billowing combover.

"No one knows what causes pareidolia," Voss said. "But researchers think that we're genetically programmed to decode patterns as facial features. They think it comes from back when people were running around with clubs and needed to be on their guard at all times. When you spotted someone out in the jungle, you needed to make a split-second decision: Is that a tiger or a tree trunk in the bushes over there, or what the hell is that? Basically, am I in danger?"

Voss waved his broad hands around in the air as he spoke.

"In other words, pareidolia is about being ready to fight. So we interpret some patterns as faces for the split second it takes us to recognize that, no, phew, that's just a coconut."

"And Lukas is—what?—a student of this phenomenon?" Schäfer asked.

"I don't know if he has studied it, but he's certainly interested in it."

"Again—he's only ten years old," Augustin said. "How is he even aware of this face thing?"

"You don't need to be a brain surgeon to know about it. Pareidolia has been trending on Instagram for several years. People take pictures of things that look like faces: electrical outlets, apples, the foam on a latte, clouds, manhole covers, *anything* at all that looks as if it has two eyes and a mouth. So no doubt Lukas just saw the phenomenon online and thought it was fun running around town finding faces with his iPhone."

"I'm still not quite following," Schäfer said skeptically, scratching his neck. "You said an apple? But apples don't have eyes or mouths."

"A perfect apple doesn't, no. But if it's lumpy and brown in certain spots, and those blemishes are positioned so that you've got a bit of a colon-hyphen-close-parentheses . . ." Voss drew a smiley in the air with a chubby pointer finger. "Then you'll interpret that as a face."

He took out his phone and typed something. Then he passed the phone to Schäfer.

"Maybe you have to see it to understand. This is Lukas's Instagram account."

Schäfer's eyes slid over the screen. He slowly scrolled down with one finger.

It appeared that the account had been created nine months earlier under the profile name *Facehunter8*. Lukas had shared a total of 227 pictures with his 198 followers. All the pictures looked like faces, and Schäfer could suddenly see the angry eyes in an Audi RS6's headlights, a cross-eyed octopus in a coatrack, a school backpack with the zipper open so that it looked like a big, shocked mouth.

His eyes stopped on the most recent picture on the page.

It had been uploaded two days earlier and depicted an old barn door with two round porthole-like windows staring like eyes and a metal bolt that looked like a closed mouth.

"Instagrammers use hashtags to help their posts surface to other people with similar interests," Voss explained. "Pareidolia enthusiasts use the hashtags #iseefaces or simply #pareidolia. There's more than a half million photos on Instagram tagged with #iseefaces."

Schäfer zoomed in on the barn door. The picture was accompanied by the hashtags Voss had mentioned, but there were also other words. Words that made Schäfer's gums itch.

#monster #die #satan #evil #Iwillkillyou

He ran a flat hand over his mouth and held the picture up for Voss and Augustin to see.

His gaze traveled from the one to the other.

"Where was this picture taken?"

18

"Is it just me or does this look like a dead body that's been lying in the water for too long?"

Journalist Mogens Bøttger prodded the overcooked ham with the metal tongs before moving on in the newspaper's cafeteria, hunting for one last addition to his lunch.

His plate was already full and looked like a brunch buffet at a suburban café: a schizophrenic hodgepodge of lackluster appetizers that did not go together at all. There was both tuna salad and warm liverwurst. Mini pancakes, blue cheese, and pineapple slices. A blob of tartar sauce and a sausage roll.

"Ah!" he said enthusiastically and helped himself to a slice of smoked salmon from the buffet.

"I'll find us a table," Heloise said and carried her tomato soup over to the open table by the window that she had spotted at the far end of the cafeteria. She sat down with her back to the room and looked down at Store Strandstræde, where people were cautiously making their way along the slick, icy sidewalks carrying bags full of groceries and steaming coffees.

Adrenaline still tingled uncomfortably in her body, like little firecrackers of indignation that kept going off at random locations in her bloodstream. She kept half an eye on her phone the whole time, but there hadn't been a peep out of Gerda since Heloise had left the barracks.

Heloise brought a spoonful of soup to her lips and blew on it. Out of the corner of her eye she spotted food critic Kaj Clevin's distended gut. He slowly limped closer with his lunch that he had brought from home, then stopped and scanned the employee cafeteria for somewhere to sit.

Heloise turned away, hoping that he would move on. The last time she and Mogens had had the pleasure of his company, he had entertained them with a *far* too detailed anecdote about a knee operation that he had recently undergone. The word "cartilage" had been uttered so many times over Heloise's slightly underdone roast pork with parsley sauce that she didn't think she would ever be able to eat pork again without thinking of Kaj Clevin's osteoarthritis.

She sensed that he had limped on and exhaled in relief.

"Well, what's up?" Mogens set his tray on the table next to theirs and started arranging his meal across the table from Heloise.

"What's up with what?" she asked, tasting her soup. It was way too sweet, a bit thin and devoid of the least bit of anything that had ever been a proper vegetable.

"How's the soldier story coming?"

"It's dead. Karen told me to drop it. She wants me to cover the Lukas Bjerre case instead."

"That makes sense," Mogens nodded and ate a pancake. It was typical of him to start with the sweets. "That story is hotter right now, a giant carrot to lure in the readers. I guarantee you that article will be number one on the website's most read list once it's published."

"No doubt," Heloise nodded. "But when did we turn into such a tabloid?"

"Since we—like all the other newspapers—started having problems with the only thing that matters: the money, honey!"

"Yeah, yeah. I know there needs to be money in the till. But don't you think it's problematic for Karen to cancel a story that's societally important and tell me I need to cover some tabloid story instead?"

"Well, I don't know. That's just the way it is." He reached for the glass of apple juice he had poured himself.

"That's just the way it is?" Heloise laughed. "Okay, what are you, a politician now? Seriously, wouldn't you be annoyed if Karen suddenly came and pulled the plug on your statistics story?"

Mogens smiled smugly. "She would never do that."

"Because you're just that good, you mean?"

He shrugged nonchalantly. "Well, that, plus I've found new sources in the police who are willing to make a public statement, naming names—sources who are high up in the hierarchy. I'm going to roast the national police commissioner over a slow fire when this story breaks—like a suckling pig with an apple in its mouth and the whole pigsty to boot! And that is exactly the kind of thing that makes Mikkelsen clap his fat little editor-in-chief hands. And if Mikkelsen's happy, Karen's happy."

"Well, good for you, kiss ass."

Mogens laughed. "Why so bitter? I honestly can't understand why you'd rather write about a couple of soldiers who lost their marbles than cover the Lukas Bjerre case."

"Don't you think it's a huge conflict of interest if I'm friends with the head of the investigation?"

"Aren't you also friends with that sex bomb lady you're planning to interview for your PTSD piece?"

Heloise received a text right then and had time to forgive Gerda a thousand times over before she had even opened the message. But once she had read it, her anger returned. It wasn't from Gerda. It was from Martin.

Looking forward to seeing you tonight. I'll pick you up at 6:30 sharp. Kisses, M.

"Everything okay?" Mogens asked.

"Yes." Heloise pushed her soup bowl away. "But is it okay if I leave you alone here with your smorgasbord?"

"Of course. Are you going to the Citadel?"

Heloise furrowed her brow. "Why? What's going on at the Citadel?"

"Weren't you going to cover the story about that boy who disappeared?"

"Yeah, it doesn't seem like I have any choice." She got up and pushed in her chair. "But what does that have to do with the Citadel?"

"One of my sources at police headquarters tipped me off this morning. They found something over there."

"Well, since you've apparently got a much better handle on the story than I do, couldn't you just write the article for me? Then I'll just go drink until I pass out."

"Hell no!" Mogens stuck his fork into a slice of pineapple. "If you're going out drinking, I'm coming with you!"

19

E VEN THOUGH CHRISTMAS was long over, the candied apples were still on display atop the counter in Nyhavn, and the sweet scent of mulled wine hung heavy in the air. Schäfer and Augustin passed the vendor booths and then waited as an armada of tourists lurched past on Segways like a flock of stray Minions. They moved in uncontrolled, random jolts, clearly inexperienced on the devices.

"Those things ought to be banned," Schäfer said.

"I hear you," Augustin nodded. "Tourists on e-bikes and Segways and whatever other oddball transportation devices—it's nuts."

"Oh, by the way," Schäfer said as they crossed the street. "When we get into the Bjerre family's home, we'll go through the boy's room and look for anything that seems like it might be important to the case. But we'll keep our cards close."

Augustin nodded.

"There's already a ton of media coverage. I don't want the leads we're looking into right now to be leaked, because you know what'll happen then."

"A waste of everyone's time."

"Exactly." Schäfer nodded.

In cases that received media attention, one of the biggest challenges the police faced was dealing with all the false confessions that popped up. Just before Schäfer's trip to Saint Lucia, he had researched a case where an elderly woman had been knocked to the ground in a laundromat in Christianshavn, a mugging that had wound up becoming involuntary manslaughter. When she fell, the woman, who had been whacked in the back with a baseball bat, had hit her forehead on the edge of a table and had ended up bleeding to death on the floor. There had been no fewer than four confessions in the case, but none of the confessors had realized what only the police and the actual perpetrator knew:

That the culprit was a woman.

Video recordings from the laundromat showed very clearly that it was a woman who had struck the elderly woman. A detail that the public never found out about, and that had made it easy to dismiss the four men who had turned up at police headquarters during the investigation looking for notoriety.

In some strange way, Schäfer had a far easier time understanding people who committed crimes than people who confessed to crimes they hadn't had anything to do with. But that's just how the world was, he thought. Crazy.

They found the address they were looking for and Schäfer pressed the buzzer with his thumb. He stood in front of the camera, which hung beside the front door, so they could identify him from their apartment. They were buzzed in and took the elevator—an old, creaky one, which looked like a prop out of *The Great Gatsby*—to the fourth floor, where they were met by an elderly woman in the doorway to the apartment.

She was a petite woman dressed in a pair of loose-fitting black leather pants and a multicolored sweater with sleeves that seemed short on her thin arms. The look in her ice-blue eyes was resolute but anxious. The gray-brown roots of her coal-black mane revealed that her hair had been dyed—and not recently.

Schäfer cast a quick glance at the last name on the brass plate next to the door and nodded politely to the woman.

"The Bjerre family?" he asked.

"Yes, please come in."

The woman stepped into the little entryway and then stepped back to let them pass.

"It's in here. I'm Marianne," she said, holding out her hand. Her voice sounded raspy, like a lifelong smoker's. "I'm Lukas's grandmother."

She led them into the kitchen, and Schäfer looked around.

The apartment was meticulously furnished, tasteful and impersonal like a display window. Plants bulged vigorously in crenellated white pots on the kitchen table next to Mason jars filled with granola, oats, and wild rice. The candles in the cubical Kubus candleholders had never been lit, and a Kay Bojesen monkey figurine made of burnished teak hung by one thin arm from the wire of the Poul Henningsen pendant light fixture over the long, white-lacquered table.

There was no indication that actual people lived here, no newspaper sections spread across the table, no wrung-out dishcloths hanging over the kitchen faucet giving off a slightly sour scent. It was a Teflon home, decorated with a lucid, watery glaze, and they were met by a couple of eyes with dark, swollen lids and moist lashes at the far end of the room.

Jens Bjerre sat on a Børge Mogensen sofa, staring into thin air in bewilderment. The academic's sofa, as Schäfer called it. Aesthetics must trump comfort when you had an MD, he thought, as his and Jens's eyes met.

He looked like a man desperately waiting to wake up from a nightmare.

His wife, on the other hand, looked as if she still hadn't fully comprehended the seriousness of the situation. Anne Sofie Bjerre perked up when she came into the kitchen and saw Schäfer and Augustin. She seemed to be clinging to the belief that the police would be able to resolve the whole thing. Like a naïve child who believes her parents can solve any problem in the world.

"Is there any news?" she asked hopefully.

"We found Lukas's jacket and some of his school things," Schäfer said.

It grew so quiet in the room that they could hear a megaphone from one of the canal tours down in Nyhavn. A lively voice boomed, welcoming new tourists aboard, and the tour guide's cheerful tone reinforced the feeling of speechless horror that filled the kitchen.

The grandmother broke the silence.

"His jacket?" Her voice was only a whisper.

"Yes," Schäfer said. "We found the items at the Citadel. The jacket was in the water there, and we . . ."

"But . . . but . . ." Jens stood up and shook his head dismissively. "But what does that mean? That doesn't mean anything. That means nothing!" He turned to his wife. "He could still have gone somewhere. He could have hopped on a train, and maybe . . . maybe he forgot his jacket at school when he left and then someone took it and . . ."

"It's below freezing," Augustin said. "We don't believe he went out willingly without his jacket on." Her tone was professional and cool.

Anne Sofie looked at her stiffly, wide-eyed. Then she burst into tears and her husband pulled her to him so that she vanished into his embrace.

"It's too early to draw any conclusions." Schäfer nodded soothingly to Jens. "Right now we'd just like your permission to see Lukas's bedroom. There could be something in there that will lead us in a new direction, a clue that we haven't found yet."

The idea was to give the parents something to cling to without promising them anything Schäfer couldn't deliver. Most of all, he needed time and space to be able to do his job.

"Come on," the grandmother said and started off down a long hallway. "It's this way."

Schäfer and Augustin left the parents in the kitchen and followed the grandmother. She showed them into a room with walls painted a shade of greenish blue. The shelves were full of board games, books, and role-play items. There was a bunk bed in the corner made of wood that had been painted black with a bed on the top level and a workspace in the little cave underneath. The desk was covered with comics, notebooks, and hand-drawn illustrations, and there were wood shavings and graphite bits from pencil sharpening spread across the whole desktop. A well-organized, cozy mess.

"Please let us know if there's anything we can do. If you have any questions about the things in here or anything . . ."

"Thank you. Marianne, that's your name, right?" Schäfer asked.

"Yes."

"Do you live nearby?"

"No, I live just outside Roskilde, but I'm here several times a month. I've been watching Lukas every other weekend since he was little."

Her voice shook as she spoke. Then she looked Schäfer straight in the eye.

"Is there something you're not telling us?" The tears welled up in her eyes. "Is he . . . is he dead?" She held her hand up over her mouth, as if it scared her to hear her own words.

Schäfer shook his head and put a hand on her shoulder.

"We're not keeping anything from you."

She released the air in her mouth, which she had been holding in. "So there's still hope? We're . . . beside ourselves with worry."

Augustin started looking in drawers and the closet, while Schäfer walked the grandmother out of the room.

"What exactly are we looking for?" Augustin asked once Schäfer had closed the door.

"We'll know it when we see it," he said and pulled out a drawer.

*   *   *

For the next half hour, they went through the things in the room with a magnifying glass, but nothing stuck out. Nothing gave them the sense that the boy had been preoccupied with anything other than superhero comics, plastic weapons, role-playing, and complicated LEGO figures, which were all perfectly assembled and lined up on the shelves and the windowsill.

"Those look more like display models than toys," Augustin noted.

Schäfer took a piggy bank down from one shelf. He pulled the rubber stopper out of the bottom and looked inside. The bank was filled with ten and twenty-kroner coins, and a 500-kroner bill and 100-kroner bill had been stuffed in through the slit. Yet another sign that the boy's disappearance wasn't planned, he thought.

Augustin lifted the mattress and looked underneath. Between the mattress and the slats in the frame there was a little notebook.

"A diary?" she suggested.

Schäfer reached for it and flipped through it. Most of the pages had been drawn on. Monsters. Random short sentences without context. In the middle of the book there was a pencil sketch of a headless person. The body stood upright, the arms outstretched to the sides, and the head sat at its feet, its mouth frowning and its eyes blazing.

"What does that say under the picture?" Schäfer passed the notebook over to Augustin.

She focused intently on the letters, which were too small for Schäfer to make out, and read out loud.

"It says, *Toke is a jerk. Ha ha ha.*" She lowered her voice and looked at Schäfer. "Maybe he isn't as gentle and compliant as his parents think, this Lukas kid."

"What do you mean?"

"I mean they seem to have this impression that he's an overly intelligent wonder kid who's always sweet and easygoing." She held the drawing up for Schäfer. "But maybe he has an internal Mr. Hyde."

"We all have an internal Mr. Hyde," Schäfer said. "It's going to take more than a drawing of a boy he doesn't like to arouse suspicion. Plus, the teachers and staff back up this impression of a quiet child, and maybe the drawing is his way of dealing with some frustrations that he doesn't dare vent in reality. The other kids in class are also scared of this Toke."

"Maybe, but if we imagine that he—"

A small piece of loose paper fell out of the notebook and Augustin froze. She picked up the slip of paper and looked at it. It looked worn, faded, and old.

"What's that?" Schäfer asked.

"It's not the same handwriting as the notebook," she said. "It looks like an adult's or an older child's handwriting."

"What does it say?"

"It says, *I'm keeping my eye on you, Lukas. —Kiki.*"

"Kiki?"

"Yes."

"Does it say anything else?"

"No."

"Hmm."

Schäfer scratched his neck and looked thoughtfully at Augustin.

"Come," he said. "Bring the slip of paper with you."

They returned to the kitchen where Jens was now sitting alone at the table. There was nothing in front of him—no phone, tablet, coffee cup, or anything else to occupy himself with. He was just sitting there in silence, staring into space.

He looked up when Schäfer and Augustin entered the room.

"Did you find anything?" he asked, getting up.

"It's hard to say at this point," Schäfer said. "But we have a question. Is there anyone in your family or in your circle of acquaintances named Kiki?"

"Kiki?" Jens furrowed his brow as he considered that. Then he shook his head. "No, I don't think I know anyone by that name. Why?"

"How about at the school? It could be a nickname or a shortened form? Maybe someone named Kirsten or Kristina or something like that?"

Jens turned his upper body toward the living room. "Fie?"

Anne Sofie appeared in the kitchen doorway. She wasn't crying anymore, but her lips and eyes were swollen and red.

"Has Lukas ever mentioned a Kristina or Kirsten from school to you?" Jens asked. "Or anyone named Kiki?"

Anne Sofie took a step into the kitchen.

"Kiki," she repeated. She walked over to the sink and filled a glass with water. She took a long drink and then turned back around to face them.

"No," she said. "Not anyone Lukas has told me about. But ask at the school—there's so many grownups over there, it's hard to keep track of all their names. Why do you ask?"

"Because he has a slip of paper from someone named Kiki in a notebook," Augustin said.

"A slip of paper?"

"Yes, a note. Someone named Kiki wrote that she was keeping an eye on him."

"Keeping an eye on him?" Jens's brow furrowed. "What's that supposed to mean?"

"That's what we're trying to figure out," Schäfer said. "But it doesn't ring any bells?" His eyes bored into Anne Sofie's.

She looked away and seemed to be groping around in the dark for something that made sense.

"It could be someone he met online," Augustin suggested. "Someone who follows him on Instagram or Facebook, or whatever he uses."

"Lukas doesn't use social media," Jens said.

Schäfer and Augustin's eyes met quickly from across the room.

"What about Instagram?" Schäfer asked.

The boy's father shook his head. "No, we have a rule that he needs to be thirteen before he can use that kind of thing."

"And you've been keeping an eye on that consistently, or what?"

"What do you mean?"

"I mean, have you made sure that he's not using social media behind your backs?"

Jens shook his head, not understanding. "We've never felt the need to check. We told him that he's not allowed to, and we trust him to follow the rules. Lukas always follows the rules."

They were interrupted when Schäfer's phone rang in his pocket. He excused himself and stepped out in the stairwell.

"Yes, hello?"

"Schäfer?"

"Yep!"

"This is Rud."

"Hi, Rud. I'm glad you called!" Schäfer said.

Rud Johannsen was an evidence analysis specialist and split his time between the Forensic Genetics Department in the University of Copenhagen's medical school and the NKC. Lukas Bjerre's jacket and the bloody sweatshirt from the trash can had been delivered to him as soon as they were found.

"Well? Is there any news?" Schäfer asked.

"Maybe . . . maybe . . ." As usual Rud Johanssen sounded as if he were wavering a bit and confused.

"Yes or no, Rud?"

"Come by later. Tonight! I'm waiting for the results from Toxicology and . . . well, it'll take the rest of the day and early evening. So, should we say around eleven PM? The results should be back by then."

"Eleven." Schäfer nodded. "I'll see you then."

He went back in to say goodbye to the Bjerre family.

"We'll keep you posted," he said. "If you hear anything at all or if you happen to think of anything, please call. But steer clear of the press. The fewer details they know about, the better."

Schäfer stuck out his hand, and Jens took it.

"What should we do in the meantime?" he asked.

"This might sound odd, but the best thing you can do is actually to try to make the time pass with normal, every-day things," Schäfer said and glanced at the grandmother, who had started making dinner at the kitchen island behind Jens. "Sitting here staring into space won't speed the inves-tigation up. So, I know it's hard, but try to grade some homework, organize some patient records, or whatever it is you usually do, and meanwhile we'll do our best. I promise you."

Schäfer and Augustin left the apartment.

As the elevator door closed and the metal cage began to move downward, lurching and creaking, Augustin glanced at Schäfer with an eyebrow raised and whispered:

"Did you see the mom when we asked about the name Kiki?"

"Mm-hmm." Schäfer nodded.

"She was lying."

"No shit, Sherlock."

"You're awfully quiet tonight."

Martin Duvall let go of the gear shift and rested his hand on Heloise's thigh. His gaze alternated between her and Vigerslev Allé, which extended ahead of them like one long, streetlight-flanked icicle, stridently cold and colorless, one of greater Copenhagen's most disheartening stretches of roadway.

He lovingly caressed the denim, following her thigh muscles with his fingers from kneecap to hip. "Are you okay?"

Heloise nodded. "I'm just tired," she said and turned her face to the passenger's side window.

She hadn't told him about the pregnancy or the argument with Gerda, but both had settled around her like a spiderweb, adhering to her thoughts.

Was Gerda right?

Was Heloise clinging to her like the last living shred of something that had once given life value?

Heloise had hidden the pill with her other medications in the drawer in the bathroom back home. She knew

Martin was going to Stockholm for work for a couple of days the following week. She would get it over with before he came home again. It would be as if it had never happened.

"Are you looking forward to seeing Connie?" Martin asked.

"Mm-hmm." Heloise pulled her leg away a little. "It sucks that it'll only be the three of us, though."

The dinner get-together had been on the calendar for months, but Connie had told her that Schäfer wouldn't be able to make it after all. The Lukas Bjerre investigation was such a high priority for the investigations unit that he needed to work around the clock. At first Heloise had suggested postponing the dinner to another night, but Connie had sounded so disappointed at the idea that Heloise had immediately said that they would come as planned.

Truth be told, she *needed* an evening with Schäfer and Connie. Whenever she stepped over their threshold, it was always like something happened to her. Her shoulders automatically relaxed, and she was able to breath more deeply, right down into her belly. It just felt . . . *nice*, like coming home.

Martin tightened his grip a little on Heloise's kneecap to get her attention as they waited at the corner of Vestre Cemetery.

She involuntarily twitched her leg. "What?"

"Don't you think we ought to take a long weekend somewhere soon?" he asked. "Don't we need that?"

"We were just at the summer house."

"Yes, and that was nice, but . . . I was thinking about a quick trip abroad, to Paris or something like that. Wouldn't that be great?"

Heloise instantly held her breath in the passenger's seat beside him.

She hadn't been to Paris since the previous year, when she had said her final farewell to her father. She had kept away from the city for years—even long before his death—because it reminded her of everything that had fallen apart in her life. When other people thought about Paris, they thought of "La Vie en Rose" and strolling along the Seine. Heloise heard the name of the city and thought: The blue pill or the red pill? Which would you choose?

But it wasn't her choice to fall into a bottomless pit. It was more like she had been force-fed a reality that she hadn't known existed and then she was suddenly left parentless. The shock and anger had left her with a new, gloomier view of the world and a heart that had been ripped in half. Nothing was the way she had thought.

Martin eyed her questioningly and his face immediately clenched up in remorse.

"Oh, sorry. I wasn't thinking. That was stupid of me."

Heloise half-heartedly shook her head and brushed his comment aside. "That's okay."

"No, that was thoughtless of me. Forget about Paris! But how about London? Or Barcelona? I bet it's warm and sunny in Spain right now. We could zip down there this spring—eat tapas, drink sangria, and shag like rabbits." He put a hand behind Heloise's head and pulled her in for a kiss. "What do you say?"

"It's green."

"I'm sorry?"

Heloise pointed to the traffic light. "It's green!"

Martin let go of her and stepped gently on the accelerator. In the middle of the intersection, they were passed on the right at high speed by a red BMW that only avoided hitting their right-side mirror by a few inches. Martin hit the horn with his fist and held it down as he exploded at the driver, who was already long gone.

"*What the hell are you doing, asshole?!*"

Heloise could see how much effort it took for him to calm himself down again. His pulse pounded visibly in his exposed neck, and he was gritting his teeth. He took a deep breath and then slowly exhaled.

"Anyway, where were we . . . Barcelona," he said, once again sounding under control and looking over at Heloise. "What do you think?"

"I've got a lot going on at work right now," she replied. "Maybe later in the year."

Heloise looked out the windshield and she could feel Martin's eyes on her for a long moment. But he didn't say anything else.

They turned left onto Strindbergsvej and were halfway down the long residential street when Heloise pointed ahead of them in surprise.

"Hey, Schäfer's car is here!"

They pulled up in front of the little house, where Martin's dark blue Tesla nearly kissed the bumper of Schäfer's battered Opel.

Heloise peered over at the house, where a warm, orangey glow spilled out of all the windows.

"I think he's home after all," she said happily.

She undid her seat belt and hopped out of the car before Martin had turned off the engine. She pushed open the gate in front of the red brick house and was halfway down the front walk when she spotted the glow lighting up the darkness on the patio. Half hidden under the cantilever roof, Schäfer was leaning against the wall. He had turned his collar up to cover his ears and had a cigarette in his mouth. He was lost in his own thoughts.

"Schäfer?" she called.

His head flew up with a start, and Heloise could see his teeth, brightening the darkness as he smiled.

"Ah, there you are!" he said. He walked over and picked Heloise up in a bear hug, so her feet dangled in midair for a few seconds.

He was a big man, a whole head taller than Heloise's five foot nine, and he smelled of cigarettes and cheap aftershave. Heloise always felt a bit tipsy in his company, safe and comfortable. You didn't need to be Freud to figure out how things stood.

"You smell like Old Spice," she said and smiled.

"Mm-hmm. The scent of a real man." Schäfer winked.

He reached out his bear paw to Martin, who had caught up with Heloise.

"Duvall," he said and nodded.

"Hi, Erik."

"It's great to see you."

"We didn't think you were going to be here," Heloise said.

"I'm home for a few hours before I head over to NKC."

"NKC?" Martin asked.

"The National Forensic Center."

"I bet it's all hands on deck right now because of that boy you're looking for," Heloise said.

Schäfer nodded and took a long drag from his cigarette.

"Shouldn't you be giving that nonsense up?" She nodded at the cigarette in his hand.

"Now don't you start, too," he said. "Connie is always after me. How about you, Duvall? You smoke, too. Do you get chewed out as well?"

"No, actually, I don't," Martin said, giving Heloise a teasing smile. "But I can't figure out if that's because Heloise loves me as I am or if she just doesn't care if I die prematurely."

"The latter," Heloise said.

It was meant as a joke, but her statement hung in the air for several seconds with a surprising bite to it, as if they both knew that it was the only honest thing she had said all evening.

"Oh, I doubt that," Schäfer said and put his cigarette out in a pail of sand that sat on the patio. "Come on. Let's go inside. Connie's pacing around in there counting the seconds. She's been working her magic in the kitchen all day." He rested his hand on the back of Heloise's head. "It was really sweet of you not to cancel. She's been looking forward to seeing you."

The front door opened just then and Schäfer's wife stuck her big, dark head of hair out.

"Heloise!" she squealed and enveloped her in a hug.

"Hi, Connie," Heloise smiled.

"Oh, it's been too long, girl! We've missed you." Her Caribbean accent flowed like thick caramel sauce over her vowels as she spoke Danish.

She released Heloise and turned to Martin.

"And who is this handsome young man you've brought with you this time?"

The question was meant as a joke. Connie had met Martin many times and had often elbowed Heloise in the side when they were alone, whispering to her that he was a keeper.

Schäfer was hardly as dazzled. In the beginning Heloise had thought that it was the packaging he took some dislike to. Martin was attractive in a way that made most men think he was either gay or someone who could use a good kick in the pants. He was simply too good looking, too . . . perfect! But for Schäfer the problem was rather that Martin had a criminal record, an old assault conviction. A thirty-day sentence for knocking out four of his ex-wife's lover's teeth, a fact that Schäfer reminded Heloise of every chance he got.

He didn't trust Martin Duvall, case closed.

Martin greeted Connie warmly and they were quickly pulled inside for the festive Cajun-Creole meal Connie had prepared. There was Caribbean gumbo with okra and tiger prawns, homemade cornbread, fried chicken, papaya salad, and a dish Connie presented as buttermilk biscuits with mushroom gravy and grated cheddar. All the courses were served in colorful, glazed tureens and bowls on the small, round dining room table. The chandelier over the table was dimmed and a pleasant, euphoric saxophone blared from the speakers.

Heloise felt completely relaxed as Schäfer pulled out a chair for her and asked her to have a seat.

They ate and talked about the food and the trip Schäfer and Connie had just returned home from. About the weather, the ungodly Danish winter darkness. About Martin's new job in the editorial offices at DR in Christiansborg, about politics, and about the cherry color Connie had painted the kitchen walls to Schäfer's profound dismay.

Then Heloise asked the question she had been working herself up to ever since she had seen Schäfer's car parked out front.

"So, how are things at work?" She looked at him over the rim of her wineglass. "Are you making any headway in your current case?"

He finished chewing whatever was in his mouth before he answered. Heloise knew him well enough to know that the long pause was not due to good table manners.

"We don't have anything concrete yet," he said.

"But I understand you had Kronprinsessegade sealed off last night and the Citadel this morning. The newspaper's sources say that you found evidence in a trash can and in the moat. Is that right?"

Schäfer stuck his fork into a prawn the size of a Shetland pony and stuffed it into his mouth. His eyes met Heloise's as he chewed. He was smiling warmly, but Heloise could see in his eyes that he was having reservations. After he swallowed his mouthful, he said nothing.

"More red wine?" Connie asked, sensing that they were moving out into an opium field packed full of land mines.

"Have you heard about Heloise's promotion?" Martin asked, holding his glass out to Connie.

Schäfer raised both eyebrows, and Connie gasped excitedly.

"Promotion?"

Heloise was just as surprised as the other two and looked at Martin.

"What?" he asked. "Am I not allowed to brag about my girlfriend?"

"Well, but . . . it's not a promotion."

"I think it is," Martin said and explained the situation to Schäfer and Connie. "They changed the workflow for the paper's investigative team, so now Heloise gets to decide what she's going to cover. Things aren't divided up as much as they were before, so she doesn't need to stick to business topics anymore."

Connie nodded with interest as Martin spoke, eager to celebrate a work change that she didn't quite understand.

"And this is something new?" she asked. "That you can cover other topics?"

Heloise shrugged. "Yes and no. I've written a lot of different things for the paper, but I've mostly covered business."

"And now you have free rein to write about whatever you want?"

"That's the idea anyway," Heloise said, thinking about Karen Aagaard's orders to cover the Lukas Bjerre case.

"So what are you working on right now?" Schäfer asked.

"A story about PTSD, about the scars soldiers carry in their hearts after they've been to war."

She regretted her lie the second she had uttered it out loud.

"That's wonderful, Heloise," Connie said. "We're so proud of you."

Schäfer nodded in agreement.

"You're sweet, but it doesn't come with any pay raise so it's no big deal."

"Sure it is," Connie insisted. "You should be proud of yourself. You're a good journalist. You know, whenever we see your name in the paper we read every word. Erik especially follows you religiously. You've practically become the daughter we never had."

"Why didn't you ever have children?" Martin asked.

"Martin," Heloise said, giving him a stern look.

"Sorry, I . . ." He looked back and forth between them. "I didn't mean to . . ."

"That's okay," Connie smiled. "It's a fair question. We really wanted to have kids, but for some reason . . . well, it never worked out."

She put her hand on top of Schäfer's. Her dark hands were slender and her nails a natural pink. She wore a gold ring on each finger. Jewelry from Saint Lucia, Heloise guessed, with Caribbean patterns and bright stones.

"We tried for many years, and I got pregnant several times, too. But then each time it was just gone before it ever really got going, so . . ." She shrugged with the kind of forced ease you develop after many years of grief. "It just wasn't meant to be."

"I'm sorry to hear that," Martin said.

"Yes, it's a sad tale," Schäfer said with a nod. "But then we have so many other good things in our lives, don't we, honey? We just returned from the most wonderful vacation. There's wine in our glasses, gumbo on our plates, and nice people over to visit." He glanced over at Heloise and Martin. "And Connie hasn't kicked me out the door yet, after twenty-nine years of living together."

He lifted her hand and gave it a kiss.

"How about you?" Connie asked. "Are kids something you're planning on?"

Heloise and Schäfer's eyes met over the table. She could see that he knew where she stood. But there was also something else in his gaze—it moved fleetingly to her belly as if he could see right through her—and she couldn't help wonder: How much did he know?

In many ways Schäfer knew her better than did the man she was with. Martin seemed night-blind in Heloise's darkness—immune to the numerous rejections that lately had gone from being subtle to big, flashing neon signs.

Martin seemed uncomfortable in his chair, filled with an expectant restlessness.

"Well, yes . . . That's something we need to get going on soon," he said and smiled.

"Duvall," Schäfer said, putting an end to the conversation by smacking the palm of his hand on the table. "Do you want to pop outside with me for a smoke before I need to run off again?"

Martin grabbed his wineglass and stood up.

The men quickly put on their coats and disappeared out onto the patio. Heloise pictured Martin standing formally out there, eager to impress, like a suitor seeking a father's blessing.

She and Connie started clearing the dishes from the table.

"He's a handsome guy, your Martin."

"He is," Heloise agreed.

"Do you love him?"

Heloise smiled. "Sometimes."

"Mm-hmm." Connie nodded knowingly and took the tray that was leaning against one corner of the sofa. "He seems very much in love with you."

Heloise glanced out at the patio but couldn't see the men out there. "Schäfer doesn't seem to like him," she said with a shrug.

"I wouldn't worry about that. Erik doesn't like lots of people."

Heloise laughed. "But you have something really special together, the two of you."

"Yes." Connie nodded. "We do."

"What's your secret?"

Connie smiled. Her teeth were a brilliant white against the pink of her gums. "Der' is no secret, girl," she declared in her lilting French-Creole dialect. "We treat each other nicely. We laugh together. We do the deed." She winked. "Dat's all!"

"Connie!" Heloise squealed and put her hands over her ears.

"Oh, please," Connie said with a smile. "Erik might not have the classic good looks your Martin does, but he is *all* man!"

"Stop, stop!" Heloise laughed. "I'm just going to go visit your restroom, and when I get back, we will never speak of this again, okay?"

Connie laughed heartily and pushed her cheerfully off toward the guest bathroom with a hand.

Heloise's smile vanished as soon as she closed the bathroom door behind her, and she anxiously touched her abdomen. She felt an ominous discomfort, as if her uterus were an old, arthritic hand trying to form a fist.

The seconds ticked by as she waited for the pain to pass.

When it was over, she washed her hands and splashed cold water on her face. She found herself looking into her own eyes in her reflection and bit her lower lip. Gerda's words echoed in her head.

You're a hypocrite, Heloise.

"Fuck you," she muttered, but wasn't sure who she was talking to. When she closed the bathroom door behind her and turned off the light, she could hear Connie singing in the kitchen and the dishes clinking against each other as she placed them in the dishwasher. She looked around the dark hallway, lit up only by a three-armed sconce mounted on the wall, which was covered with a wallpaper with a large floral pattern.

Then she spotted it.

The case file.

It sat with Schäfer's car keys and police badge on a cream-colored table with curved legs in the middle of the hallway.

Heloise peered out at the patio and listened carefully. She could hear Martin's laughter out there, obtrusive and too loud, and Schäfer's mellow chuckle. Connie was still clattering around in the kitchen at the other end of the house and humming along to an old Dionne Warwick number that was playing on the sound system.

Heloise debated with herself in the mirror on the wall over the case file. For and against, back and forth. Then she turned off the voices in her head and hastily decided. She could *help* Schäfer if she knew a little more about the case.

She held her breath and opened the folder.

Her heart pounded in her chest, like accelerating beats on a bass drum, as she flipped through the papers. She skimmed the pages in the soft light and latched onto individual words and sentences. She tried to memorize what she saw, tried to decode Schäfer's chicken scratch:

> *Jacket found at the Citadel. iPhone . . . Pareidolia. Who has a motive to kill or kidnap? . . . Who is Kiki—is there a conflict? . . . Anne Sofie Bjerre, alcoholism . . .*

Alcoholism, Heloise thought. Did Lukas's mother drink? Gerda had never mentioned that.

She heard a sound from the front door and looked up with a start. When it didn't open, she quickly went back to flipping through the file.

Come on, come on. Give me something, she thought, something concrete.

Then she stiffened.

On the very last page of the case file there was a picture of an old, dilapidated barn door that looked like a creepy face. The picture triggered a strange, silent echo in her, a delayed glimmer of light that seemed as if it had traveled across an inner galaxy.

She read Schäfer's notes under the picture:

> *Where is this place? Lukas is hunting for faces, pareidolia. Whose face does he see here? His attacker's?*

Pareidolia, Heloise thought. What did that mean again . . . something about faces? She vaguely remembered having seen the term on Instagram at some point. She took a picture of the barn door on her cell phone. Then she closed the file and walked quickly back to the living room.

". . . not a darn thing." Schäfer laughed as the front door opened.

"You're wrong," Martin protested. "He's the only one at Borgen who knows what he's doing, and he's one of the good guys: right wing when it comes to the redistribution of income and wealth, left wing when it comes to the climate. The best of both worlds."

"He's a politician." Schäfer spat the word out like a clump of infected mucus. "Makes him a douchebag in my book."

"Time-out," Heloise laughed and walked into Martin's embrace. "You can't talk about politics anymore or we'll never be invited back."

"They don't understand what's going on out in the streets," Schäfer continued, unmoved. "Send all the politicians to Vollsmose after dark and let them try to implement their so-called integration plans. Let the Alternative dance boogie-woogie down Blågårdsgade blowing bubbles with their noses. I'd like to see if a politician like Uffe Elbæk still thinks the whole thing is hilarious once he's taken a cobblestone in the head."

"There, there, baby." Connie came into the living room. She was carrying a pineapple cake and a pitcher of coffee on a tray. "Don't scare our guests away now."

"It's okay," Heloise said. "I stopped engaging in politics a long time ago. It's all bullshit anyway."

"It's not bullshit," Martin protested.

Schäfer smiled indulgently and patted him on the shoulder.

"You mean well, Duvall, and you get points for that. But I'm afraid that I have to agree with Heloise." He took out his phone and read a text that he had just received. Then he reached out to Heloise and pulled her into a goodbye hug. "Take care of yourself, okay?"

"Always," she said, hoping that he couldn't see through her deceitful smile to sense her guilty conscience.

Schäfer kissed Connie goodbye and then drove away for his late-night work appointment. Heloise and Martin stayed for another hour while they ate cake and looked at vacation pictures from Saint Lucia on Connie's phone.

"It looks amazing," Heloise said.

"It's the most beautiful place in the world." Connie nodded. "You have to come visit us over there someday. We have a little guest room you can stay in."

"We'd love to," Martin said. "Wouldn't we, Helo?"

Heloise smiled but didn't respond. Instead, she set down the phone and said, "Thank you so much for this lovely dinner, Connie. It was wonderful to see you."

They said their goodbyes and Heloise promised to stop by again soon.

As soon as she sat down in the car with Martin, and they pulled away from the curb, headed back toward downtown, she pulled out her phone and found the picture of the barn door. It felt as if the temperature in the car dropped as she stared at it and her fingertips began to throb.

Those round porthole windows, that pursed iron mouth.

She recognized the place.

She had been there.

CHAPTER

21

Schäfer sucked the glow so far down into the filter that he nearly burned his fingers. He hurriedly flicked the cigarette butt out the window and exhaled the smoke in a single, hard breath. Then he parked his car on the narrow street between two rows of long, low buildings and slammed his door shut behind him.

Rævegade was hands down the darkest and most dismal street in downtown Copenhagen. It wasn't because it was in a bad neighborhood. The narrow street was right next to Saint Paul's Church, surrounded by ambiance and picturesque little streets. Every once in a while, a joyful cheer could be heard from Borgerkroen, the bar over on Borgergade, but Rævegade was empty and deserted. Dead, really. It made you want to kneel down in the middle of the street and administer mouth-to-mouth resuscitation.

Nothing green grew here. There weren't any potted plants or trees. There were no benches in front of the row of houses the way there were on other streets in the area, no bicycles leaned up against the walls. There was only cold asphalt and snow between the dirty brick buildings, which had gloomy, dark brown shutters alongside their windows. Here—in the middle of the breathing space that was Frederiksstaden—the street sat like a hideous dead end from some poor, hooligan-filled neighborhood in suburban England. Schäfer half expected to see a couple of young lads with crew cuts, wearing Billy Bremner jerseys and dribbling down the street.

Go, Leeds!

He double-checked the address in the text he had received from the investigations department before he had left home. A teacher from the Nyholm School had come by police headquarters earlier in the evening to talk to Schäfer about the Lukas Bjerre case. Lene Nielsen was her name. She had said that she had information about the boy, but the colleague who had sent the text didn't know any more than that. The woman had left her address and her phone number, and Schäfer had tried calling from the car, but the call had gone directly to voice mail.

Schäfer found the woman's address in the middle of the block. The windows were dark, and Schäfer glanced quickly at his watch. It was 10:17 PM, so maybe she had already gone to bed.

He rang the bell. Then he knocked firmly on the door, three quick raps with his knuckles.

It took a second and then the lights came on inside. Schäfer heard a wary female voice through the door.

"Who is it?"

"It's the police."

The door was opened. The chain was still on, and through the crack Schäfer could see a short, rumpled-looking woman in her pajamas. She looked at least ten years older than sixty-one, the age the national registry reported, and she was scrunching up her eyes in a way that made it clear that her vision was poor.

"The police?" she asked.

"Yes, good evening." Schäfer held his police badge up, even though it seemed unlikely that the woman would be able to see it. "Erik Schäfer, Copenhagen Police. I'm looking for a Lene Nielsen."

"That's me," she said with a nod.

"I'm sorry to bother you so late. I'm in charge of the Lukas Bjerre investigation, and I understand that you have some information you'd like to share with me. You stopped by police headquarters earlier?"

"Yes, just give me a moment," the woman said and closed the door.

A few moments later, he heard the chain being undone. Then the woman opened the door.

"Come in," she said and pointed to the kitchen, which was to the right of the front hall. She had put on a dark green velour bathrobe and a pair of glasses with lenses so thick they must be murder on the bridge of the nose.

Schäfer didn't offer to take off his shoes. He never did. Instead, he wiped them thoroughly on the doormat and ducked his head as he stepped through the low doorway into the kitchen. The room had a lot of atmosphere, a dark cave with blue and white grandmother plates and a German pendulum clock on the wall. The dining table was set with a red Christmas tablecloth with snowflakes embroidered on it, even though they were a month and a half into the new year.

"Coffee?" the woman asked, roaming a little randomly around the kitchen, as if she didn't quite know what to do with herself. "Or perhaps you'd prefer tea? I also have an apple pie I could warm up in the toaster oven?"

"No, thank you. Nothing for me."

The woman walked over and sat down at the table, where her knitting sat in a braided basket, and looked expectantly at Schäfer.

He pulled a notebook and a pen out of his inside pocket and nodded to her.

"I understand that you stopped by police headquarters this evening?"

"Yes," she said and nodded. "I teach the 3X class. I know Lukas." She fidgeted with the ribbed wrist cuffs of her pajamas, which stuck out of the sleeves of her robe. Her bedhead and disproportionately large eyes behind her glasses made her look like a bird that had just fallen out of its nest.

"So, Lukas's class," Schäfer noted. "How many third-grade classrooms does the school have?"

"Two."

"And why is yours called 3X?"

"I . . . I don't understand your question?"

"When I was a kid, if there were two third-grade classrooms, we called them 3A and 3B," Schäfer said. "I actually thought all Danish schools did it that way."

"Yes, that's how they do it most places, but at Nyholm we don't like the insinuation encoded in the traditional lettering system. We don't want half the children to feel like they're on the B team while the other half is on the A team. It has such a negative ring to it, and we don't go in for signaling inequities in that way. So our two classes are X and Q."

If life were a sitcom, Schäfer would have glanced wryly into the camera. Instead, he asked, "What do you teach?"

"Music, science, and technology."

"And did you teach on Monday when Lukas disappeared?"

"No, and that's also why I didn't contact you until now. I did a professional development course in Odense for three days and just got home. Of course, I've been following the news and I've spoken with my colleagues about the case, but something just occurred to me today."

"What occurred to you?" Schäfer glanced at the pendulum clock above her. He had an appointment to meet Rud Johannsen at NKC at eleven PM and needed to leave in ten minutes if he was going to make it there on time.

"It was something that happened at one of the recesses," the woman said. "Based on the school rules, the younger kids from kindergarten through sixth grade are supposed to stay in the schoolyard during recess. It's a paved area that faces Øster Voldgade."

"Where the jungle gym is?"

"Yes," she said with a nod. "The older students—the seventh through ninth graders—are supposed to stay out behind the school or around the gym."

"Behind the school? So, out by the train tracks?"

"Yes, and the students are actually very good at following these rules. The older ones don't like to be with the littler ones anyway, and the little ones are often afraid of the big ones, but . . . every once in a while we'll still find that one of the younger kids has wandered around behind the school."

"And?" Schäfer nodded impatiently.

"And today it hit me that I've seen Lukas back there twice, on the wrong side of the school. And both times he was talking to some woman and he seemed very upset. He was sorry about it, but . . . he also seemed scared."

Schäfer furrowed his brow. "You said he was talking to a woman?"

"Yes, both times I saw them standing a good way down the path, in the direction of the National Gallery. I didn't think so much about it at the time. I just assumed it was someone he knew . . ." She shrugged apologetically and did not volunteer anything more.

"What did you do then?"

"Well, the first time I called him back to the school. I asked him if anything was wrong. He denied that, although something was clearly bothering him. But we see that all the time at school, especially with the boys. They're not so forthcoming when they've been beaten up or teased. So I just reminded him that he wasn't allowed to be back there and then sent him back around to the schoolyard in front again."

"And the second time?"

"The second time I actually scolded him a little." She said that as if it were highly controversial. "But the place where they were was actually quite far from the school—three more paces in that direction and Lukas would have been off school grounds entirely, and we can't have that. So, yes, I scolded him!"

"Did he say anything about who the woman was?"

"No, but I also didn't ask."

"Was it the same woman that you saw him talking to, both times?"

"Yes, I think so. Tall, blonde. Sort of a bit rustic to look at."

Schäfer looked up from his notebook. "Rustic?"

"Yes, sort of a little . . . rural. She was wearing rubber boots and an oilskin jacket. She wasn't *chic* or whatever you'd call it. More . . . yes, *rustic*."

Schäfer bit his lower lip as he thought. "And it wasn't his mother, the woman you saw?" he asked. "It wasn't Anne Sofie Bjerre?"

"No, I know her."

"When did this take place, did you say?"

The woman sighed, thinking back. "I can't remember the exact dates, but it was this school year. The last time was probably right before Christmas I would think."

"And how much time was there between the two instances?"

"A couple of weeks, maybe a month. Somewhere around there."

Schäfer noted that in his notebook. Then he looked up and nodded encouragingly. "Did anything else happen?"

The woman shook her head, embarrassed. "I know it doesn't sound very important, now that I say it out loud, but I would feel awful if I hadn't said anything and then Lukas . . ."

"You did the right thing," Schäfer said. "This woman you saw Lukas with . . . Do you think you could identify her if you saw her again?"

The woman pursed her lips together and wrung her hands. "Oh, I don't know . . . Maybe?"

Schäfer looked at her thick eyeglass lenses.

Hmm, he thought. Maybe not.

22

O N THE STROKE of eleven, Erik Schäfer pushed open the glass door into the National Forensic Center with an Ecco shoe that was worn to the point of being shiny. The center, commonly referred to as NKC, was in an old ramshackle building in Værløse. The center should have been torn down long ago and operations moved into new, state-of-the-art offices in Ejby, but a fire had put a temporary halt to the move.

He looked around in the empty, late-night lobby and discovered that Gloria—the old receptionist who had worked there for all the years Schäfer had been coming there—had been replaced. Or maybe this was just a temp. At any rate, a young, redheaded woman Schäfer didn't recognize was sitting at the desk.

"Erik Schäfer," she said with a smile as he approached the front desk.

He nodded contentedly. "Good evening."

"You look tan," the woman commented. She put both elbows on the counter and rested her chin on her folded hands. "Have you been off traveling?"

Schäfer raised an eyebrow and scratched his chin with his left hand. An automatic reaction; a quick *flash* of his wedding ring. "Mm-hmm."

The woman nodded but didn't say anything else. She didn't look away, either.

Schäfer cleared his throat and pointed to the lab hallway with his thumb.

"Uh, um . . . Is Rud here? I have an appointment."

She reached out and picked up her phone with a slender hand.

"Yes, hi. I have Erik Schäfer out here at the front desk for Rud Johannsen." She hung up and nodded to the glazed double doors at the opposite end of the lobby. "He's in Lab 4. You can go right in."

Schäfer gave the counter a pat in thanks and unconsciously sucked in his gut as he walked over to the doors.

He found Rud Johannsen sitting at a desk covered with X-ray images, photos, tissue samples, and test tubes full of fluids of various colors. He was wearing a pair of black magnifying loupe glasses with a forehead light, and his shoulder-length, pigmentless hair looked as if he had just stuck a pair of chopsticks into an electrical outlet.

Schäfer smiled at the sight and gave him a friendly thump on the back.

"What's up, Doc? Have you gotten your flux capacitor working?"

Rud Johannsen pushed the magnifying glasses up onto his head, looking confused.

"My what?"

"Your flux capacitor. You know, *Back to the Future*! You look like Doc Brown with that seine net of hair up there."

"What kind of net?"

"Never mind," Schäfer said, shaking his head. "What've you got for me?"

Rud Johannsen got up and left the room without saying a word. Schäfer had worked with him long enough to know that he should follow him.

He caught up with Rud partway down the lab hallway and they turned right into the anteroom of the forensic department's evidence room, where they put on protective suits and face masks.

When Rud opened the door into the clean room where the evidence was kept, there was a sucking sound, as if the room took a breath. There was a large table in the middle of the room. The lights underneath the white glass tabletop lit up the surface and the object that was on it—the jacket that had been fished out of the Citadel's moat.

"There are three interesting findings on the jacket," Rud began, holding one bony index finger up in the air. "One: Traces of blood. Here on the right side of the collar."

He turned off the ceiling lamps, plunging the room into darkness, and turned on a UV light. He sprayed luminol on the collar of the jacket and aimed the light at the area where a few small spots fluoresced, lighting up like blueish white fireflies.

"Do you see?" he asked and pointed. "There is smudging here . . . and here . . ."

Schäfer nodded. "How about DNA? What's the time frame?"

"We collected samples—both from the jacket and from the sweatshirt from the trash can—and they've been submitted for rapid testing. So we'll know something when we know something. I can't tell you any more than that."

Schäfer grumbled, disgruntled.

"It could be that we get the results tonight. It could be that we get them in the morning," Rud said. "And, yes, it definitely is a pain having to wait, but every other test has been put on standby for this. We're doing our best."

"I know that." Schäfer nodded. "And I appreciate it, Rud. What else have you got? You said there were three findings on the jacket?"

"Yes." He turned the overhead lights on again and pointed to a microscope on a counter at one end of the room.

"Number two: We found a few hair fibers. Uniform, blond strands of hair, which have also been sent for DNA testing. They were stuck in the Velcro of the jacket's hood closure."

He switched on the microscope and gestured with his hand for Schäfer to take a peek.

Schäfer leaned forward.

The hair, which was magnified seventy-five times, looked like a blurry, golden-brown piece of straw.

"The structure and color indicate that the hair comes from the boy, so that doesn't give us that much, but let's wait and see what the DNA shows," Rud said with a shrug of his shoulders. "I could be wrong. It doesn't happen that often, but it happens."

"All right. What else have you got?"

"Number three!" Rud flung his long arms out theatrically and raised one eyebrow. "There are traces of a rodenticide on one of the jacket sleeves."

Schäfer straightened up. "Rat poison?"

"Yes, and an interesting type too."

"What do you mean?"

"There are three main types of rat poison, which each work via a different mechanism to exterminate the pests. One is a neurotoxin, bromethalin, which kills a rat a few hours after it's been consumed, usually via respiratory failure."

"In other words?"

"The central nervous system collapses and the rat suffocates."

Schäfer moistened his lips and nodded. "What else?"

"The next—fumarin—is a poison that is absorbed through the skin. It kills like this!" Rud snapped his fingers. "And it is one nasty way to go, causing acute nosebleeds, bloody urine and stools, bleeding gums, edema, fluid in the lungs, and so on. Capisce?"

"Capisce!" Schäfer nodded.

"The third most common rodenticide is called warfarin. Warfarin is similar to fumarin in the sense that it's an anticoagulant, so the rat bleeds to death internally, and at extremely low doses it's actually also used as a blood thinner for humans. It's a poison that's both odorless and tasteless, and unlike the other two types of rat poison, it's slower acting—a stealthy son of a bitch that causes a prolonged, painful death."

Rud pointed to the jacket sleeve.

"And here—on the ribbed cuff of the left sleeve—I found traces of a rodenticide that I wasn't initially able to identify. But the results just came back from Toxicology."

He pulled out an envelope, pulled the results out, and handed them to Schäfer.

"Formula: $C^{19}H^{16}O^4$," he announced. "It's warfarin."

Schäfer skimmed the pages. "So you say this is used in medication as well? Which means it would be something that a doctor would have access to?"

"Well, a doctor would have access to *medical grade* warfarin, but that's not what's on the jacket. What the boy was exposed to was a highly concentrated version. Pure rat poison, and any idiot can get his hands on that. Does the family live in a house? Do they have a rat problem?"

"No, in an apartment. On the fifth floor."

"Then it's *very* concerning that there's rat poison on the jacket, I'd say."

Schäfer folded the document up and put it in his inside pocket.

"Because you think that it indicates that . . . what? . . . that someone is killing the boy with this stuff?"

"I estimate that if nothing else, it's *plausible* that you have yet another deadline hanging over your head if you want to find this boy alive."

Schäfer looked over at the child-sized jacket on the light table and speculated on what kind of a monster would hurt a child. In his thirty years on the force, he had investigated almost 600 homicides, and an ordinary person had been hiding behind every single beast. In most of the cases he had been able to see the situation through the killers' eyes, and it wasn't hard to understand motives like revenge, jealousy, money, and sex. But—no matter what glasses Schäfer put on—there was no part of him that would ever understand how a person could make himself hurt a child.

He turned to Rud.

"Have you ever had a case where someone was killed with this stuff?"

"I've had cases where people have unintentionally ingested warfarin, but I haven't personally worked on a homicide case where that happened. But conspiracy theorists believe that Stalin was killed with warfarin, that he was poisoned, murdered!"

"Stalin?"

"Yes, but don't let the color of my hair fool you." Rud smiled and ran a hand through his white mane. "That was long before my time."

23

THE HARD SPRAY from the shower head stung Heloise's skin. She quickly lathered herself, rinsed, and five minutes later she was in her bathrobe, seated at the breakfast table with a towel around her hair and all the day's newspapers in front of her.

Martin sat in the chair beside her in a freshly ironed shirt and suit. Neat and clean, swathed in a cloud of fashionable aftershave that smelled like a surprising blend of leather and cedar. Heloise alternated between loving and hating the scent. This morning it didn't bother her.

He folded up the copy of *Politiken* he had been reading and leaned against her.

"Have a good day."

"Are you leaving already?" Heloise asked and kissed him.

"Yes, I've got to go." He drank the rest of his coffee and stood up. "The prime minister just announced that he's holding a press conference in an hour and a half, and we don't know yet what he's planning to talk about. So I need to go gather the troops before it starts."

He put on his camel hair coat and buttoned it.

"I'll see you later, right?"

"Yeah." Heloise smiled.

After Martin left, she threw on a pair of faded jeans and a gray striped sweater and sat down at her desk in front of the living room window. From the little penthouse apartment, she had an unobstructed view of the Marble Church's big, verdigris dome. Today it looked like an enormous soft ice cream cone that had been dipped in white chocolate. All of Copenhagen was a dazzling white, all the roofs and branches beautifully covered with snow.

She created a new document on her computer and drummed her fingers a little on the desk as she thought. Then she took out her phone and called Morten Munk in *Demokratisk Dagblad*'s Research Department.

He answered the call with a theatrical, "You may speak!"

"Hi, it's me," she said. "Are you up for some work?"

"Why do you think I'm here?"

They usually bantered like this. Heloise could hardly remember a conversation with Munk that hadn't begun with an exchange like this.

"Well, Milady?" he said. "To what do I owe this honor?"

She could hear that he was eating something as he spoke, and his voice sounded strained and a bit winded. Munk's New Year's resolution had been to go on a diet this year, but it did not appear to be in effect now, two months later. He wasn't yet over thirty, and Heloise was afraid that he wasn't going to make it to his next birthday if he didn't turn things around.

"Lukas Bjerre," she said. "The missing kid."

"What about him?"

"Could you please gather everything that's been published about the case and send it to me? All the details that have been made public, personal data, status of the investigation, and so on."

"Are you prepping a Britney?" Munk asked.

A Britney was newspaper slang for a prewritten obituary that you kept in a drawer, just in case. The procedure, which journalists used to call a Keith Richards, had been named in the years when Britney Spears had seemed to be on the verge of dying of an overdose or suicide. It was basically about being three steps ahead—good old common sense. But it still always felt a little morbid to write a commemorative piece in honor of someone who was still breathing.

"Yes, just a short one," Heloise said. "But most of all, I just want to get up to speed on the case."

"You don't sound that enthusiastic," Munk commented.

"It's commissioned work."

"Isn't everything in the end?"

He had a point, Heloise thought, feeling annoyed. She hung up and found the picture she had taken of the barn door in Schäfer's case file. She transferred it onto the computer so she could enlarge it. Her internet was acting up and the file took a long time to upload, so the picture gradually resolved in small, pixilated pieces like an unfinished puzzle.

When it was finally there on her screen and in focus in front of her, she had that same strange feeling of déjà vu that she had had at Schäfer's house.

She was certain that she had been there, that she had recently stood in front of that barn, and that she had had the same thought she was thinking now: that the old, dilapidated façade looked like a cagey, eerie face.

She picked up her phone again to send the picture to Munk and opened her photo library. She scrolled too far back in the archive and came to a halt when she saw the series of pictures she had taken at the summer house in Rørvig.

There were photos of Martin swimming naked and laughing hysterically in the middle of winter in the blue-black Kattegat Sea. Photos of sand dunes and rice pudding pancakes, and one of a little fallow deer that had appeared in the yard early one morning.

But it was the pictures Heloise had taken on her walks alone in the orchard that made her stop. She had seen many beaten-up old houses in the woods on those walks and remembered one in particular: a dilapidated cabin that she had thought was the sort of place kids would be afraid of. A place that would send their imaginations into overdrive, coming up with monsters, witches, and beasts.

Heloise, on the other hand, had tried to imagine what it would be like to live in such an isolated place, in peace and quiet—free from the outside world. She had walked around the property and had taken only one photo of the main house. But hadn't there been a barn around the back? Was that where she had seen the face on the barn?

She typed in the number for the reception desk at *Demokratisk Dagblad* and waited as it rang.

"Hi, this is Heloise Kaldan," she said. "Is there a car available this morning?"

CHAPTER

24

GRADUALLY THE WORLD had stopped swaying beneath Erik Schäfer's feet. After three days on Danish soil and a couple of nights of shallow sleep, he felt more or less like himself again. Now a completely different sort of discomfort took over: the feeling of not being able to make a breakthrough in the investigation.

He sat heavily in his desk chair at police headquarters and looked at the file in front of him. Lisa Augustin sat on the other side of the desk. The coffee between them had grown cold while they had tried to knead the different clues in the case together into one coherent mass. No matter how they looked at it, they could not find a common thread.

There were 227 pictures in Lukas Bjerre's Instagram account and from those 227 pictures, there was only one recurrent theme that appeared multiple times.

The barn door.

Lukas had shared the picture four times over nine months, but there was no pattern to the timing of when he had done it. There were 23 days between the first and second times, 173 days between the next two, and 55 between the third and final times, when he had uploaded it the day before he disappeared. They had noted the dates and checked if anything in particular had happened in Lukas's life on those days, but neither the school nor the boy's parents could account for any outings or events that had taken place on the dates in question. The police had obtained access to both Jens and Anne Sofie Bjerre's calendars and the school's old weekly schedules, and Lukas's class had just had regular school on all four of the dates and no coincidences among the after-school activities.

While all the other photos in his profile were tagged with words that had to do with the subject matter (#banana, #outlet, #clouds, #mud, etc.), all four of the photos of the barn door were accompanied only by hostile, aggressive hashtags (#die, #Imgoingtokillyou, #satan, #youwilldie).

There was no doubt in Schäfer's mind. It was critical to the investigation that they find that barn.

He was putting together a summary of all the rural areas on the island of Zealand, where they knew for sure that the boy had been in the last year, either on school field trips or with his family, places where it was plausible that one might run into a barn like the one in the picture.

Schäfer looked at the map of Zealand hanging on the wall. Red pins marked places they knew the boy had stayed. He had visited his grandmother near Roskilde several times, both on his own and with his parents. He had gone to camp with his class in a little hamlet in Odsherred, and other field trips had taken them to the forested area of Hareskoven, just northwest of Copenhagen, to the Faxe Limestone Quarry, and to the Knuthenborg Safari Park drive-through zoo. Augustin had downloaded pictures from the field trips from the school's intranet, but so far there wasn't anything that seriously triggered Schäfer's radar.

Where the hell was this kid?

Schäfer needed someone who could help interpret the psychological evidence in the case, to read the things between the lines that he didn't have the expertise to decipher on his own. He cursed Michala Friis for having resigned from her position with the investigative unit. Her successor didn't possess a tenth of her skill at spotting critical details.

"Have we heard anything from Joakim Kjærgaard?" Schäfer asked.

Joakim Kjærgaard was the police psychologist, who had taken over Friis's job when she transitioned to the private sector.

"Not yet," Augustin said. "I talked to him last night and he still seemed to be stuck at square one."

"Why am I not surprised?" Schäfer asked and looked down at the paperwork again.

Augustin got up and stretched her neck from side to side. Her vertebrae made a loud crunching sound and she sighed heavily.

"Lunch?" she asked.

Schäfer shook his head without looking up.

"I'm just going to grab a bagel from the cafeteria. Can I bring you anything?"

He shook his head again and Augustin left the room.

"All right," Schäfer said to himself, rubbing his palms together. "Let's start from the beginning."

He started listing facts, muttering, and concentrating:

"The boy collects faces. There's one motif that recurs: that barn door. And then there's the warfarin on his jacket . . . Did someone poison him? How did the jacket end up at the Citadel? And who's the Apple Man?"

Schäfer looked at his notes, groping around in his mind.

"Argh, damn it!" he mumbled, running his hands up and down over his cheeks. He leaned back in his chair with his eyes closed. He didn't open them again until the phone on the desk in front of him started ringing.

"Hello?"

"Ah, hello hello."

"Rud?" Schäfer's voice sounded hopeful through the phone. "Tell me you've got something."

"We got the results back on the DNA, and I'm sending them to you . . . now."

The computer in front of Schäfer dinged as a new email arrived in his inbox.

He clicked on the link and opened the email.

"What am I looking at?" he asked.

"The first test results are from the swab from the sweatshirt you found in the trash can. There is only one blood type—one person's DNA."

"And? Do we have a match?"

"We have a match."

Schäfer closed his eyes. "Is it the boy's blood?"

"No, it belongs to a Thomas Strand, age twenty-nine," Rud Johannsen said.

Schäfer opened his eyes again, his brow wrinkled. "Who's he?"

"Born in Haderslev, lives on Sølvgade in Copenhagen. He's a sergeant major and has worked for the Danish military since 2010. But they kicked him out just after New Year's, because he was charged with assaulting a civil servant."

"Is that all we've got on him?"

"No, he's got a few priors and quite a few charges that were filed but then dropped for one reason or another. All of the cases involved violence or threats of violence."

"Against children?"

"No, nothing like that. He's mostly been in bar brawls, but there have been quite a few of them."

Schäfer could hear fingers moving quickly over a keyboard.

"And then there's the DNA results from the boy's jacket," Rud said. "Those little bloodstains."

"Yes?"

"The results are the same. Same person."

"Thomas Strand?"

"Yes."

Schäfer thanked Rud for the call. He hung up and yelled to everyone in the department.

"Time to roll!"

25

WHEN THE SIGNAL was given, the battering ram splintered the frame. The door flew open with a bang and the next few seconds were a cacophonous inferno of shouting and heavy boots stomping into the apartment.

Eight SWAT team officers in tactical gear moved quickly, searching the small apartment room by room with automatic weapons in their hands.

"ALL CLEAR!" a voice yelled from the far end of the apartment.

Schäfer quickly followed the sound. It was freezing cold in the apartment and his breath lingered in the air behind him like smoke from a steam engine. He walked down the narrow hallways with his service weapon raised in front of him. The gun felt cold to the touch, familiar in his hands.

"Schäfer!" one of the officers called. "In here!"

Schäfer turned a corner and entered a bedroom with dark curtains drawn over the windows. There wasn't any toppled furniture or any other signs of a struggle in there, but a faint odor of death had settled like a thin membrane over the room.

Thomas Strand lay in his bed.

The pillow under his head was black with congealed blood and his bald head was tipped backward at a violent, unnatural angle. A bullet hole the size of a blueberry went in through the left side of his lower jaw. It looked like he had been shot at close range—probably while he was asleep.

An assassination, Schäfer thought.

Lisa Augustin appeared beside him, considering the body.

Thomas Strand's eyes were closed, and his facial features were distorted by the bullet that had ripped through his facial muscles and cranium beneath the skin. Blood had trickled out of all the bodily openings in his head, caked now in coagulated stripes down the man's face, while yellowish blobs that looked like little marzipan stars had exploded over the body and the bedding.

Augustin stepped closer to the bed and squinted her eyes. "What is this stuff that's all over everything?"

"I'm guessing mashed potatoes," Schäfer said.

Augustin turned her head to give him a bewildered look. "Mashed potatoes?"

"Yeah, it's an old trick. If you don't have a professional silencer, you can use a large potato. You hold it in front of the muzzle, watch the angle, and then fire the bullet through the potato. It works nearly as well."

Augustin smiled. "An old wives' trick for murderers?"

Schäfer nodded. "Something like that."

"How long do you think he's been lying here like this?"

He shrugged, his eyes running up and down the body. "It's hard to say. We need to wait for Oppermann."

"And the boy?"

Schäfer shook his head. "He's not here."

* * *

The kitchen looked lonely, unused, as if Thomas Strand had never made a meal there. There were only drinks in the fridge: a six-pack of beer, a bottle of vodka, a shelf full of Red Bull. Most of the cupboards were empty. So was the dishwasher. And the trash can contained a couple of takeout containers and used disposable utensils.

"We need to find out how long he has been living here," Schäfer said. "What did the neighbors see? Who came and went to the apartment? Have they seen any kids in the stairwell, and so on."

Lisa Augustin nodded.

They moved on into the bathroom, where the unflattering hippie color scheme revealed that it had last been renovated sometime in the eighties. The walls over the checkerboard linoleum floor were covered in crackled tiles, and the shabby toilet was at least eight different shades of brown.

Schäfer leaned in over the edge of the moss-green bathtub, looking for any traces of blood. There were little dark, curly hairs on the drain cover and the bottom of the tub was dirty. A sharp sewage smell rose from the drain. It didn't look like anyone had bothered to remove any evidence.

"There's something here on the windowsill," Augustin said from behind him.

Schäfer turned around and saw a thin streak of dried blood on the edge of the sill, as if something had grazed it very lightly. Something bloody.

Augustin pointed with her foot at a roll of black trash bags lying under the radiator on the floor by the window, which was ajar.

"Wasn't the bloodstained sweatshirt found in a bag like that?"

Schäfer squatted down and looked back and forth between the roll of bags and the bloodstain.

He stood back up and put on a pair of latex gloves. He opened the mirrored cabinet over the sink and surveyed the contents. The shelves contained the usual toiletries: some deodorant, a disposable razor full of stubble, a toothbrush, toothpaste, aspirin, and mouthwash. There was a box on the bottom shelf, a white box of pills with a prescription label. The label sticker had been put on crookedly, so it was wrinkled, which made it hard for Schäfer to read the text. He held the box out to Augustin.

"What does this say?"

She took it and squinted. "It's something called almotriptan. It says it's for migraines." She gave Schäfer a wry look. "I don't think it's going to help the headache he has right now."

"Whose name is on the prescription?"

"Thomas Strand."

"No, I mean: Who's the doctor? Who wrote the prescription?"

"Oh, it was a . . . Jørgen Juul-Hansen at someplace called Havnegade Medical Practice."

"Damn it!" Schäfer said, running his hand around the back of his neck.

"Were you hoping it would say Jens Bjerre?"

"Yes, it would really help the situation if we could find something to connect the various pieces of this crummy case."

"Maybe Thomas Strand is a friend of the family," Augustin suggested.

"Maybe." Schäfer nodded.

They were interrupted by a forensic technician from NKC who wanted to enter the small bathroom.

"Can I come in?"

"Yes, we'll give you some space now," Schäfer said and herded Augustin out of the room.

They moved into the living room and looked around. There was an open pizza box on the coffee table with a couple of slices of pepperoni pie in it. There was also a box of Cocoa Puffs on the table and a bowl, which was glazed with chocolaty milk residue and dried pieces of puffed chocolate rice.

Schäfer carefully tilted a milk carton that sat on the parquet floor next to the table. He could tell that there was still milk in it.

"The victim ate his dinner in front of the TV and then went to bed without cleaning up," Augustin suggested. "And then someone broke in overnight and what? Shot him?"

Schäfer growled evasively.

"How did the killer get in?" he asked. "Was the door unlocked?"

"No."

"So whoever did this closed the door on their way out, but how did he get in, through the bathroom window?"

"He or she," Schäfer corrected.

"Maybe they knew each other. Maybe the victim let the killer in before he went to bed." Augustin slapped her upper arms to try to warm up. "Holy cow, it's freezing in here."

Schäfer didn't say anything. He stared at the things on the coffee table.

"What are you thinking?"

"Cocoa Puffs," he said. "Who likes Cocoa Puffs?"

"Kids."

Schäfer nodded slowly. "Kids."

"Do you think the boy's been here?"

Schäfer didn't answer that question. Instead, he asked a new one: "How did Thomas Strand's DNA end up on Lukas's jacket?"

Augustin bit her cheek as she considered that.

"Thomas Strand kidnaps Lukas, maybe as part of some plot involving a third person," she suggested. "The third person kills Thomas Strand—and maybe Lukas as well—and then runs off. Or he kills Thomas Strand, kidnaps Lukas, and runs off."

Schäfer didn't say anything. There were too many unknown factors. Too many pieces that didn't fit together.

A crime scene investigator came into the room. "It looks like the heat in the apartment was turned off," he said. "All the radiators are cold as ice."

Augustin shrugged. "Maybe they don't work. It is an old building."

Schäfer walked over to the nearest radiator and turned the thermostat to the left with his glove-clad hand. He heard the water running into the pipes right away and felt the heat spreading from the top of the radiator. He turned it off again.

"They work."

Augustin looked puzzled. "Who the hell turns off the heat in their apartment in the middle of the coldest winter in a hundred years?"

"What makes a worse stink in an apartment building?" Schäfer asked. "A body in a heated apartment or in an unheated one?"

"So you think the killer turned off the heat to cover up the smell?"

"To make sure that the body wouldn't be found for a while." he said with a nod and turned to the investigator. "Make sure to dust for prints on the thermostats and check all the rooms and all the cupboards and drawers in the place for a poison called warfarin."

The investigator got to work, and Schäfer turned to Augustin.

"We have the turned-off radiators and something that looks like a textbook assassination in the bedroom." He pointed toward the room with his thumb. "We have the victim's blood on Lukas's jacket, and if we assume for a moment that the killer was the one who nabbed the boy from the school, then he did it without attracting attention to him or herself. That seems disturbingly professional, well thought out."

They could hear voices out in the stairwell; cheerful greetings that echoed up the stairs.

Medical examiner John Oppermann appeared in the front doorway and Schäfer's eyebrows shot up his forehead.

"What the hell, John?" he blurted out. "You shaved your mustache?"

Oppermann, who had been sporting a Thomson and Thompson style mustache for at least thirty years, smiled and ran his fingertips over his bare upper lip. Then he put on his work glasses.

"Well, which way to the main character here?"

* * *

Schäfer sent Augustin off to ring doorbells and question Thomas Strand's neighbors in the building. In the meantime, he put on a protective suit and face mask and went into the bedroom where Oppermann was examining the body.

The scene of the crime was already contaminated by the numerous snow-wet combat boots that by now had plodded through every room in the apartment, but that's how it went with these types of raids. There was a "shoot first, ask later" mentality in the SWAT team that the boys at NKC always bitched about.

An officer pulled the heavy curtain in the bedroom carefully aside to avoid sending too much dust around the room. The blazing white light from the sky pierced the room and made Thomas Strand's contorted face look even more grotesque and waxy.

Oppermann took the body's temperature and Schäfer averted his gaze. No matter what people had been subjected to in their final hour—whether they were mowed down by an AK-47, cut into little pieces, or dumped naked in the middle of street, there was nothing so humiliating as having a thermometer stuck up your butt without your consent. Schäfer felt that he owed every crime victim the respect of looking away.

"Hmm," Oppermann muttered and shook his head. "It's hard to establish a time of death when the body has been kept this cold. The body's temperature is the same as the room's so that doesn't tell us anything other than that he's been dead for at least twenty-four hours. Rigor mortis is also unreliable because of the cold. Livor mortis observed . . ." He paused and used his shoulder to scratch the mustache that was no longer there. A habit that would probably take a year to break.

He shrugged. "Twenty-four to seventy-two hours is my best estimate. So the time of death would be sometime between Sunday and Tuesday. You probably won't be able to do much with that, but I can't be any more specific right now. It's going to be incredibly difficult to pin it down any more than that."

"The earliest he could have been shot is Monday after eight PM," Schäfer said. "His blood was found on a jacket belonging to the boy who went missing from Nyholm School Monday morning. So we can rule out Sunday."

"Well, unless the deceased was shot Sunday and the boy got the blood on his jacket then."

"You mean *before* he went missing?" That was a possibility Schäfer hadn't considered.

"I don't *mean* anything," Oppermann said. "I'm just telling you what I see here, namely that the time of death is sometime between Sunday and Tuesday."

* * *

Once Oppermann had finished his initial examinations, Thomas Strand's dead body was moved into a body bag and transported to the Department of Forensic Medicine.

"I'll start the autopsy as soon as I get back to the department," Oppermann said.

Schäfer nodded. "I'm right on your heels."

He turned to the window and looked out over the Rosenborg Castle Gardens, which were across the street. The castle rose majestically in the middle of the snow-covered park and made the whole area look like a Disney screensaver. Like something right out of a fairy tale, beautiful.

He turned to the bed and stared at the pool of blood that had seeped down into the mattress. There were bits of brain and potato on the headboard and on the floor were the clothes Schäfer presumed Thomas Strand had removed before getting into bed.

A pair of worn blue jeans, a black T-shirt, and dirty athletic socks turned inside out.

Schäfer sighed heavily as questions accumulated in his mind, like blood in a clogged artery.

If Thomas Strand had kidnapped Lukas Monday morning, had someone then assassinated him that same night and taken the boy? If so, what would be the motive for that? Who was the third party involved?

And more importantly still . . .

Where was Lukas now?

26

THE DRIVE UP to Rørvig took an hour and a half, which was significantly longer than it had taken in Martin's Tesla on a snow-free highway the week before.

Heloise had picked up the Ford from the newspaper's vehicle pool at around ten and was now slowly rolling through the neighborhood of summer vacation homes looking for something she couldn't quite put her finger on, just *something* that would make all the pieces in her thoughts fall into place.

There was more snow up here than in Copenhagen, and most of the small wooden houses looked as if they had been closed up for the winter, dark and deserted. Several of them had shutters over their windows, and there were no footprints to be seen in the snowy front yards. Only prints from roe deer hooves, mouse feet, and hare paws.

Heloise drove up and down the narrow, bumpy lanes for an hour and was losing her enthusiasm when she came by an uneven forest road on her right side. She hit the brakes and looked down the road, which curved a little farther in, heading into the dense, coniferous forest, which began right behind the set-back properties. It was hard to see what was hiding at the end of the road. The snow hadn't been plowed and there was a sign by the entrance.

Private property. No access.

Heloise remembered having seen the sign the previous weekend and ignoring its prohibition. She had turned onto the road anyway. Was that where she had seen the house with the barn?

She turned off the engine and got out of the car. The snow crunched loudly beneath her boots as she walked, and the dark branches above her stole the light from the sky as she made her way farther into the woods.

Heloise spotted a house wrapped in overgrown ivy and years of dirt, and she scanned it for signs of life. All the windows in the main house were covered with red linen curtains and nothing was visible through the cracks other than coal-black darkness.

Heloise looked at the name that hung on the door.

Van Dolmens, it said, a Dutch-sounding last name.

She started walking around toward the backyard and had made it to the corner of the house when she heard a voice behind her.

"What do you want?"

Heloise turned with a start toward the front door, which was now ajar. She could see a thin strip of an elderly woman's face. The woman's one visible eye stared coolly at Heloise.

Heloise nodded politely. "Hi there! I was just walking by and saw that—"

"Didn't you see the sign out by the road?" the woman asked. "This is private property. You're trespassing."

Heloise continued unabashedly. "There's a barn out back, isn't there?" She pointed around behind the house and took a couple more steps in that direction.

The woman opened her door a little farther. She was wearing a light gray terrycloth bathrobe, and a Norwegian forest cat rubbed playfully against her bare ankles. From somewhere inside the house, Heloise could hear the faint tones of an old Supremes song.

Baby, baby. Baby, don't leave me. Please don't leave me. All by myself.

"It's not a barn," the woman said. "It's a shed."

"Okay, we'll call it a shed." Heloise smiled. "Could I see it?"

The woman's eyes narrowed, and she tilted her head back. "Can you *see* it? Why?"

"I take pictures of old barns. I'd really like to take one of yours . . . of your shed. If you don't mind?"

The woman reluctantly eyed her up and down. "But you don't have a camera with you . . ."

Heloise pulled her iPhone out of her pocket. "I use this."

The woman hesitated for a second and then shook her head. "The shed collapsed. The snow was too heavy and . . . Bad construction, old piece of junk."

"Could I just go around and see?" Heloise took another couple of steps farther from the house.

"No, I'm going to ask you to move on. This is private property."

Heloise ignored the woman's wishes and proceeded around the house.

"Hey!" The woman leaned out the door and called after her. Then she rustled around in her entryway and put on a pair of boots. "Hey, you there!"

Heloise quickly rounded the corner of the house. Then she slowed down.

There wasn't much to see back there. What had once been a shed now looked like a pile of pick-up sticks, dropped by a careless hand. The boards lay jumbled in a big pile and were covered with snow. It was impossible to tell what the building had looked like before it had collapsed, and Heloise looked for those two round windows she had seen in the picture in the case file.

She walked over and started lifting off boards and brushing aside snow, but before she had time to find a line or detail in the wood that she recognized, the woman caught up to her and grabbed her upper arm.

"This is private property," she repeated. "Get out of here!"

Heloise pulled her arm back and showed her a picture of Lukas Bjerre on her phone.

"Have you seen this kid?" she asked. "He's missing."

The woman looked at the picture. Then her eyes softened a little.

"Is that why you're here? You're looking for that boy?"

"He took this picture the other day." Heloise showed her the picture of the barn. "And then after that he disappeared, and now coincidently your shed has collapsed . . . His name's Lukas Bjerre."

"Yes, I know who he is."

Heloise's heartrate sped up. "You know him?"

"Are you with the police?"

"No, I'm a journalist."

The woman was quiet for a moment. Then she nodded. "I've been following the case. Come inside and I'll show you what the shed looked like before it collapsed. I have a couple of old pictures of it in the house somewhere."

Heloise cast a hesitant glance at the main house. She stood in the snow up to her mid-calves and her feet wouldn't budge.

"It's all right," the woman said, holding out her hand. "I'm Rita."

Heloise took the woman's hand. "Heloise Kaldan."

"I didn't mean to be rude just now, but I thought you were from the municipality."

"The municipality?"

"Yes, from the permit office. They've started dropping by and calling nonstop with their tape measures and building codes. What do they care if my house sticks out ten inches too far in one direction or the other? It's been like this for thirty years. And who's it going to bother anyway? There's no one around!" She flung out her arms and started walking back to the front door. "You comin'?"

The woman left her door open as she disappeared into the house.

Heloise looked around for a moment and then followed her.

She took off her winter boots in the front hall and followed the woman into the living room in her socks. It was nice and warm inside, cramped and dark in a way that made Heloise think about the forts she used to build as a kid out of sofa cushions in her dad's apartment on Suensonsgade. She would lie inside in the darkness with a flashlight and read comic books and eat cookies while the other neighborhood kids played outside. Heloise had opted out of the sunshine and the rest of the world—and loved it.

"Now, let me see. Where did I put those pictures?" the woman said. She opened the curtains and let the winter light into the room. She walked over to a tall bookshelf, its shelves filled with stacks of books, binders, knickknacks, and ceramics, and pulled an old wooden beer crate off the bottom shelf.

"I bet there's something in here," she said and dug through its contents. She pulled a Kodak photo envelope out of the crate. She handed it to Heloise and then went out into the kitchen, where a coffee maker had started making hissing and gurgling noises.

Heloise opened the envelope and browsed through the pictures. They were photos of family life, and she recognized the woman of the house in her younger years. She paused at a picture that looked like it was taken on a summer day on the patio behind the house. A man was sitting at a picnic table—a middle-aged man in shorts, a polo shirt, and baseball hat—and a lanky teenage girl in a Metallica T-shirt with long, henna-red hair. Heloise could see from the date stamp on the back of the picture that it had been developed in 1999, the same year she had graduated from high school. Memories of that day flashed through her mind: the victory dance around the statue in the center of Kongens Nytorv with Gerda. Cans of beer, laughter, and Pearl Jam on repeat.

Dreaming about the life that awaited them . . .

"I've been following the case in the news," the woman said with curiosity. She had reappeared beside Heloise. "Do you think the boy is in our neighborhood? In a barn?"

"Is this your family?" Heloise asked instead of answering her question. She held out the picture.

The woman smiled. "Yes, that's Diederik and Stine, my husband and daughter."

Heloise looked around the room for signs that the woman lived with someone. "Does he live here, your husband?"

The woman set the coffee pot down on the table and reached for the stack of photos. "No, Diederik passed away in 2008. Prostate cancer. I've been on my own ever since." She started flipping through the pictures.

"And your daughter?" Heloise asked. "Does she live in Rørvig?"

"No, Stine works for the Danish embassy in Mozambique. So she lives in Maputo—that's the capital down there. She's been there for, what, I guess it's been eleven or twelve years now." The woman pointed to the mantle, where there was a picture of three boys with dark skin and longish hair. "That's Zas, Bryce, and the little one with the ring curls is Alick, the youngest of my grandkids."

She pulled a photo out of the stack.

"Ah, here it is. See, this is what the shed looked like before it collapsed. I would have cleaned up the mess out there, but what's the hurry, right? Now I'll wait until the snow is gone." She handed Heloise the picture.

It was the right kind of wood, Heloise could see, but there were no windows in the barn door. No iron clasp that looked like a mouth.

"I'm sorry, Rita," she said and set the picture down again. "I must have been wrong. This wasn't where I saw the barn I'm looking for."

"No need to apologize. I'm sorry, too, that I was so rude earlier. I don't get very many proper visitors out here, so . . . coffee?"

"No thanks, I'd better be going."

The smile lines around the woman's eyes faded some and Heloise thought that maybe it wouldn't be as nice to live out here all by yourself as she had imagined. She looked at the woman's grandchildren again on the mantle.

Wasn't one of the arguments for getting married and having kids that you wouldn't have to be lonely in your old age, that there would be someone to take care of you, someone to share your life with? But what guarantee was there that your life would have a happy ending, Heloise thought. The woman across from her appeared to have played by the rules, done what was expected, lived a traditional, bourgeois life. But now her husband was six feet under, and her daughter lived on another continent while she sat here, disappointed and lonely, in a hovel with a cat as her only company.

Heloise was prepared for the loneliness. She was at peace with it. But she never wanted to put herself in a situation again where she risked being disappointed by someone or something.

She looked at the woman. "Do you know of any other places in the area where I could find the barn I'm looking for?"

"Hm, there are a lot of houses out here in the woods along the coast, but unfortunately I can't point you in the right direction. I don't get out that much anymore."

Heloise thanked her for her help and walked back to her car with a strange lump in her stomach.

She got in her car and was about to turn the key when her phone rang. The caller ID didn't display a number.

"This is Kaldan," she said.

"It's me." Gerda's voice sounded tense.

Heloise closed her eyes for a second, simultaneously relieved and angry.

"Hey," she said.

"Hi. Listen, I know you're mad at me, but I don't have time to talk about that right now, and that's not why I'm calling."

"Then why?" Heloise looked puzzled.

"I need a favor."

Heloise waited to hear what Gerda wanted without saying anything.

"Something has come up here at work and I can't leave. But I can't get ahold of my mother. She's not answering her phone and Christian is in the U.S. and . . ."

"I'll pick up Lulu," Heloise said.

She heard Gerda exhale in relief.

"Thank you."

"I'll bring her home with me after work and she's welcome to spend the night if it gets late."

"Thank you," Gerda said again. "I don't know when I'll be able to leave."

"What happened?"

"I can't tell you, not right now, anyway. I don't have a handle on the situation yet, so . . ."

"Okay."

"You just need to trust me when I say that—"

"Okay," Heloise repeated. "I trust you, of course I do."

Heloise hung up and turned the car key in the ignition. She looked down the bumpy wooded lane one last time. Rita stood in the snow watching Heloise.

There was something about the place that felt familiar and yet not.

Heloise *knew* that she had seen that barn. If it wasn't here, then where was it?

She put the car in reverse and turned to look out the rear window.

CHAPTER

27

S CHÄFER SCANNED THE row of white rubber boots lined up below a garland of chainmail gloves. Various names were written with a Sharpie on the ankles of the boots, and he reached for the pair on the far right.

They were labeled *Erik Schäfer.*

He slipped the boots on and walked down the long hallway of the autopsy room. He passed the isolation room, where some poor guy who had died of meningitis or the plague or some other barbaric bacteria was being autopsied. The next four tables in the autopsy room were empty and clean, and Oppermann stood at the fifth and last one up to his elbows in Thomas Strand's internal organs.

"Well, Doc, what do you say?" Schäfer came to a stop next to the autopsy table and nodded at the bullet hole in Thomas Strand's face. "Did he die of natural causes or what's your verdict?"

John Oppermann looked up from the open ribcage without lifting his head.

"Very funny."

"You know I admire you for the way you don't cut corners." Schäfer smiled. "Even when a man's been shot in the face, you won't determine a cause of death until he's been checked for pneumonia and syphilis. I mean, that's thorough!"

Oppermann ignored him and continued working in silence.

Schäfer watched the man's experienced hands and recognized the procedure: Oppermann made a Mercedes incision over the victim's heart, three incisions that met in the middle, like the car logo.

"What are you looking for?" Schäfer asked.

"Scars in the heart."

"Scars in the heart," Schäfer repeated and happened to think of what Heloise had said about soldiers with PTSD. Those were the words she had used to describe their situation, that they had *scars in the heart*. But wouldn't anyone have scars in their heart if you looked closely enough?

Scars from trauma? Scars from grief?

He knew that if he dissected his own heart, it would be full of scar tissue, old scars from old battles.

"Some scars are visible to the naked eye," Oppermann explained, as if he could read Schäfer's mind. "It could be from an old blood clot or other heart disease. Other scars are harder to see. It could be like the ones that . . ." He paused for a moment, trying to find the right way to express it.

"Like the ones that we have, from Kosovo?" Schäfer suggested.

"Yes," Opperman agreed somberly. "Like the ones we have from Kosovo."

Opperman moved on to the head. He made an incision with the scalpel from ear to ear over the crown of Thomas

Strand's head and everted the skin forward. Then he began sawing the cranium open.

Schäfer's gaze fell on the bloody blob at the top of Thomas Strand's neck, where his face had been turned inside out, and he thought of Lukas Bjerre's Instagram photos.

"Are you familiar with something called pareidolia?" Schäfer had to raise his voice to be heard over the wail of the Stryker saw Oppermann was using to cut the cranium open with.

The medical examiner stopped the saw and looked up at Schäfer. "What was that?"

"Pareidolia," Schäfer repeated. "Does that mean anything to you?"

"You mean like when you see faces in different things?"

Schäfer nodded, impressed. "Yes! How the hell did you know that?"

"I remember we discussed it back when I was in medical school." Oppermann opened the top of the cranium, like the flip top on a tube of toothpaste. "People who are resuscitated after having been dead for a minute or two sometimes say that they've seen a face surrounded by a luminous glow. Then of course they always start talking about life after death and that sort of thing. They become tremendously religious. Really, it's more likely that what they saw was just some random light incursion. In the final seconds before death occurred, the eye took in random patterns, which the brain subsequently decoded as facial features. And then that's the sight they remember when they wake up again."

"So you don't think they had a quick gin and tonic with the Lord?" Schäfer asked with a smirk.

It was an inside joke. What Schäfer and Oppermann saw in their jobs did not leave any room for religious fantasies.

John Oppermann raised a bushy eyebrow and allowed a snort to escape his nose. "Hardly. But it is actually quite human."

"What is?"

"Trying to find some meaning in things."

"Believing in a higher power, you mean?"

"No, I'm talking about pareidolia. It's really about our need to understand the world we live in. We're so preoccupied with labeling the things around us that we misinterpret what we're seeing."

"Academics think it has to do with being prepared to fight," Schäfer said. "That we're so on our guard that we see the face of the enemy everywhere—even in places where there is no enemy."

"That makes sense." Oppermann nodded thoughtfully. "It's always wise to take precautions. What's that old scouting motto . . . better safe than sorry?"

"Be prepared."

"Potato-potahto." Oppermann blinked and lifted the brain out of Strand's skull with a practiced motion and a loud, wet squelch.

* * *

After John Oppermann had washed and changed his clothes, he and Schäfer left the department. They stopped briefly on Simon's Bridge. The sky bridge was named for one of Oppermann's predecessors and connected the autopsy rooms to the rest of the department.

Schäfer leaned against the glass wall and looked at Oppermann. "So he was shot. It was an assassination, right?"

Oppermann nodded. "One bullet from what looks like a nine millimeter." He pointed with his thumb at his lower jaw where the entry wound had been.

"Can you tell me anything else right now?"

"You know the procedure," Oppermann said elusively. "The blood tests go to Toxicology. Ballistics will look at the bullet wound and the bullet. Fingernail scrapings will be sent in for examination, even if there's no current indication that he fought his killer. There are no signs of defensive injuries on the deceased, no cuts or marks on the arms from any kind of struggle." He shrugged. "We'll have to wait and see."

The deceased, Schäfer thought.

Oppermann had once confided in him that he never learned the names of the people he autopsied. He did his work and when he was done, he hung up his lab coat along with his memories of the milky-white dead eyes that he had looked into over the course of the day.

He didn't take his work home with him. He didn't let his emotions stew, not anymore.

Schäfer sometimes envied him.

But then again, not . . .

He remembered the name of every single victim in every single murder case he had ever investigated, and he remembered them best if their cases were never solved, the ones whose killers were never caught.

"All right, John." He shook Oppermann's hand. "Let me know if anything turns up."

28

THE SCISSORS SLID through the paper as if it was made of whipped cream. Finn carefully followed the contours with the sharp metal edge and took extra effort around the boy's hair. And around his ears. When he was done, he held the newspaper clipping up in front of him and looked at those watchful blue eyes. The few, almost invisible freckles on the nose. The mouth that curled upward into a cautious smile.

The sight really put Finn in a good mood.

He could remember the first time he had seen the boy over at the school and the first time the boy had come into the store on his own. That was how Finn preferred it: When they came by themselves, without their parents.

Finn had offered to let him take an apple from the pile, and the boy had reached for a dull red one. That was an unusual choice. All the other kids always picked the shiniest apples and always the green ones, but not this boy in the picture.

Finn had known right away that he was something very special, that he was different. Like Finn. But perhaps no one would find that out now, he thought, and put the newspaper back on the stack on the table.

The door to the staff room opened and Anja with the eyelashes came into the room.

Finn quickly folded up the clipping and hid it away.

"Your break is over, Finn."

She walked over and pushed a button on the coffee dispensing machine. It spat out a white plastic cup and filled it with a stream of instant coffee.

"Malik says customers are complaining about the cucumbers. They're too soft, so you need to sort through them right away, okay?"

Finn nodded.

He got up and put the newspaper clipping in his employee locker and then locked it.

Anja sat down heavily at the staff table and reached for the day's *B.T.* from the stack of newspapers. The front page promised macabre details about the Lukas Bjerre case in a six-page article inside the paper, and her fingers purposefully flipped through to it.

Then she stopped.

"What the hell? Who cut up the newspaper? Did you do this, Finn?"

Finn shook his head and hurried back out onto the floor.

29

"WHERE'S MOM?"

Lulu looked up in surprise from the canvas in front of her. She was painting an eye that was crying grayish green acrylic tears, which dripped down onto the floor in front of her stocking feet.

"Your mom had to work late today, so you're coming home with me," Heloise said and flung her arms up in the air. "Surprise!"

"Yay!" Lulu threw her arms around Heloise's neck so her long chestnut-brown curls flew into the air.

They found Lulu's coat and backpack in the entryway at the rec center and walked out onto the schoolyard hand in hand, past the basketball court, and then stopped at the intersection in front of the school.

"Well?" Heloise asked and gave Lulu a loving bump with her elbow. "Did you have a good day?"

"Mm-hmm," Lulu said.

"What did you do?"

"Nothing."

"Nothing?"

"Nah."

"Not a single thing? You've been at school for—what?—eight hours and you haven't done a thing?"

Lulu giggled. "Well, yeah, I have, but I don't want to go into it."

"Oh." Heloise nodded in agreement. "That's a totally different matter."

The light turned green, and they started crossing the street.

"What about you? What did you do?" Lulu asked.

"Nothing."

"No way. You did too do stuff!"

"Sure, but I don't want to go into it," Heloise said, shaking her head in mock somberness. Then she smiled.

Lulu laughed and looked up at her, her eyes twinkling with delight.

"What do you want to have for dinner?" Heloise asked.

"Spaghetti and meat balls!"

"Well then that's what we'll have." She gave Lulu's hand a squeeze. "I think I have most of the ingredients at home, but we are going to need to pick up some meat and a few other little odds and ends."

"Where?"

"We can get them at Føtex Food."

"Can't we just buy one of those jars with the meatballs already in it? Mom usually buys those."

"What kind is that?"

"I don't know. They keep it in the ready-made section. It's in a glass container. It tastes a lot better than when you make it yourself."

"Okay," Heloise said. "On one condition."

"What?"

"You pick out some candy for us while I find the other things."

Lulu cracked a grin.

Heloise watched her in secret as they walked along Grønningen. The little girl she had known since she had been a newborn, a pink lump with a monk's hairdo and a hormone rash. She had gotten so big—so *pretty*. Eight years old and heartbreakingly optimistic, secure in her belief that the world was a good place.

Someday it would let her down, Heloise thought and felt a pang in her heart that almost made her double over.

When they entered the store, Heloise pointed to the wall with the pick-and-mix candy bins.

"Knock yourself out, beautiful. I'll find the spaghetti sauce you like and then we'll meet back here at the self-checkout in a few minutes, okay?"

Heloise grabbed a basket and headed over to the refrigerated section at the far end of the store, where she found the display fridge with the prepared meals. She grabbed a jar of Bolognese sauce from the top shelf. She also added some Parmesan cheese, parsley, and a package of fresh linguine noodles to her basket.

Just as she had selected a bottle of chardonnay from the chilled wines, a text arrived from Martin.

Would you like to have dinner together? Restaurant Frank at 8?

Heloise called him and he answered right away.

"I have Lulu tonight," she said. "Gerda had to work and couldn't find a sitter, so I'm bringing Lulu home to my place. We're going to have dinner there."

"That sounds great!" His voice sounded exuberant. "Can I come over or is this a girls' night?"

"You're welcome to join us if you want to. But if Lulu spends the night, you're going to have to go home after dinner."

She turned around to look for Lulu over the shelves in the wine section. She spotted her dark curls and eyes, which lit up with excitement. Heloise saw her laugh and she took a step to the side so she could see all the way down the aisle with the spices and baking supplies to where Lulu was.

Lulu was at the end of the aisle, weighing a bag of candy. A man was squatting next to her, a skinny man, pale as wax, with silvery gray titanium glasses and short, dirty blond hair that was receding a bit at the temples. He gazed at Lulu, mesmerized, enthralled, eager as a dog whose owner had just walked in the door.

His enthusiasm sent a chill down Heloise's spine.

Heloise hurriedly concluded her conversation with Martin and walked quickly over to Lulu and the stranger.

She stepped in front of Lulu right as the man held a chartreuse-green apple out to her. Heloise put her hand on the apple and pushed the man's hand away, forcefully.

"No thank you."

The man got up and nervously adjusted his glasses. He was the same height as Heloise, and even though they were standing face to face, his eyes were still on Lulu.

"Can I help you with something?" Heloise eyed him stiffly.

"I . . . I just wanted to give her an apple," the man said, holding the fruit out in both hands like an offering.

"No thanks," Heloise repeated and took Lulu by the hand. "You just stay far away from her, you hear?"

The man avoided making eye contact with Heloise. He nodded strangely agreeably, awkward and confused, and then quickly vanished around the corner, heading toward the fruit section.

"What's wrong?" Lulu asked once they had left the store.

"Nothing," Heloise said, trying to smile. "It's just . . . You shouldn't take things from strangers. You know that, right?"

"But I always get a free apple when we go to Føtex. Mom says it's okay."

"From that guy?" Heloise pointed at the store. "You usually get apples from him?"

Lulu nodded. Her brown eyes were wide and questioning.

"Hmm," Heloise said and zipped Lulu's jacket up to her chin so she wouldn't get cold. "That's not a great idea."

Heloise knew she was overstepping the lines of what she should say to someone else's child, but she didn't care.

"People can seem nice even when they're not. Do you understand?"

Lulu shrugged.

"You can't trust everyone. Your mom and dad, grandma and me—you can always count on us. But when it comes to other people, it's a good idea to be a little skeptical, okay?"

"Skeptical?"

"Yes. I mean it's totally fine to hope for the best, but you always need to take precautions and be prepared for the worst. Some people are kind of messed up in the head."

Lulu looked puzzled and then smiled. "Well, you're a little messed up in the head too."

"Yes." Heloise smiled. "You may be right about that."

"But you do know that I'm eight, right?"

Heloise nodded.

"I'm not a baby anymore."

"I know that."

"Next year I have to start walking home from school by myself."

Heloise nodded in surrender. "Yes, yes, and soon you'll move away from home and be hired to do some big, impressive job at NATO and before we know it, you'll start walking with a cane, *but* . . ."

Lulu giggled.

"Just remember to take care of yourself along the way is all I'm saying. Okay?" Heloise reached out and brushed a couple of strands of dark hair off Lulu's face.

Lulu rolled her eyes. "Yeah, yeah. Did you find the spaghetti sauce or what?"

Heloise raised the plastic bag in confirmation. "Let's go home and have some food. Are you hungry?"

Lulu nodded, and they started walking.

"Hey, who's this Tristan guy you're so crazy about?" Heloise asked.

"Where'd you hear that?"

"Your mom."

"He's in fifth grade." Lulu smiled. "He plays basketball."

Heloise whistled, impressed. She looked back and discovered that the man with the apple was standing in the store's sliding front door watching them.

Heloise shot him a warning look, but he didn't notice her.

He saw only Lulu.

30

T HERE WERE SIX surveillance cameras along each of the four tracks in Østerport Station. That meant that the police needed to plow through twenty-four videotapes, each one twelve hours long, to see if they could spot Lukas Bjerre in the crowd of almost 100,000 people who had gotten on or off the trains at the station on Monday. It was like looking for the infamous needle in a haystack.

Michael Voss scratched the back of his head with the eraser end of a pencil. He shook his head and looked tiredly at Schäfer, who had just come back from police headquarters after his visit to the Pathology Department.

"This is like *Where's Waldo*," he said. "I mean, if you image a black and white version of *Where's Waldo* where the pages of the book are 100 by 100 yards. We've cleared the first six hours, so we're halfway there."

Voss and his team in Computer Forensic Investigations had been working around the clock since they had received the tapes on Monday evening. An almost endless row of computer screens lit up the dark room inside police headquarters. IT specialists sat in a line, alternately pressing *play* and *pause*, as they reviewed each frozen frame for anything that stuck out.

"What have you found?" Schäfer asked.

"So far we haven't found shit and now it's almost crap o'clock again." Voss looked at his watch. "It's going to be another long night in here."

"All right. Let me know if you find anything," Schäfer said and headed for the exit.

"Yo, Voss!" One of the men in front of one of the computers called out. "You might want to come and look at this."

Schäfer stopped.

He followed Voss over to the guy who had called out. He was quite young. Schäfer thought he looked like a big kid—a kid who was suffering from a serious vitamin deficiency, lanky and sallow, pale in that way that only gamers who live off potato chips and soda look.

"Well?" Voss crossed his arms and nodded at the screen. "What are you working on?"

"The recordings from Monday between four and seven PM."

"Why the hell are you looking at those?" Voss raised his arm as if he wanted to give the boy a disciplining swat to the back of the head. "Those weren't the ones I asked you to check, you ninny."

"No, but I've already checked the others, and there wasn't anything, so I thought I would go ahead with . . ."

"Your job isn't to think. Your job is to follow orders," Voss said. "What did you find?"

"Check this out." The guy typed something on his keyboard.

Schäfer stepped over to the screen. "What are we looking at?" he asked.

"Track 4, Monday, 6:13 PM."

The playback was set to a sort of choppy slow-motion, which made all the movements in the image look robotic. Schäfer saw the B train pull up to the platform. People in shades of gray crowded together by the train doors. Passengers got out; new travelers boarded. Then the doors began to close.

"Now look . . . ," the IT specialist said and pointed.

A man appeared on the right side of the screen and put his hand into the gap between the automatic sliding doors. The doors opened again, and the man boarded the train. Then the doors closed behind him and the train left the station.

Voss shrugged. "So?"

The young guy rewound the tape, going back a couple of seconds, and then hit *play* again. This time he paused the playback right when the man stuck his hand between the closing train doors with his back to the camera.

Schäfer felt his cheeks grow hot and the hair follicles at the back of his neck tingled in that familiar way.

The man on the platform was wearing a backpack. It was impossible to make out the color from the recording, but the LEGO Ninjago logo was clear on the side of the backpack. As was the Stormtrooper reflector that hung from the zipper.

"I'll be damned," Schäfer mumbled.

"The boy's backpack," Voss said, clasping his hands together in satisfaction behind his head. "It's like I always say. If there's video evidence, we'll find it!"

"Can you zoom in on him?" Schäfer asked.

The IT specialist typed something and enlarged the man's image.

"But that's the only angle we have of him," he said. "We don't have anything that captures his face."

Voss leaned closer to the screen, scrunching up his eyes. "What kind of a weird outfit is he wearing?"

Schäfer closed his eyes tight and the blood in his veins started to boil.

Damn it!

He had had him. He had had him and he had let him get away.

Schäfer opened his eyes again and looked at the man on the screen.

"It's a pilot's suit," he said.

"UNO!"

Lulu held her last card up in front of her mouth and looked triumphantly across the dining table at Martin.

"What the heck, you little rascal?" he laughed. "How did you get rid of all your cards already?"

Martin drew three more from the deck, got a wild card, and played it. "Change to red!"

Lulu threw a red eight down on the table and thrust her arms up. "Ta-da!"

"That's the third time in a row!" Martin said, skeptically shaking his head. "I think you must be cheating."

"No way." Lulu tossed her hair and started gathering up the cards from the table.

"Yes way. You must be," he joked.

"No, I'm not. Heloise, Martin says I'm cheating."

"He's just a poor loser." Heloise smiled, setting the tray with the plates down on the table. "Could you two please set the table? Dinner's almost ready now."

Heloise could hear Martin and Lulu laughing together as she returned to the stove to get the pots with the pasta and sauce. It was nice to have them both in the apartment, but it also made it clear to Heloise that this was the closest they were ever going to come to resembling a real family: Heloise, the boyfriend, and the godchild. A mock version of the nuclear family that she would always keep at arm's length.

"What did you do today?" Martin asked once they were all seated.

Heloise took the pasta fork and asked Lulu to hold out her plate.

"Karen Aagaard foisted a story off on me, so I've been working on that," she said and spun a ball of linguine onto Lulu's plate.

"Foisted?" Martin asked. "What do you mean by that?"

"I was working on something with Gerda, which Aagaard vetoed because she wanted me to dig into something else."

"What does she want you to dig into?"

"That case the media is all crazed about right now. You know the one." Heloise gave him a look.

Martin glanced over at Lulu, who was pouring sauce on her pasta, and then asked in English, "About the missing kid?"

Heloise nodded and opened the bottle of wine.

"Uh, you know I can speak English, right?" Lulu said, twirling linguine around her fork.

"You can?" Martin asked.

Lulu shoveled the bite into her mouth. "Mm-hmm."

"How did you get to be so clever?"

"I'm eight years old!"

"Yeah, but when I was eight, I wasn't as bright as you are," he said. "How can you already know how to speak English?"

"Netflix," she said and swallowed. "Plus, we take English at school. Are you writing about Lukas?" She looked at Heloise.

Heloise ran her fingers through her hair. "Well, that's what my boss wants me to do, so . . ."

"Because you think he's dead?"

"Whoa, hey!" Martin put his hand on top of Lulu's. "No one thinks he's dead. The chances are still really good that the police will find him soon. We actually know the lead detective working on the case and he is incredibly good at what he does. He'll find Lukas. Isn't that right, Helo?"

Heloise looked down at her plate to avoid making eye contact with Lulu.

"Mm-hmm," she said and nodded. "He'll find him . . . One way or another."

"Yes, it'll end well, the whole thing," Martin said. He winked at Lulu and took a mouthful of pasta.

Heloise cleared her throat and reached for her wineglass without looking at either of them.

"Or maybe it won't," she mumbled. "You never know. I think it's a good idea to be realistic about this."

Heloise noticed Martin's jaw muscles stop chewing. He gave her a look that indicated she could sugarcoat things a little more.

Heloise squirmed in her chair. "But no matter what, you'll be fine," she told Lulu. "You've got a lot of people looking out for you, beautiful."

Lulu looked at them in turn. Her eyes were suddenly serious.

"I think he's dead."

Heloise looked puzzled. "Why do you say that?"

"I don't know. He's just . . . weird."

"Weird how?" Heloise set down her silverware.

Lulu shrugged, searching for words. "I don't know, like . . . Sometimes he's a lot of fun. He kids around with me and stuff. But other times he seems so . . . so *angry*."

"In what way?"

"Well, I think he likes me," she began.

"Of course. Who doesn't?" Martin smiled.

"But then the other day I passed him on the stairs at school. At recess, you know?"

Heloise nodded to get her to continue.

"I bumped into him and then he went completely nuts."

"Why?"

"How should I know?!" Lulu shrugged theatrically. "He just flipped out. He was yelling and screaming and then Patrick came over to comfort him, but . . ."

"Who's Patrick?"

"One of the recess monitors. He just wanted to help us solve the conflict, but Lukas kicked him and hit him in the stomach and then Patrick got, like, super mad."

"What happened then?"

"Then Lukas got in *big* trouble. Patrick dragged him down the stairs and tossed him out into the schoolyard. I've never seen Patrick so angry before."

"Who did you say he is, this Patrick guy?"

"One of the teachers."

"What's he like?"

"He's all right, but he spends most of his time with the boys," Lulu said. "They do role-playing and fencing and stuff like that, and they're always outside—even when it's cold. He's not so good at girl stuff."

Martin looked at Heloise. "Does this Lukas kid have a diagnosis or something like that?"

Heloise shrugged. Then she looked at Lulu. "Have you seen Lukas flip out other times?"

"Yeah. There's a kid in Lukas's class named Toke. Everyone's scared of him except for Lukas. One day they were out in the schoolyard arguing and then I heard Lukas tell Toke that he was going to kill him."

Martin raised his eyebrows and glanced briefly at Heloise. Then he turned his attention back to Lulu. "Kill him? Did he really say that?"

Lulu nodded.

"What did the grownups say about that?"

"Nothing. They didn't hear him say it. And Toke didn't say anything either, because he always gets the blame whenever there's trouble, so probably nobody would have believed him. All the grownups really like Lukas, because he's usually quiet and because he's super good at every subject, but, well . . . *I* heard it."

"Did you tell your mom about this?" Heloise asked.

Lulu shook her head and took another bite of pasta. "I was right, wasn't I? This sauce is crazy good."

Heloise nodded slowly as she thought about what Lulu had said.

When the doorbell rang, she got up. Her stomach dropped when she saw Gerda's face on the video display. She buzzed her into the building and opened the door of the apartment for her.

"Mom, why are you here already?" Lulu said when Gerda walked in.

"Hi, honey . . . uh, it's nice to see you too," Gerda said, taking off her army green rubber boots. She walked over and kissed her daughter on the top of her head.

"Yeah, hi, but seriously—why do we have to go home so soon? Couldn't I spend the night with Heloise?"

"Not today, honey."

"Please?"

"Not today, Lulu."

"But couldn't I just stay and watch a little bit of *Kung Fu Panda 3*? We bought candy and we were going to watch a movie. So can't you just have a cup of coffee or something before we leave?"

"Sure." Gerda nodded. "One cup. Okay, so off to the living room with you and then we'll go home in half an hour."

"Martin, don't you want to come watch the movie?" Lulu asked.

Martin gave Gerda a hug. Then he disappeared into the living room with Lulu.

Gerda sat down in the empty chair next to Heloise and put a warm hand on her back.

"Hey," she said, and just like that all the hard feelings between them were gone. "Thanks for your help. Did you have a good time?" She unzipped her black leather jacket and wriggled out of it.

Heloise nodded. "A great time. How about you? Did you get a handle on whatever situation you needed to get a handle on?"

"Yes and no. Can I have a sip?" Gerda reached for Heloise's wineglass.

"Yes. I'm assuming that you don't actually want coffee?" Heloise smiled.

"No, thanks," Gerda said and drained the wineglass. "One of my former clients has been killed."

"In Afghanistan?"

"No. In Copenhagen. Can you believe it?"

"Really? Just now? In a training exercise?"

"No, in his bed. Shot in the head."

"What?" Heloise raised both eyebrows in surprise. She filled the wineglass again and handed it to Gerda.

"I know. right? It's crazy," Gerda said. "So we spent the whole day sorting through the entire course of his therapy. We turned over every stone."

"We?"

Gerda's and Heloise's eyes met. "Yes, another trauma psychologist and myself. The client was in therapy with me up until a year and a half ago. Do you remember the guy who had the crush on me and started stalking me online?"

Heloise nodded. "It was him?"

"Yes. He became practically obsessed. It was creepy. So I got one of my coworkers to take over his therapy at that point so that it wouldn't turn into an even bigger problem."

"I remember that," Heloise said. "But I don't remember your actually being afraid of him."

"No, not *afraid*, but . . . He was an unsavory guy."

"In what way?"

"In every way! Most of the soldiers I see for therapy have been through so many awful experiences during their deployments, things they need to process. It's often that they've lost buddies. They've had friends blown up by road-side bombs and had to gather up the bloody pieces so the soldier's parents back home would have something to bury. Horrifying!" Gerda rubbed her eyes tiredly. "And of course my clients need to process all that. But another thing that weighs on them is that they have killed people. In some situations, killing the enemy doesn't affect them very much, but . . ."

"Like when?"

"Like when it comes to members of ISIS or the Taliban who are firing an AK-47 at our troops. Then it's kill or be killed. That's not something they generally lose sleep over. But when it's a civilian who gets killed—especially if it's a child—many of them have a hard time with that later."

"And your former client? Was he affected by that?"

"No, that's what was so creepy. He was almost *proud* of the notches he had in his belt. I happen to know that on one tour of duty in Afghanistan he shot a whole family when he was clearing a house in a village. Children, uncles, aunts, grandparents—everyone. The BDA reported it as a legitimate enemy killing, but in therapy he admitted that they were unarmed."

"The BDA?"

"Yeah, it stands for Battle Damage Assessment. The soldiers keep a log of who and how many people they've killed and under what circumstances. And in the log this particular episode was described as a by-the-book combat situation, but in reality he made the family line up in a row and then he . . ." She made the shape of an automatic weapon with her hands and then squeezed the trigger. "And he *smiled* when he described it."

Heloise narrowed her eyes in disbelief. "He really told you that?"

"No, he didn't tell *me* that story, but I know it from my coworker."

Heloise hesitated for a moment but couldn't help but stick with the topic. "The one who took over the client from you?"

"Right," Gerda said evasively. She took a sip of the wine. "One of the other trauma psychologists at the barracks."

Heloise had no doubt whom she was alluding to.

"And now he's dead?" she asked. "The client?"

Gerda nodded.

Heloise shrugged. "Well, that's how karma works. Have you told the police?"

"Which part?"

"That he killed a bunch of civilians in Afghanistan."

Gerda shook her head. "The military is responsible for communications with the police. I just attended the in-house meeting at the barracks. Besides, like I said, it wasn't me that he told his story to."

"No, it was your *coworker*." Heloise nodded sarcastically and bit her lower lip. "Why did he share the story with you?

Isn't the idea that that sort of thing is meant to stay between the psychologist and their client?"

Gerda eyed Heloise for a long moment without saying anything.

"Because he trusts me," she said. "Like I trust you."

"Hmm," Heloise said. She didn't notice that she had rested her hand on her abdomen until she instinctively removed it again. "I think you ought to tell the police what you know either way."

Gerda leaned forward in her chair in a way that signaled that the conversation was over.

"Lulu," she called. "It's getting late, sweetie. We have to go home now."

Gerda's resistance made Heloise think of the barn door and the woods in Rørvig, and she decided she was going to need to come clean to Schäfer. If her intuition was right, she couldn't keep hiding it from him.

They got up from the table as Lulu walked in from the living room.

"Can I bring the rest of the candy home?"

"Yes, of course." Heloise smiled and gave her a long hug.

"Oh, you got candy?" Gerda said. She took Lulu's down jacket down from the row of hooks in the front hall and retrieved her backpack from the floor.

"Yup!"

"Wow, you lucky duck. Did you say thank you?"

Lulu nodded and put on her jacket. "Heloise totally freaked out at the Apple Man at Føtex, though."

"Freaked out?" Gerda repeated. "Why?"

"Well, I didn't exactly freak out," Heloise protested.

"She basically told him to take his yucky apples and scram." Lulu laughed.

Gerda eyed Heloise indulgently.

Heloise held a finger up to object. "That is not what I said."

"That was what you meant," Lulu said.

Gerda didn't say anything. She just nodded and gave Heloise a hug. "Thanks for all your help today."

"Any time!"

Heloise could hear Lulu and Gerda laughing all the way down the stairs. She closed and locked her door and turned around. Martin had sat down at the kitchen table and was watching her. He looked like a cat who had just swallowed a canary.

"What?" She smiled.

"You're good at that."

"At what?"

"Being with Lulu. She loves you."

Heloise's smile stiffened. This was not a conversation she was interested in having.

"Do you know what *you're* good at?" she said instead.

She got up and grasped him by his shirt collar and slowly pulled him up off the chair.

"Come on," she said.

She took him by the hand and led him into the bedroom.

"WE NEED TO get this to the media right away." Schäfer handed Lisa Augustin a picture of the man in the pilot's suit from Østerport Station.

He glanced at the clock on the wall. It said 8:11 PM.

"We need to get this on the evening news shows. Maybe a viewer can identify the suspect from his clothing."

Augustin set down her phone and picked up the picture. "Did IT find anything else?" she asked.

"Not yet. The S train he boarded was headed west. The B line stops at fourteen stations between Østerport and Høje Taastrup, so he could have gotten off anywhere. They're gathering surveillance footage from all the stations now, but it takes time. So let's just go big with this shit in the papers and on TV. Now!"

Augustin nodded. "They just called from Forensics."

Schäfer stopped. "Anything new?"

"Yes, they found a handprint that doesn't belong to the murdered soldier on one of the thermostats in the apartment on Sølvgade."

"Who does it belong to?"

"We don't know yet. They're running the fingerprints through the system now. We need to wait and see if there's a hit, but that print could have been left by anyone—his mother, his girlfriend if he has one, his cleaning lady . . ." She shrugged.

"So you think that apartment looked like it was professionally cleaned every now and then?" Schäfer gave her a teasing look. "Have you ever considered going into detective work, Augustin?" He put his finger up alongside his nose. "You're sharp as a whip!"

"All right, smart ass, so not a cleaning lady then, but maybe a prostitute, or whoever."

"That sounds more likely." He nodded. "Anything else?"

"Yes. There isn't anyone named Kiki or anything like that."

"What?"

"I've gone through all Lukas Bjerre's family members, teachers, other school staff, and classmates, and the only person who has a name that's anything like Kiki is a Kitzer, a woman who used to work in the school cafeteria." Augustin yawned without covering her mouth or stopping talking. "But she moved to Sønderborg a year and a half ago, so whoever she is, it isn't of any interest to us."

"And what about that troublemaker kid's family?"

"Toke?"

"Yes. Did you get hold of his parents again?"

"Yes, this afternoon. I stopped by their apartment on Classensgade."

"And?"

"And they seem a little loopy. The father is just an extra in that house. The mother is the one running the show. And she seemed a little bit too excited to have the police pay her a visit, if you know what I mean. Like, now she has something to tell the other gals at the salon."

"The salon?"

"Yeah, she's a hairstylist. She works in some sort of celebrity salon down on Gothersgade. But she didn't say anything that would be of any value to the investigation."

"What about the boy?"

"Toke?"

Schäfer nodded.

"He was climbing the walls while I was there. Apparently he has a bunch of diagnoses. His mother rattled them all off, but I tuned out after the third abbreviation. I tried to talk to him about Lukas, but when I asked a question in the west, the boy answered in the east. It was a complete waste of time."

"So you don't think there's anything to pursue with *anyone* in that family."

Augustin shook her head.

Schäfer received a text message and pulled his phone out of his back pocket. It was from Heloise Kaldan.

Can you meet me tomorrow morning? It's important!

Schäfer furrowed his brow as he typed back on his screen, his rough-skinned fingers fumbling.

Are you OK?

Yes, everything's fine. Bistro Royal at 9 A.M.? Just for a quick cup of coffee. It's important.

Sure! 9 A.M. See you then.

He put his phone back in his pocket and looked at Augustin.

"Will you make sure that the media get this picture right away?"

"Yes, sir! How about you? Are you on your way home?"

"Yes, but I'm gonna swing by the parents' place first," he said and headed for the exit. "I don't want them to hear about this latest evidence from the news."

CHAPTER

33

SCHÄFER PULLED THE old elevator door open and saw Anne Sofie Bjerre standing in the doorway to her apartment.

She looked exhausted. The skin around her eyes was puffy. Her dirty blonde hair was flat and dull, and her sweatpants drooped from her boney body.

In only a couple of days she seemed to have wasted away, and the weight loss made her look both ancient and far too young at the same time. Almost too young to be anyone's mother, Schäfer thought, and it struck him that he could easily picture what she had looked like as a kid. But they didn't look like each other, she and Lukas.

"Is there any news?" she asked, hugging her arms together tightly.

"We haven't found him," Schäfer hurried to say. "But there is another development in the case that I'd like to discuss with you."

Anne Sofie pulled the door open all the way and then stepped back into her front hall. She gestured with a nod for him to follow.

Schäfer walked into the kitchen and looked around. The large oval top of the dining table was covered with photo albums. They were all open, and Lukas stared up at Schäfer from their pages.

There were pictures of Lukas in a baby carrier, pictures of Lukas at Legoland, Lukas's first day of school, Lukas at the summer house, Lukas wearing a hat that said "Happy New Year," new soccer cleats, wearing a costume for Carnival.

"I didn't know your generation kept physical photo albums." He smiled warmly to Anne Sofie. "I thought everything was online these days."

She attempted a smile. It looked more like a facial tic.

Schäfer peered into the living room. "Where's your husband?"

"He took your advice."

"My advice?" Schäfer asked, looking into her eyes.

"Yes. You said we should try to work. Grade papers, organize patient records . . ." She leaned against the doorframe, focusing on a point just over one of Schäfer's shoulders. Then she shook her head and closed her eyes. "But I can't."

"Is he at the clinic?"

She nodded. "I don't think he can stand being here. We just sit around waiting, and . . . every minute that goes by, some of our hope fades away, some of Lukas fades away." She looked around and flung up her hands. "But he's everywhere here in our apartment. The smell of him in his bedding. His books, his things. I can hear his voice when I close my eyes." She sounded stuffed up as she spoke, stumbling over a couple of her s's. "I don't dare go out. Because what if when I come back he's really gone?"

"Do you drink?"

She turned her face toward Schäfer, her eyes suddenly guarded.

"What do you mean?"

"I mean: Do you *drink*? Do you have a drinking problem?"

She made a small, indignant sound in her throat and shook her head. "No."

Schäfer regarded her for a moment. The red eyes. The slightly slurred speech.

It was understandable that people tried to soothe their pain during a crisis by imbibing, shooting stuff into their arteries, or whatever else they might come up with. He couldn't imagine anything worse than being in Anne Sofie's shoes right now. But she had smelled like alcohol even at their first meeting and not just from her breath, but from her pores, from her sweat glands.

Schäfer had been several years younger than Lukas when he had realized that his mother wasn't like other mothers. None of his friends were ever asked to pick up wine or beer on their way home. They didn't hide bottles when people came over, didn't sweep up broken glass and help their mother into bed when she was too drunk to get there by herself. They didn't live—as he had—in homes where everything looked great from the outside and chaotic on the inside.

Schäfer knew what it would mean to hide an addiction—because he had done it for years, *her* addiction.

"Does Lukas know that you drink?" he asked.

"I don't drink!" Anne Sofie looked defensively at Schäfer. Then she took a deep breath and let it out slowly. "I . . . have an occasional drink every now and then."

She looked like she was making an effort to appear calm, but Schäfer could hear from her voice that she was starting to choke up.

"I don't drink," she repeated.

"Are you drunk right now?" he asked softly.

"I am not *drunk*. I am *devastated*," she said. "Don't you know the difference?"

Schäfer nodded. "I do know the difference. But being one doesn't rule out the other."

Anne Sofie walked over to the kitchen table and started closing the photo albums one by one. She hesitated when she came to the last album and stared at a picture of Lukas standing next to a sandcastle on the beach. He had a look of pride in his eyes.

Her fingers grazed his face. Then she looked at Schäfer.

"I'm really trying to stop . . ." Her eyes misted over, and her chin began to quiver. "I promised Jens that I *had* stopped but now . . . with all this that's happened . . ."

Her tears overflowed and ran down her cheeks.

"Please don't say anything to him," she pleaded. "He can't take any more right now."

"What about Lukas? What does he say about it?"

"He doesn't know." She shook her head insistently. "I haven't done much drinking in front of him, and we don't keep any alcohol here in the apartment anymore. I made a deal with Jens."

Schäfer considered telling her that she was wrong. Most alcoholics couldn't see their own addiction when they stared in the mirror, but children could identify an alcoholic from miles away.

Instead he asked, "Have you had anything to drink today?"

She nodded just once.

"Marianne," she said. "My mother-in-law. She brought a bottle of cognac with her when she came over this afternoon. I think she thought I needed something to numb myself with. She doesn't know that I . . ." She ran a hand through her hair. "We had a couple of drinks together, and I . . . I poured the rest of the bottle down the kitchen sink after she left."

Schäfer looked closely at her. He wondered if there was anything else in her life that she was hiding from her husband.

"Anne Sofie, if there's anything at all that you can tell me that could help us find Lukas, anything at all, it would be a huge help."

She shook her head, confused. "I don't know what you . . ."

"Who's Kiki?"

She opened her mouth, but nothing came out. Then she slowly shook her head without batting an eye. "I . . . I don't know."

"I think you do," Schäfer said.

"No," she said. "I don't!"

She started stacking up the photo albums into a pile and carried them over to a shelf in the corner of the kitchen.

"Is that why you came?" she asked and set the stack down forcefully. "Because I've already told you that I have no idea who that is so if you—"

"What about this guy?"

Schäfer reached into the inside pocket of his bomber jacket and pulled out the picture of the man in the pilot's suit.

"Do you know him?"

She took the photo. Then her hand flew up to cover her mouth.

"Oh God," she whispered. "That's Lukas's school bag!"

Schäfer nodded. "Do you recognize the person?"

She stared at the picture.

"It's hard to say. I . . . When was this taken?"

"At about six PM on Monday at Østerport Station."

She looked up, her eyes wide and full of fear. "Who is he?"

"That was what I was hoping you could help with . . ."

Schäfer heard the front door open. Jens walked into the kitchen with all his cold weather gear on and two grocery bags in his arms. Small snowflakes sat in his blond hair. The color drained from his face when he saw Schäfer.

"Is there any news?"

"We haven't found Lukas yet," Schäfer said. "But we found something else."

He took the picture out of Anne Sofie's hand and handed it to her husband.

"And there's more." Schäfer nodded toward the dining table that they should take a seat. "I have a couple of questions."

Schäfer set his case file on the table.

Jens and Anne Sofie had sat down side by side, and Schäfer had intentionally positioned himself across the table so that he could see them both.

He could tell that Anne Sofie was holding something back. But he didn't know if she was doing it on purpose or if she hadn't realized that she was holding cards in her hand that might be crucial.

He opened the file and took out a photo of Thomas Strand. The picture had been taken in Helmand province a few years earlier. The picture had been cut off just below Strand's camouflage pants. He was wearing a tight-fitting black T-shirt and stood with his arms crossed, leaning against a wall that was dusty with desert sand. Tribal tattoos ran like a wildfire up his forearms and his dog tags hung between his pronounced pectoral muscles.

He looked sunburned, smug and smiling, with a haughty look in his ice-blue eyes.

Schäfer pushed the picture across the table.

Jens picked it up, and Schäfer didn't detect any recognition in his expression.

"Do you know him?"

Jens shook his head and looked at his wife. She leaned in closer to the picture and scrunched up her eyes.

"I don't really know . . . ," she said.

"Who is he?" Jens asked, looking over at Schäfer.

"His name is Thomas Strand. Does that mean anything to you?"

Jens gave his wife a questioning look. "Do *you* know him?"

She shook her head uncertainly. "No. I don't think so." She took the picture out of her husband's hands and looked at it more closely. "But . . . you see this type of person on the streets pretty often. You know, bald with those gang-like tattoos on their arms. I mean, I can't say for sure that I haven't seen him here in Nyhavn. The cafés and bars on the other side of the canal are full of his type."

She looked up at Schäfer again.

"Why are you asking? What does he have to do with us?"

"That was what I was hoping you might be able to tell me," Schäfer said. He leaned back in the chair and regarded Anne Sofie, trying to provoke a reaction.

She shook her head blankly. "Me?"

Jens glanced back and forth between Schäfer and his wife. The look in his eyes seemed stiff, lost.

"Does he have something to do with Lukas's disappearance?" he asked. "Tell me what's going on, Fie!"

"Well, *I* don't know!" she said, throwing up her hands. She glanced at Schäfer. "Who is he?"

"He's a soldier. Or rather, he *was* a soldier. Sergeant Major Thomas Strand."

"Was?" Jens asked.

"Yes, he's dead, shot in his bed sometime between Sunday and yesterday morning."

Jens looked as if Schäfer had started rattling off random prime numbers.

"But what does that have to do with Lukas? We have no idea who that is . . . who this *person* . . . is." He nodded at the picture of Strand. "We've never met anyone who . . ."

"The connection to the case is that this guy here," Schäfer put his index finger on the picture. "His blood is on the jacket that we found at the Citadel, Lukas's jacket."

Jens's chin dropped, and Anne Sofie covered her mouth with her hands.

"His blood?" she whispered.

Schäfer nodded.

"So Lukas has been missing since Monday morning." Schäfer held up a finger for each item he listed off. "Thomas Strand was shot. His blood ended up on Lukas's jacket. And the jacket was found at the Citadel. That indicates two things to me: (1) The cases are connected, and (2) there's a third party involved."

Anne Sofie lowered her hands from her mouth. "A third party?"

"Yes, we assume that Lukas wasn't the one who shot Thomas Strand. My guess is that this guy had something to do with it."

He set the picture of the man in the pilot's suit next to the picture of Thomas Strand.

"So the question is: Who is the man, who got on a train Monday evening wearing Lukas's school backpack? And what connects Lukas—or you—to him and to Thomas Strand?"

"Where does he live?" Jens nodded at the picture of the soldier. "Where does he go?"

"What do you mean by 'where does he go?'"

"I mean, does he have kids at Nyholm School? Could he be someone I know from when I was a kid in Roskilde? That kind of thing!"

"He was born and grew up in Sønderjylland. He doesn't have a wife or kids, but he lived on Sølvgade not far from Nyholm. Does any of that ring any bells?"

They both looked silently at Schäfer. Anne Sofie shook her head.

"Is he . . ." Jens looked like he was going to throw up and swallowed audibly. "Is he a pedophile?"

"There is no indication of that," Schäfer said. "There's nothing in his criminal record to suggest that, and there was nothing in his apartment to indicate that he's interested in children in that way."

Something occurred to Schäfer, and he looked around the kitchen to see if he could spot any cereal boxes on the shelves. He noticed the Mason jars of raisins and healthy grains next to the toaster.

"Does Lukas like Cocoa Puffs?"

Anne Sofie raised an eyebrow in surprise. "Cocoa Puffs?"

"Yeah, you know, that chocolaty sugar cereal kids eat for breakfast."

She shrugged. "He probably would, but . . . that's not something we usually get. Why do you ask?"

Schäfer frowned and shook his head. "I'm just trying to get the pieces to fit together."

Anne Sofie looked down and stared at the picture of Thomas Strand for a long time.

Schäfer saw a flicker of something in her eyes. She had noticed something.

He sat up straighter. "What?"

"This picture," she said. "Where was it taken?"

"At Camp Bastion in Afghanistan. Why?"

Jens immediately looked up and glanced over at Schäfer. "When?" he asked and took the picture out of his wife's hand.

"I don't know. Strand was deployed multiple times, so I don't know when this photo was taken. Why?"

"When were you there?" Anne Sofie asked, looking at her husband.

Schäfer's brow creased. "When were you *where*?"

He had already checked as to whether Jens and Thomas Strand might have crossed paths in the military and knew that they hadn't. No one in the Bjerre family had done any military service.

"In Afghanistan," Jens said. "I've been there numerous times, but it's been several years now since the last time. Is that where you said the picture was taken?"

"Yes."

"At Camp Bastion?"

Schäfer jutted out his chin and studied Jens. "I didn't think you had served in the military."

"I didn't. But I've done a number of stints for Doctors Without Borders."

Schäfer's palms tingled. "You've worked in war zones?"

He nodded.

"What countries have you worked in?"

"Besides Afghanistan I've been to Sudan, Nigeria . . . Zambia . . . one quick trip to Syria before it got so hard to enter the country with emergency aid."

"Sierra Leone," Anne Sofie added.

He nodded. "Yes, Sierra Leone."

Schäfer mentally crossed off the African countries. He knew that Thomas Strand had been to Afghanistan several times and Iraq but doubted he had been to Syria as well.

"Afghanistan. Let's just stick to that," he said. "When were you there?"

"I've been there several times. I think the last time was 2013. Right?" He glanced at his wife. "It was before Lukas started school, because I remember that he drew a picture of me wearing a military uniform when he was in nursery school. Some of the older kids there had heard that I was in Afghanistan, and they had put the idea into Lukas's head that I was there as a soldier. Do you remember that?"

Anne Sofie smiled at her husband and nodded.

"What happened while you were there?" Schäfer asked.

"What happened?" Jens stared vacantly at him. "Have you ever been in a war zone?"

Schäfer nodded. "Yes, and it's a real shit show. But what I meant was, did anything happen that could have somehow involved this guy?" He nodded to the picture of Thomas Strand. "Have you been to Camp Bastion?"

"Yes, a couple of times," Jens said. "We went to visit the Danish troops, just to say hello, to see other people from home. But we didn't stay there. Doctors Without Borders had a hospital in Kunduz in northern Afghanistan. That's where I was working while I was there."

"And you don't recall having met him?"

Jens took the picture again and studied it intently. "No, I . . . Well, they do all look alike in their uniforms and so many of them have their heads shaved or wear crew cuts and have tattoos. It could well be that I've met this guy, but I don't remember him."

"Did anything in particular happen the times you visited the camp?"

"Such as?"

Schäfer flung up his hands. "Did you get into any arguments with anyone? Was there any conflict between you and any of the soldiers?"

"There were the usual political disagreements between us and the boys in uniform, but it's always like that when we're out in the field. It's not anything we shout from the rooftops, but everyone has their own ideas and I'm sure they sense that too."

"Political disagreements?"

"Yes." Jens nodded. "We go there to save lives. They go there to kill."

A warm wave of irritation ran up Schäfer's neck, and his old soldier buddies—the living as well as the dead—flashed through his mind, soldiers he respected, soldiers he cared about.

"I think a lot of people would consider that to be a pretty inflammatory opinion," he said in a measured tone.

"Perhaps." Jens set down the picture of Thomas Strand. "But that doesn't make it any less true."

HELOISE SECURED HER bra clasps behind her back and stuck her feet into her blue jeans. She pulled the pants up, hopping a couple of times to pull them up to her waist, and buttoned them. It was almost as if they had already started to feel a bit tight. Or was she just imagining that? She found a gray hoodie and pulled it on over her head.

"Is it too cold in here?" Martin asked. "Do you want me to close the window again?"

He was sitting on the wide windowsill, wrapped in one of Heloise's white down comforters, exhaling smoke through the cracked-open window in an attempt not to stink up the room.

It didn't make much of a difference, Heloise thought. The whole apartment smelled like his cigarettes anyway.

"No, that's okay," she said. "But I'm just going to pop over to the newspaper office."

Martin looked puzzled and glanced at his watch. It was almost midnight. "What, now? I thought we were going to bed."

"Well, you are very welcome to sleep here. But I forgot my computer on the passenger's seat of the company car I borrowed today, so I just want to run in and pick it up."

"Couldn't you just do that tomorrow?"

Heloise shook her head. "I don't dare risk its being stolen. I won't be able to fall asleep now anyway, so I'd just as soon do a little work. You know how I am—when the words want out, they want out."

The truth was that Heloise didn't have any words at the moment. Normally they were like air bubbles underwater inside her; they found their way to the surface, wanting out. Up and out!

She felt more like a quiet swamp now. Dead. Fallow. It was an unfamiliar feeling, and she didn't like it.

"Okay." Martin flicked his cigarette out the window and stood up. "Where's the car parked? I'll go get the computer for you."

Heloise shook her head. "You can't."

"Why not?"

"Because the car key is on my desk in my office, so I need to go grab that first."

"But it's the middle of the night. Can you even get into your office at this hour?"

"Yes, of course." Heloise smiled half-patronizingly. "There are people at the news desk around the clock. Did you think we all went home for dinner and just let the news handle itself or something?"

Martin shrugged. "I mean, you never know with you news people."

"You and all those politicians are just annoyed that you can't control us from inside Borgen."

"I can *easily* control those idiots running around inside Borgen," he said, leaning over to Heloise. "You're the only one I have trouble controlling."

"Shh! Do you hear that?" Heloise pretended to hear something and held her index finger up in front of her lips.

Martin pulled his head back. "What?"

"Listen!"

The wind wailed and tugged at the roof, and there were a few loud bangs from the balcony.

"Ugh, it sounds like the windbreak came loose out there," Heloise said, miming to him that she was contemplating what to do. "I have an idea! There's some zip ties in the drawer in the kitchen, and if you could be a dear and secure the windbreak while I'm gone, then we won't have to listen to that racket all night." She smiled sassily. "Smart, right?"

Martin raised a sarcastic eyebrow. "Huh, so I'm good for something? I'm just a handyman you have fix up your house while you're at work? I have feelings, too, you know."

Heloise laughed out loud, grazed his lips with a kiss, and left the apartment.

35

CONNIE PUT HER hands on Schäfer's shoulders and massaged his sore neck muscles in long, firm strokes. It had been a half hour since he had come home from seeing the Bjerre family and he was sitting at his little black lacquered desk in the living room reviewing the case details one more time.

He let his head loll back and closed his eyes.

"How can a person need a vacation only a few days after coming home from one?" He sighed.

"It's the winter darkness here in Scandinavia," Connie said and kissed him on the forehead. "It sucks the life out of you, babe."

"Hmm," he mumbled. "Let's go back."

"We could go back in October. And maybe a short trip over Easter?"

"No." He turned in his desk chair and put his hands on her hips. "I mean, let's move there! Let's sell the house here, say to hell with it, and go."

Connie sat down in his lap and took his face in her hands. His stubble scratched loudly against her soft skin. She smiled and ran a finger over his lower lip.

She smelled like eucalyptus and vanilla, Schäfer thought. Deep, delicate notes of safety. And warmth.

She kissed him fleetingly. "Is it that time of the year?"

"What do you mean?"

"Christmas is over, winter vacation is done, and now there will be at least two months where you mope around hating everything."

"I don't hate you."

"I don't hate you either."

"And then they lived happily ever after." Schäfer smiled.

Connie leaned against him. "We can't go, and you know that perfectly well, babe."

"Why not?"

She nodded at the case file and all the papers on the desk in front of Schäfer. "Because right now you might think that you want to leave all this behind, but . . . you don't. At least not yet."

Schäfer rubbed his eyes and yawned. She didn't need to say anything else. They both knew she was right.

"What's that?" Connie put her hand on the stack of photo albums on the desk.

"That's the Bjerre family's photo albums from the last five years."

"Did you get them from the boy's parents?"

Schäfer nodded. "Borrowed them, yeah."

"Are they nice?"

"Who?"

"The boy's parents."

Schäfer shrugged. "I suppose so. It's hard to get a proper impression of people who are going through a crisis, but the father is a little full of himself in terms of how he looks at the world, I think."

"In what sense?"

"He's a professional do-gooder. He thinks he has the right view of the world, you know. The *one* right view." He said the last sentence with a sneer. "The kind who doesn't want to admit that sometimes the world is black and white and that there are certain conflicts that can't be solved by sitting in a circle and singing 'Imagine.' He said that he thinks our soldiers are tax-financed murderers."

Connie raised her eyebrows. "Really?"

"Well, maybe not in those exact words, but it was pretty clear that that's what he meant."

She folded her hands behind Schäfer's head. "What does he do for a living?"

"He's a doctor," Schäfer replied. "He works with Doctors Without Borders."

She didn't make any effort to hide her smile. "A hero, in other words? You're annoyed at a *hero*."

"A self-righteous academic type, who—admittedly—saves lives, and thank you very much for that, but that doesn't give him the right to put down our soldiers. They're risking their lives for this country."

"Okay, okay." Connie smiled. "What about the mother. What's she like?"

"The mother drinks. And you know how that automatically throws up a red flag for me." He gave Connie a knowing look.

She ran her fingers through her hair, hesitating before answering. Then she said, "That doesn't necessarily make her a bad person, you know."

Schäfer didn't reply. He didn't want to get into that, not tonight.

"Are you coming to bed?" Connie asked, getting up.

"I'll be in a little later. We just sent a picture of a suspect to the media, and the phones have started ringing, so . . ."

"Is it paying off?"

"Not yet. We've only heard from the usual crazies so far, so there hasn't been anything useful yet, but . . . a guy can hope."

Connie kissed him good night and walked down the hall to their bedroom, her hips swaying.

Schäfer turned back around in his desk chair and looked at his notes. Nothing fit together on its own, so he spent the next hour trying to force the pieces to add up. He sat holding the picture of the barn door in his hand and flipped through all the family's photo albums, comparing the surroundings in the picture with what he saw in the albums, trying to find a match.

Then he opened his computer and googled "pareidolia." He clicked on the first hit that showed up and read:

Pareidolia is a psychological phenomenon in which random elements appear to have significance. It's a form of optical illusion: The eye recognizes a pattern, where there isn't actually one, and draws hasty conclusions.

Schäfer set the photo albums on the table and rested his forehead on his knuckles as he thought.

Was that what was going on now?

Was he trying to find a pattern where there wasn't one?

Was he so eager to see a connection that he was looking in the wrong places?

He reached for the case file and started over again.

36

Heloise pulled a knit cap down over her ears and put on a pair of leather gloves. Then she set out toward the newspaper office on foot.

She turned right on St. Kongensgade, which was deserted in the nighttime darkness. One lone car cautiously rolled down the snow-slick street. Every time its brake lights lit up, the car slid off to the side and bumped into the curb. Then it slowed down, stopped, and started again.

There were no other cars on the street, nor any people.

Heloise paid her regards to the Marble Church as she walked by it. A loving nod to an old friend. She had visited the church once a week since she was a child but realized that it had been a month and a half since she had last been there. At the Christmas mass, she had delivered her customary gift of port wine to Bobo, the old custodian who worked in the church, but she hadn't gone up the tower. She hadn't been up there a single time since last year.

Bobo had welcomed Heloise warmly and remarked in a heart-to-heart voice that she didn't come to the church that often anymore.

"If I didn't know any better, I'd think you'd forgotten us," he said, half in jest, with a shy smile.

Heloise looked up at the tower sticking up on top of the big domed roof. Her and her father's initials were scratched into the oxidized copper up there somewhere, like her memories of a happy childhood were engraved on her soul, a childhood that now served as a counterweight to an adult life where nothing fit together.

"I haven't forgotten," she whispered and picked up her pace.

The lights were on in the lobby at *Demokratisk Dagblad*, the newspaper where she worked, but the reception desk was deserted. Heloise swiped her access card over the electronic lock and entered.

She opened the door to the newsroom on the first floor and looked over at the night team at the far end of the floor. There were three journalists, a photographer, and the night shift manager. A couple of them were leaning back, their legs up on their desks, coffee cups in hand. Several TV screens were mounted above them, set to various news stations: TV 2 News, CNN, BBC, and Al Jazeera.

None of the journalists noticed Heloise. They were absorbed in the overhead screens.

Three of the channels were muted, but she could hear that the BBC's volume was turned up. A breaking news story about an earthquake in Pakistan—7.4 on the Richter scale. Karachi lay in ruins, and people were running around in the streets covered in dust and blood, panicked, while thousands of others lay dead or trapped beneath the rubble.

A few seconds later, Al Jazeera interrupted its broadcast with the same news update. Then CNN joined in.

Heloise looked over at Denmark's TV 2 News. They were broadcasting a story about the crown prince and some honorary award he had received for some community-minded thing he'd done.

She waited for ten heartbeats.

Then that story was replaced by an update on Helicopter Gate, a case about whether it was fair to use tax money on a new medical helicopter for the southern Denmark region. A couple of politicians with opposing political views gesticulated angrily on the muted screen, and a few words from a local farmer were also included. He was subtitled so Copenhageners wouldn't be confused by the man's dialect.

The earthquake was given all of seven words of space in the rolling text at the bottom of the screen along with the other secondary news of the day.

Heloise shook her head.

Denmark was a postcard country plagued by first-world problems, she thought. Someday the real world would come knocking. It wasn't going to be pretty.

She left the newsroom and continued up the stairs to the third floor, where the investigative team, the culture desk, and the lifestyle journalists worked.

She opened the door to the landscape office and looked around. All the lights on the whole floor were off. Only the streetlights out on Store Strandstræde shone faintly through the windows.

Heloise strode over to her desk in the dark and switched on her desk lamp. The keys to the Ford were sitting next to her computer. There were also a couple of messages on her desk, and there was a yellow Post-it note on her keyboard. It was from Mogens Bøttger.

My story breaks tomorrow. Champagne at Clarrods & Co. at 5 P.M., Kaldan. Be there!

Heloise smiled.

Over the years it had become a tradition for her and Mogens to toast the publication of their big stories together, always at Clarrods & Co., the wine bar across the street from the paper, and always with champagne.

It wasn't something they did every time their byline appeared in the paper, because that was part and parcel with their job. But the stories that could shift something in society—the revelations that had the potential to result in political reforms—were always marked by a visit to the wine bar. Although over the last year it had become more the rule than the exception that it was Mogens—and not Heloise—who had written the story, but it hadn't always been like that.

She turned on her computer and logged into the newspaper's intranet, where the next day's articles were already in the system and the pages of the paper were laid out. She found Mogens's article and read it.

He hadn't been exaggerating. It was a monster story.

Heloise felt the familiar sensation that always flared up in her when she read one of Mogens's articles: impressed admiration with a knife-tip stab of envy.

The article reminded her that she was feeling some work-related impotence lately. Her PTSD story had been officially axed, and she still hadn't written a word about the Lukas Bjerre case. She had no Britney ready to go in her drawer, and she hadn't finished writing the background article either. She had sat down at her computer several times, tried to force the words out, but she still didn't have anything interesting down on paper. The only thing she could even come close to allowing herself to categorize as investigative journalism was her trip up to Rørvig, and even that hadn't amounted to anything.

Heloise shook off her self-pity and sat up straight.

For crying out loud, pull yourself together. Dust yourself off, go get your computer, and get started on that story!

She sent Mogens a text praising his work and promised that she would swim in a waterfall of vintage bubbly with him as soon as the story was printed. Then she logged off her computer and stuck the car keys into her jacket pocket.

As Heloise stood up, a quick jolt of pain shot through her stomach and down into her pelvis. She doubled over and put a hand on her stomach.

It felt as if there was a battle raging inside her, like something was drastically wrong.

She stood there for a moment and took several deep breaths until the pain subsided. Then she turned off the light on her desk and started walking toward the stairwell at the end of the room.

On her way down to the dark editorial hallway she slowed. She took a couple of steps as she listened.

Then she stopped altogether.

A presence in the room sent a cold chill down her spine.

Was that a sound? Had she heard something somewhere in the room? Or seen something move?

Heloise turned her head, her eyes scanning the dark office landscape. She recognized the empty cubicles, separated by low partitions and bookshelves.

She didn't detect anything moving. Nothing caught the light from the street outside.

"Hello?" she called into the room. "Is anyone here?"

She swallowed hard and took a couple of steps farther out into the room, moving among the desks and bookshelves. She could feel her pulse throbbing in her ears, but beyond that she couldn't hear anything except for the radiators humming and gurgling along the exterior wall and the sound of a woman's laughter, which echoed loudly from somewhere on the street below.

Heloise quickly strode over to the switch and turned on the lights. Hundreds of halogen spotlights immediately lit up the large editorial office space.

Her eyes flickered over the deserted department. Nothing stuck out.

Then she heard the sound again, an oddly *wet* sound.

She held her breath and looked in the direction the sound had come from. The lifestyle editor's area at the far end of the room.

That area was partially secluded behind a large, wheeled whiteboard, and Heloise couldn't see what was behind it. But it was there, from behind the whiteboard, that the noise had come. A pouring sound, like a container that was slowly overflowing.

She looked around and spotted a letter opener on one of the desks. She grabbed the sharp implement and clutched it in her hand.

"Hello?" she called again as she stepped farther into the room.

Then she saw the feet. Two fleshy feet in leather shoes came into view under the rolling whiteboard. They were surrounded by a reddish puddle, some type of liquid dripping down from somewhere above.

Heloise walked over to the whiteboard and pulled it aside with her weapon raised.

She stared straight ahead in shock. Then she lowered her arm.

Food critic Kaj Clevin lay in front of her, lifeless, splayed forward on his work desk. His eyes were wide open, staring in horror at Heloise.

It was obvious that he was dead. Even so, she walked over and pressed two fingers to his neck. His skin was still warm, his stubble poking her fingers.

There was no pulse.

Heloise looked around. There were eight open bottles of red wine from various wineries on the desk in front of Kaj and eight more or less half-empty glasses. A couple of the bottles had tipped over and were pinned underneath Kaj's heavy torso. His white shirt had soaked up the spilled wine so the fabric down his chest was wet and dark red. The rest of the grape blood had formed a lake on the desktop around him and was dribbling off the edge of the desk, down onto his slacks and from there onto the floorboards in a slow drip.

He must have died a few minutes before Heloise arrived.

On the computer screen in front of Clevin, the cursor sat blinking in an open document with headers and short sentences describing the different wines. The last line he had written was a review of a 100-kroner bottle of Shiraz.

An appallingly bad wine from California, without a doubt a regular proletariat pleaser. Waste of money, waste of life.

Heloise wiped her nose with the back of her hand and looked around the department.

There was only one thing to do.

She pulled out her cell phone.

"Hello, my name is Heloise Kaldan. I'm a journalist at *Demokratisk Dagblad*. I just found one of my colleagues at the newspaper, Kaj Clevin, our food critic. He's dead."

Her eyes slid over Clevin's hefty body.

"I don't know," she said. "But if I had to guess, a heart attack."

Heloise gave the dispatcher the address and hung up. She sat down in the desk chair next to Kaj Clevin and slowly swiveled from side to side while she watched his dead body. She happened to think of the grandchild he had brought to work with him the previous week. Heloise knew that Kaj had four adult children. Four families, who would all receive the dreaded call from the police in the middle of the night.

Again she felt a painful twinge in her stomach and put her hand on it. This time she had no doubt what it meant.

Heloise got up and moved over by the window to watch for the ambulance.

By the time it pulled up in front of the paper, she had begun to bleed.

"WHAT'S UP, ERIK? Long time, no see."

Schäfer looked up from his papers and pulled his chin back in surprise. Former police psychologist Michala Friis stood in front of him, holding out a paper coffee cup so that the loose Rolex watch on her wrist slid down toward him.

As usual she was wearing black. Schäfer had never seen her in anything else. Her jeans fit like they had been painted onto her slender legs. Her long hair was half tugged into the collar of her turtleneck sweater under her trench coat.

"What the hell!" he said with a smile. He got up and accepted the coffee. Then he stuck out his paw. "Wow, it's been ages!"

Friis smiled and shook his hand. She scrunched up her eyes. "But not long enough, or what?"

Schäfer shrugged and adjusted his belt. "That depends on whether you're just stopping by to say hi or if you're here to stick your nose into my case."

Friis set her own coffee cup down on the desk. She unbuttoned her coat and tossed it onto the empty desk chair across from Schäfer.

Augustin wasn't in yet. It was only just past seven. It was early even for Schäfer, who had been at it for a couple of hours now. It was more than conspicuous that Friis hadn't just randomly stopped by with an extra cup of coffee. Schäfer guessed that Commissioner Per Carstensen had brought her in without consulting the head of the investigation.

Friis met his gaze and nodded. "He thought you could use my help."

She ran a hand through her hair. It had gotten longer since he had last seen her, Schäfer noted. And blonder.

He raised an eyebrow. "He? Who's he?"

"Carstensen."

"Right." He nodded. "But do you even have time for this sort of gritty work? Isn't there some investment banker or real estate guy out there who urgently requires your assistance?"

Friis smiled knowingly.

She was willing to take a few jabs if that's what it took to break the ice—and it was. Schäfer wasn't going to let her waltz into his investigation without giving her a couple of verbal volleys as welcome. But he was in no way sorry to see her. Surprised, yes, and a little wary, but he knew better than anyone else that having Friis on your team in a murder investigation was entirely a good thing.

She was one of the country's foremost experts in psychological profiling for criminals and murder victims and people in general, and until recently Schäfer had had more respect for her than he had for the rest of his colleagues in the investigative unit combined. Their paths had crossed many times over the years when she had worked full-time as a police analyst, and they had cooperated on almost every major murder case Schäfer had been involved in for the last ten years.

But these days Friis primarily worked freelance and primarily in the private sector. She still occasionally analyzed and profiled for the police but devoted most of her energy to big corporations that wanted to assess a potential client, a competitor, or what have you. There was more money to be made in the private sector—*far* more—and maybe that's what bothered Schäfer. He had trouble understanding how a woman as talented as Friis could waste her efforts on those sorts of champagne-swilling geese and Cohiba-smoking assholes. Plus, her exit from the police had meant that for most murder investigations he was now forced to make do with the second best in the field, and Schäfer had a hard time not holding that against her.

"Anything else you need to get off your chest?" She smiled and held her arms out to the sides as if she were open to more abuse. "Any more insults? Let's hear them. You'll feel much better afterward."

Schäfer shot her a wry look. "Nah . . . I imagine the fact that you sleep poorly at night due to your career choices is punishment enough."

"I sleep fine."

"Well, you're lucky, then. I usually sleep like crap."

Friis took her coffee cup from the desk and raised it to his in a toast. "Okay, are we done with this, then? Cheers!" She set her cup down again and raised both eyebrows. "Shall we get started?"

Schäfer made a sweeping gesture with his arm over toward the crowded bulletin board, which covered the back wall of the office.

"Mi casa es su casa."

* * *

An hour later Schäfer had given Friis a thorough summary of the case. He had shared with her everything he knew about Lukas Bjerre, about finding Thomas Strand, the man in the pilot's suit, the clues that connected them, the Apple Man, pareidolia, Doctors Without Borders—the works.

Friis sat in Augustin's chair now with her hands clasped behind her head, looking at the bulletin board behind Schäfer.

"What does your gut tell you?" he asked. "Who's behind this?"

She was quiet for a moment.

"My first thought is that you're looking for a perpetrator who's between thirty and forty," she said. "Someone who's experienced some form of trauma in their life."

"Argh, isn't that a little too easy?" Schäfer eyed her indulgently. "I mean, don't they all have that?"

She ignored his comments.

"Maybe he grew up in an orphanage. Maybe he lived alone with a sadistic or dominating parent. One way or the other, there was some sort of defect in his life."

"Do any of the people we're looking at speak to you more than others?"

Friis got up and walked over to the board, where the picture of the man in the pilot's suit was posted. She stood with her arms crossed, staring at the picture for a long time.

"We know that there must be a third person involved in the case," Schäfer said. "The boy disappeared, Thomas Strand's blood is on his jacket, and the man who got on the train Monday night was wearing Lukas Bjerre's backpack— and it was the same guy that I saw at the Citadel the day we found the jacket. Is he our perpetrator? Did he kill Strand and kidnap Lukas?"

She shrugged. "He could easily fit the profile, but I need to know more about who he is and what circles he travels in to be able to say anything more."

"What do you think the school backpack means?" Schäfer nodded at the picture. "Why did he dump the contents at the Citadel and then take the empty backpack with him?"

"Who says it's empty?" Friis turned her head and looked at Schäfer over her shoulder.

"The boy's schoolbooks were in the bushes."

"Maybe he emptied the books out of the backpack because he needed room in there for something else."

"Such as?"

"I don't know." She shrugged. "But I do know that it's always a bad idea to make a categorical statement about something you don't know for sure. You see a school backpack here and a bush full of books there and conclude that therefore the bag must be empty. And you could be right about that, too. I'm just saying: Maybe it's *not* empty. Maybe the bag is serving some particular purpose. Maybe there's an object inside it that needs to be transported from point A to point B without attracting much attention for some reason we're not aware of yet. You know what they say about assumptions . . ."

"They're the mother of all fuck-ups."

"Nothing less." Friis nodded.

Schäfer took a deep breath. He crossed his arms and leaned back in his chair. "Then there's the question of the woman Lukas Bjerre met a few times out behind the school."

"What about her?" Friis asked.

"Well, for starters, who is she? And what makes you rule out a female perpetrator?"

"I'm not ruling anything out at the present time," Friis said. "I'm just telling you what my first impressions are."

"Okay. What else are you picking up on?"

She ran one thumb over her lower lip as she thought. "You're working on the theory that someone abducted the boy from school on Monday morning, correct?"

Schäfer nodded. "Pretty much, yes."

"That means you don't think he ran away?"

"Like you, I'm not ruling anything out. But if someone's going to run away from home, there needs to be a good reason for it and there needs to be a . . ."

"His mother being an alcoholic could be a good reason, couldn't it?" Friis suggested.

"Well . . ." Schäfer's expression was skeptical. "I know kids who grew up in families where the alcohol abuse was far worse, but they didn't run away. In my opinion, that would take more than what's going on in the Bjerre household."

"Okay. What else?" she asked. "I interrupted you before . . ."

"Yes, one other thing that sticks out to me is that there's no trace of the boy at Østerport. If you want to run away and you're only a few yards away from a place where you can catch an express train to Timbuktu every two minutes, that's the most obvious escape route. Plus the piggy bank in his bedroom was full of money. There must have been 700 to 800 kroner in it. And people don't plan to run away without money in their pocket. And: where the hell would he go?"

"I don't know, but there's something about his going missing from school that doesn't add up."

"And that is?"

"According to all the statements obtained, Lukas is a highly gifted child. He's not the type to voluntarily walk away with someone he doesn't know. No one has described him as stupid or gullible, the sort of little boy that you could just lure away from the school with some candy or free apples, as you suggested earlier. Every indication is that intellectually he's way, way ahead of his peers. He knows very well that he shouldn't walk off with a stranger. So I simply don't believe that some person he doesn't know was able to lure him away from the school."

"So he was taken from the school by force?"

"No, I think that's also unlikely. Picture a perpetrator showing up at a school attended by—what—just shy of 600 students? And how many teachers and instructional assistants are there? Forty or fifty? If Lukas was grabbed by someone who wanted to drag him away, he would have yelled, and someone would have heard him. And he's too big for someone to have been able to do a Disneyland maneuver on him."

"What's a Disneyland maneuver?"

"A Disneyland maneuver." Friis flung out her arms as if this should be self-explanatory. "There have been many instances in amusement parks in the U.S. where little kids were kidnapped in broad daylight. Typically, the kidnapper hides in a public restroom and when some random kid walks in to go to the bathroom, they quickly subdue the child with chloroform or a similar substance."

Friis rattled off the procedure as if she were reading a recipe out loud.

"They cut off the kid's curls and change the kid's clothes. In other words, in just a couple of minutes they transform a girl with long hair in a pink dress into what looks like a boy in jeans and a white T-shirt. Then they put the unconscious child into an umbrella stroller that they have brought with them and roll it right past the mother and father who are standing outside the restroom waiting."

Friis sat back down in Augustin's chair and clasped her hands behind her head again.

"Typically, it's a father standing outside waiting, because he doesn't feel like he can accompany his daughter into the women's restroom."

Schäfer shook his head in disgust. "What the hell kind of world are we living in?!"

She agreed, her eyebrows raised.

"Do you think someone drugged Lukas with something at school? Maybe poisoned him or knocked him out?" Schäfer thought about the warfarin stain on the jacket. Could rat poison be used like an anesthetic?

"And what?" She smiled. "Rolled him out of the school-yard in a wheelbarrow? Hardly. That was exactly my point: He's way too big for a stunt like that, so I think it's unlikely that anyone snatched him from school against his will."

Schäfer reached for the latte Friis had brought him and took a sip.

"So maybe he voluntarily went along with someone?"

"Maybe."

"What about this Kiki, who wrote to the boy?" he said. "What do you think about her?"

"I could be wrong," she said. "But my sense is that that person doesn't have anything to do with the case."

"Why not?"

"Because you said the boy had hidden the note you found, that it was inside a diary. Wasn't that what you said?"

"A notebook. It was hidden under his mattress."

"Children don't hide letters and notes from people they don't like or people they're afraid of. If Lukas kept this note, then it's because it meant something to him. Because *she* meant something to him. So, since we don't know who Kiki is, we need to ask ourselves the following question to proceed: Who is Lukas Bjerre?"

Friis stood up.

"What's going on inside *his* head?" she asked.

Schäfer walked over and stopped in front of the bulletin board with his hands at his sides. He nodded to the picture of the barn door. "He's very preoccupied with those faces I told you about."

She nodded. "Pareidolia."

"Yes. What do you think about that?"

"I think that he seems like an inquisitive child. He's very aware of the world around him—and watchful! Pareidolia is interesting specifically because the phenomenon is related to the Rorschach test. The one where you look at different random inkblots and describe your associations, whether you see a bat, a face, a woman's spread legs, or what have you. It's a test that reveals people's innermost and maybe even subconscious thoughts. Their secret, deviant desires. Their biggest fear. Their dreams—and so on."

Schäfer listened attentively.

"Similarly, pareidolia reveals something about our thoughts and about our personality," she continued. "We all have the ability to see these faces, but how *developed* that ability is varies quite a bit from person to person and depends on the life we lead. People who are generally comfortable and optimistic and rarely worry about anything find it harder to decode these patterns as faces. But if you're suffering from anxiety or are particularly sensitive, then you see faces as signs of danger all over the place."

"But there's no indication that the boy suffers from anxiety or anything like that," Schäfer said. "On the sensitive side perhaps, but his teachers and parents describe him as a child who functions at a really high level."

Friis was quiet, thinking. She turned her back to Schäfer and studied all the pictures hanging on the wall, one by one. They were pictures Schäfer had taken out of the family's photo albums and hung up.

When she finally spoke, it sounded as if she were talking to herself, in a whisper.

"He's not a happy child."

"I'm sorry?" Schäfer looked at Friis's back, his brow furrowed.

She turned to him. "He's not happy."

Schäfer shook his head, not understanding. "What are you talking about?"

He gestured over at the board that was covered with pictures of Lukas in every conceivable photo op situation. He was smiling in every picture.

"The kid is like a Kellogg's Corn Flakes spokesmodel incarnate," he said. "I have statements from everyone he associates with—his teachers, family, friends, and so on. Everyone describes him as a sweet, *happy* boy, a fun, clever kid."

Friis walked over to the board and pointed at one of the pictures. "Who took this one?"

Schäfer shrugged. "As far as I can remember, it's from a family vacation."

He pulled the thumbtack out of the photo and read what it said on the back. It said *Summer house life. Klint, July 2017.*

"It was probably one of his parents who took it. Or his grandmother," he said.

"It's the only picture we have of him where he's smiling," Friis said.

Schäfer stared at her blankly. Then, slightly irritated, he pointed around at the rest of the board without breaking his eye contact with her.

"Do you see all the pictures here? I count at least twenty pictures where the kid is smiling."

She shook her head. "No, you count nineteen where he's *faking* a smile, and this one . . ." She slapped the picture from Klint with her palm. "This is the only one where his smile is genuine."

"Elaborate," Schäfer said with a wave of his hand.

"There are thought to be about eighteen different types of smiles, but only one of them is an expression of joy."

"Eighteen types of smiles?"

"Yes. Some smiles occur because of pain or fear. Other smiles are due to people finding themselves in an embarrassing situation. There are also other people who express indignation, anger, or speechlessness with a smile, and people sometimes smile when they're lying or confused."

Schäfer looked puzzled. "Who in the world expresses anger by smiling?"

"Well, *you* did when I walked in the door. You gave me a smile that said: What are you doing here, you traitor? I don't trust you, because you'd rather earn money than catch criminals."

"Fair enough. Then what does this smile mean?" Schäfer looked at her, his teeth clenched and his lips apart in a defiant smile.

"That you grudgingly acknowledge that I know what I'm talking about, and that you're not at all as clever as you think you are." She pointed at the bulletin board. "Lukas is smiling in all these photos because he *decided* to smile. That's a 'say cheese' smile, not a genuine smile. There is only one genuine smile: the so-called Duchenne smile."

"What's that?"

"It's the only smile that is an expression of true joy. It can't be forced. It can't be faked. It's named for a French neurologist who was responsible for the first documented smile studies, done in the early 1800s. His name was Guillaume Duchenne. By electrically stimulating the facial muscles, he learned to distinguish between genuine, happy smiles and other types of smiles."

"And how do you tell the difference?"

"In general people can only *rarely* tell, but I can. Specialists who know what they're looking for can."

"And what do *you* look for then?"

"During a genuine smile, the corners of the mouth move up and back. The fleshy part of the eye between the eyebrow and the eyelid tilts downward, while the innermost part of the eyebrow lowers. That's what creates the crow's feet by the eyes known as laugh lines," she said and pointed to her eyes. "When a person feels happy and smiles, then there's both a voluntary and an involuntary contraction by two muscles: the zygomaticus major muscle—that's the one that raises the corners of the mouth—and the orbicularis oculi muscle, which lifts the cheeks and produces the laugh lines around the eyes. The first is controlled by the frontal lobe. That's where the voluntary, conscious movement takes place. The other muscle is controlled by the emotional center in the brain. Do you follow?"

Schäfer nodded.

"You can't activate that latter one on your own," she continued. "It only responds to emotions. In other words, you can't *fake* your way into making the laugh lines around your eyes appear. So, with a fake smile—which we also refer to as a Pan Am smile, named for the airline's cabin crew— the smile doesn't reach the eyes. Only the corners of the mouth come up."

Schäfer nodded. "So what you're telling me is that you can't make anyone get those Duchenne smile wrinkles by their eyes by holding up a camera and asking them to smile?"

"Well, you could if the person were already happy. Someone optimistic, who thinks the world is a wonderful place. In that case it doesn't take very much to trigger a genuine smile, especially not in kids, who are generally more in touch with the joy of living than adults are. But this kid," she pointed to Lukas. "He's not joyful."

Schäfer massaged his stubble as he contemplated this.

"What are you thinking?" she asked.

"I'm thinking that it's been a long time since I last had a case that made so little sense. Here I've got a boy who's missing, a dead soldier, and an unidentified man in a pilot's suit. These three people are connected, but no one can tell me how. To the contrary, everyone says that the boy is practically traipsing through life happy as a clam, and now you tell me that he's not."

Friis looked at her Rolex with a look of disappointment.

"What is it?" Schäfer asked.

"I have another meeting in half an hour, so unfortunately I'm going to have to run."

Schäfer remembered his own meeting with Heloise and looked at his own watch, a cheap Casio he had had since the early nineties.

Friis put on her coat and gathered up the copies Schäfer had made for her. She put them in her big leather shoulder bag and looked up at him.

"I'll look at the case again tonight and let you know if I find anything else."

Schäfer held out his hand to her. "Thank you, Michala. I really appreciate it. And, hey, we miss you around here. If you ever decide to come back full time . . ." He held his arms out to the side to signal that she was always welcome.

She nodded. "Maybe someday . . ."

On her way out she turned around in the doorway and looked at Schäfer.

"Hey, I didn't have a chance to ask you. How are things with Connie?"

Schäfer looked up, his eyebrows raised. "Connie? She's doing great, thanks. Everything's great."

"Still the One?"

He nodded slowly, surprised at the question.

"Still the One," he replied.

Friis smiled slightly. "I'll see you around, Erik."

Schäfer watched her long blonde hair disappear down the hallway and thought about those eighteen types of smiles.

Which type had she just given him?

H ELOISE HAD RETURNED home around two in the morning after the EMTs had driven away with Kaj Clevin's body. Martin had been snoring away in the double bed when she silently let herself into the apartment.

She had taken a long, scalding hot shower, washed off the blood, and felt relief running through her body like fine-grained beach sand through her fingers.

The whole thing had resolved on its own. Even nature could tell she wasn't cut out to be anyone's mother.

After her shower she had felt as if life had given her a much-needed revitalizing saline drip. Her words had returned to her, her desire to work had welled up within her. She had spent the rest of the night writing the articles about the Lukas Bjerre case that she had been putting off for the last twenty-four hours and she was still sitting at the computer when Martin woke up.

She told him about Kaj Clevin and nonchalantly brushed off his concern for her. "People die, life stops. That's the way it is! You don't need to worry about me. I'm fine."

Martin shook his head at her and went into the kitchen. When he returned to the living room ten minutes later, he brought a tray of breakfast items. Toasted rye bread, soft-boiled eggs, coffee, orange juice, and the day's papers.

"You haven't slept at all," he said and started setting out the meal around Heloise. "Aren't you dying from exhaustion?"

She smiled at his word choice and shook her head. "No, but I could definitely go for a cup of coffee."

He sat down across from Heloise and poured her a cup of coffee. He handed her the cup.

"Are you sure you're okay? That must have been quite a shock."

"I'm fine." She turned back to her computer again and continued writing. "And I wouldn't exactly call it a *shock* when people who eat and drink their way through life keel over dead. It's sort of in the cards, you could say."

"Well, yeah, but . . . still," he said. "What about everyone else at the paper? Have you talked to any of them?"

"I called Mikkelsen last night and he came in right away. He was completely devastated. They've worked together for thirty years or something, so . . ." Heloise shrugged. "He just sent me a text saying the funeral will be Saturday."

"*This* Saturday? As in the day after tomorrow?"

Heloise nodded absentmindedly as her fingers danced on the keyboard.

"Where will it be?"

"At the Marble Church. A big circus followed by a reception with hors d'oeuvres and beer at AOC. Just what Kaj would have wanted," she said. "Could you hand me my phone?" She pointed over at the coffee table, her eyes still on the computer screen.

"Sure," he said and reached for it. "Here you go!"

Heloise looked up and saw that Martin was holding a little jewelry box out to her.

She looked at the box but didn't reach for it.

He opened it and held the contents out to her. There was a ring inside. An understated circle of forged fine gold without stones or whimsical details, very simple and clean. Just as she would have wanted it. If she had wanted a ring.

Heloise met Martin's gaze. His eyes were wide and full of anticipation.

"I couldn't lure you to Barcelona, and now I can't wait any longer, so . . ." He set the open jewelry box on the desk and pushed it closer to Heloise. "What do you say, Helo?"

Heloise closed her eyes for a moment. When she opened them again, the look in his eyes was unchanged. Still just as hopeful.

"Martin," she said, putting a hand on his cheek. "Listen, I . . . I'm not the person you're looking for, the one who . . ." She nodded at the ring. "It's never going to happen."

"It is, Heloise." He nodded insistently. "You're the only one for me. I know it!"

"No, I . . . Maybe if we had met each other in another life, but . . ."

"In another life? What do you mean?"

"I mean—it's been fun, and . . ."

"*Fun?*" A groove appeared above the bridge of his nose.

"Yeah, we've had fun together, and I wish we could continue like that, but . . . we don't want the same thing, you and I. You want to get married and have children, and I don't want that. In fact, I've known that all along, so it's not fair for me to keep . . ."

"Wait . . ." He shook his head, not understanding. "You've never dreamt of raising a family?"

"There are lots of things I've dreamt of at some point that I no longer want."

"I don't understand."

"The things that have happened in my life in the last few years . . . Everything is different now."

"Why? Why is everything different now?"

"It just is. *I'm* different. I can't be the things you're looking for. The mother of your children—that's not going to be me."

Martin closed the jewelry box and leaned back.

"But you can still do your job." His voice sounded hollow, hurt. "You can still be Gerda's friend, and get drunk on white wine, and run large companies into the ground on the front page of the newspaper. But this . . . you can't do this. You're just not up to kids after what you've been through, is that what you're telling me?"

Heloise nodded. "That's what I'm telling you."

He leaned forward and took her hand. "Heloise, you're one of the strongest people I know. Of course you can figure out how to be a mother."

She shook her head. "You're misunderstanding me. I'm not saying that I've become weak or that what's happened in my life has broken me. But . . ." She searched for the words. "It . . . it feels kinda like an internal 9/11."

He furrowed his brow. "9/11?"

"Yes. When those airplanes hit the towers that morning, they changed something, irrevocably. New Yorkers rebuilt their city and what happened made them stronger—more resilient. But . . . it's a different city now. It will always be marked by what happened that morning."

Martin eyed her without saying anything. She could tell he was desperately searching for an angle to approach this from, a point that would yield to pressure, somewhere he could set his thumb and press.

"I lived a life before that was good," she continued to get him to understand. "Not a perfect life, but a good one.

And it was shattered to smithereens when I lost my dad. I've found a place to moor again that I'm happy with, and . . ." She shrugged. "I don't want to rock the boat. And I do *not* want to pass down his genes."

"But you can't let what happened to your father color the rest of your life. He was *sick*, Heloise. But it's not contagious. It's not *heritable*."

Heloise didn't say anything. Martin's words bounced off her like projectiles off bulletproof glass.

He put his hand on hers again. "I saw how you were with Lulu last night, how much you care about her. If you had your own children to—"

"We live in a fucked-up world," Heloise snapped. She felt suddenly annoyed to have to spell it all out. She stood up and started clearing off the desk even though they hadn't eaten yet. Plates and glasses clinked loudly against each other. "People out there are sick in the head. Why the hell do *you* want to bring children into this world?"

"Oh, for crying out loud, because they're the whole *point* to everything!?" Martin raised his voice, following her into the kitchen.

Heloise set the plates down on the kitchen island and shook her head.

"For you, maybe. But not for me."

"So you don't want to have kids because the world is shit, and you're—what?—afraid of dying?" He flung up his arms, upset.

"No." She shook her head. He didn't understand anything. "I don't want to have kids because I'm *not* afraid of dying, not now, not the way my life is set up. I don't depend on anyone, and no one depends on me. And the thought of someone . . ."

"What, needing you?"

Heloise stared at him blankly. "That's not a responsibility I want in my life. I'm not even sure I would be able to *feel* what you're supposed to feel. It's like there's something broken inside me. When I found Kaj yesterday—it seriously didn't affect me. The EMTs put him in a body bag and rolled him out of the building and I felt nothing. Nothing! Do you understand what I'm telling you? My alarm system went off, but I didn't *feel* anything. I don't think I even have it in me anymore."

"You say that now, but I know you would feel differently if you got pregnant." Martin's voice was thick with emotion. "The second you knew that there was a life, that it was a baby—*our* baby!—you would love it right away. It would change your whole—"

"It wouldn't change a thing."

"Yes, I *know* it would, Heloise. If you just gave it a chance. If you opened your heart to . . ."

"I went to the doctor the other day for an abortion."

The words tumbled coldly from her lips. There was no compassion in her voice, no desire to meet him halfway.

Martin looked as if she had just informed him she was terminally ill.

"You did *what*?" he whispered.

"Monday." Heloise nodded. "I went to the doctor on Monday, because I wanted to get an abortion."

Martin took a step away from her. He sized her up, his eyes coming to rest on her belly.

"You're pregnant?"

She considered her words for a split second and then shook her head. "Not anymore. But I was and my point is that it didn't change anything. I didn't want it."

Martin's shoulders sank and his face slumped forward. Then he directed his gaze at Heloise without lifting his head.

"You went to the doctor for an abortion without talking to me first?"

"Yes."

Heloise felt the back of her head hit the doorframe before it dawned on her what had happened.

She collapsed on the floor while her left eye started closing all on its own. Every nerve quivered, like one big bundle of pain.

Martin stood over her, his hands clenched into fists. His face was cold, his eyes black with rage.

"You murdered our baby?" he yelled. Tears welled up in his eyes. "How could you do that?"

Heloise tried to get up, and he pushed her back down onto the floor again. She raised one arm and held it defensively over her face.

Martin grabbed it tightly, his fingers digging into her skin.

"How could you be so fucking cold, Heloise?"

"Martin, let go of me!" Heloise's voice trembled with rage and shock. "*Let me go!*"

She felt dizzy, her vision blurred as if she were looking through a fogged-up windowpane.

Martin, suddenly frozen, stared down at her for a long moment without letting go of her arm. The black, glazed look suddenly disappeared from his eyes again.

He let go of her.

"*Get out of here!*" Heloise yelled, pushing herself away from him with her feet.

Her left eye throbbed violently and felt like it was exploding in her skull. She could taste blood in her mouth.

"*Go away!*"

"I'm sor—sorry." Martin dropped to his knees in front of her. "I'm sorry, Heloise. I'm sorry, I . . ." His tongue ran over his lips as he fumbled for the words and tried to make sense of what had happened. "I don't know what got into me. I didn't mean to . . ."

"If you don't get out of here right now, I'm calling the police," Heloise said, unsteadily getting to her feet.

Martin took a step toward her, and she reached for her phone.

"Heloise, wait. I . . ."

"Hello? Is this the police?" Heloise's voice shook as she spoke, angry tears pouring down her cheeks.

Martin's arms dropped to his sides. The light in his eyes went out.

"Heloise," he whispered.

She shook her head. The dispatcher asked the nature of her emergency.

"Last fucking warning," Heloise said, gesturing to the front door with her chin.

Martin nodded, crestfallen, and turned around.

The ring was still sitting on the dining table when the door shut behind him.

39

"A CUP OF COFFEE, please. With a little milk on the side."

Schäfer gave a friendly nod to the girl who took his order.

He had been seated at a window table in the bistro on Kongens Nytorv and was now looking out at the construction mess by the subway station across the street where a large, reddish-brown crane towered up from the roadway like a brachiosaurus.

Trucks loaded with oversized metal cylinders and strange-looking plastic things coughed their way into and out of the construction site, splattering slush toward the tourists—who were the only people it occurred to to go anywhere near the site. There were a few barricades left on the south side of the square, but there—in the middle of it all—for the first time in years you could see the equestrian statue.

At long last.

Beautiful and majestic, like an old friend the city had been deprived of for ages.

Schäfer smiled at the sight. It was like seeing Atlantis rise from the sea.

The waiter set his coffee in front of him and handed him a menu.

"Thanks, that's okay," Schäfer said, holding up one hand. "Just the coffee."

"Are you waiting for someone?"

Schäfer nodded and looked at his watch. It was 9:08, and Heloise hadn't shown up yet. It wasn't like her to be late without letting him know. Plus, she had emphasized in her text that this was important.

Schäfer called Heloise, but the call went straight to her voice mail. He asked her to call him back.

By the time he finished his coffee, it was 9:21, and he was starting to have a nagging feeling—the kind that whispered to him that something was wrong.

He tried to catch Heloise by phone again, without any luck.

Then he asked for the check.

* * *

The front door to her residential building on Olfert Fischers Gade was open and Schäfer swore softly. He had told Heloise that she should make sure to get the lock mechanism fixed so every conceivable suspicious character couldn't just waltz in and out of the building. It sometimes seemed like she was completely immune to common sense.

He made his way up the creaky old stairs and was out of breath by the time he reached Heloise's apartment on the fifth floor. He cleared his throat to get that tobacco tickle under control and knocked on the door.

He waited for a long moment and then knocked again.

"Heloise?" he called. "Are you in there?"

The door opened a crack, and Heloise looked out, looking like someone who had just woken up. She was wearing jeans and a black T-shirt, was barefoot, and her hair was uncombed.

"Hey," she said. Her voice was shaky and standoffish.

Schäfer flung out his arms in annoyance. "I've been waiting for you for half an hour. What happened? Are you sick?"

"I'm sorry," Heloise said and took a step back in her entryway so that he could come in. "I had completely forgotten we were supposed to meet. Sorry about that."

Schäfer opened the door to the living room, so the morning light hit Heloise's face. The skin around one of her eyes was swollen and red, and a little blood was trickling from her eyebrow.

"What the hell?" he exclaimed. "What happened to you?"

"Nothing." Heloise averted her gaze.

"What do you mean, 'nothing'? You're a total . . ." Schäfer stopped himself. Then his eyes widened. "Did Martin do this to you?"

Heloise held up a hand defensively. "He didn't mean it."

"I'm going to fucking kill him!" Schäfer seethed. He started pacing back and forth in the room. "I knew this would happen one day. I *knew* it!"

"He didn't mean it," Heloise repeated placatingly. "I pushed him away and then he lost his temper . . ."

"Do you hear yourself?" Schäfer pointed to one ear with an angry finger. "You sound exactly like those women we come out to see after some asshole of a husband has beaten the crap out of them."

"I'm not like those women," Heloise said, irritated.

"You're defending him!" Schäfer bellowed. "What the hell is the difference?"

"I threw him out, okay? It's over! I threw him out."

"You need to report him." Schäfer put his hands on his sides. "He needs to be punished for this."

Heloise turned away from him. She walked off into the kitchen and threw a pod into the coffee machine, which spat a stream of black liquid into a little porcelain cup.

She turned back toward Schäfer and crossed her arms, waiting for his next outburst.

"You need to file an official report against him," he said, now with more composure.

"No, I don't want to."

"Why the hell not?"

"Because I'm simply not up to the whole production, and because . . ." She shrugged. "I provoked him. I was intentionally trying to push him over the edge, so I wouldn't have to be the only bad guy. So part of it was my fault."

Schäfer's lower jaw fell a couple of inches, and he looked at her, dumbstruck.

"How in the world can you believe that what you did— whatever it was—could justify his behavior? This business is never okay. *Never!* Just *look* at yourself for Pete's sake!" He stepped over closer to her, studying her face with an expression of concern. "Can you even see out of your left eye?"

Heloise pulled away, positioning herself with her side to Schäfer, so he couldn't see her swollen eyelid.

"I'm not condoning his behavior, but . . . I haven't been honest with him. From the very beginning of our relationship, he's said that he wanted to start a family, that that was a deciding factor for him. And for a year and a half I've let him think that that was a possibility with me, so . . ."

Schäfer shrugged unsentimentally. "So what?"

"And so I said some things that were mean. I hurt him."

"Mm-hmm, and this is the world's smallest violin playing in honor of Martin Duvall." Schäfer rubbed the tips of his thumb and index finger together. "That's life, right? We don't always get what we want. Our hearts get ripped to pieces and then they heal again. We don't start punching each other with our fists."

Schäfer was seething with rage. He blamed himself for not being more attentive to Heloise. From the beginning he had known that Martin Duvall was a loose cannon, a crummy wolf in permanent press trousers. No matter how impressed Connie was by the man's straight teeth and long eyelashes, he couldn't control his inner Neanderthal.

Schäfer's hand grazed the handcuffs that hung from his belt. His fingers itched to slap them onto Duvall's wrists, and Heloise's leniency really irked him.

"Martin has always had a hard time controlling his temper," she said. "But deep down he's a good person."

"No, you need to wake the hell up now, Heloise!"

"All right, *stop!*" She held up her hand. "It's sweet of you to get so upset on my behalf, and I appreciate your being here, I do. But you're not my dad, okay? I can take care of myself."

"I'm not your dad, but if I were, you would darn well be grounded for your behavior."

"Are you mad at me?"

"Yes, damn it, I'm mad! You need to get that eye checked out. That doesn't look good at all."

Heloise nodded. "All right, I will."

"Come on. I'll drive you to the doctor."

"No thanks. I can do it myself."

Heloise took the full coffee cup from the machine and handed it to Schäfer.

He hesitated a moment. Then he accepted it, took a sip, and tried to stabilize his breathing.

There was a long silence between them. Heloise walked over and sat down at the kitchen table.

"Well," Schäfer said and sat down next to her. "What was it that was so important when you wrote to me yesterday?"

He looked at her one eye, where blood had accumulated, discoloring the white of her eyeball. He winced compassionately and cautiously touched her chin to rotate her head so that he could better examine her injuries.

Her left eyelid was swollen and red, her eyebrow split near the bridge of her nose. Luckily it was just a little gash, and it was hidden in the eyebrow hairs. It wouldn't leave an ugly scar, Schäfer thought. Not on her face, anyway.

"Why did you text me last night?" he asked again. "What was it that you wanted to tell me?"

Heloise looked up at him and blinked a couple of times.

Schäfer could see that she was hesitant to say whatever it was that she had on her chest. He returned her chin to its previous position and eyed her calmly.

He knew that look in her eyes. He had seen it before.

"Heloise," he said, shaking his head and closing his eyes for a second. "What have you done *now*?"

She got up without saying anything and walked into the living room. When she returned, she set down two sheets of paper on the kitchen table in front of him. One was a printout from Google Maps, an overview of small roads, paths, and forests in an area of Odsherred with a lot of summer vacation houses. One of the neighborhoods had been outlined with a red Sharpie. The second page was the picture of the barn door from Lukas Bjerre's Instagram profile.

Schäfer gave her a piercing look. "What is this?"

"That's the place you're looking for." She pointed to the picture. "That barn there. I think it's somewhere in this area."

She pushed the map closer to him.

Schäfer didn't say anything. He just stared at her as a knot of anger grew in his stomach.

"I *know* I've been there," Heloise said. "I've stood in front of that barn recently. And I haven't been anywhere except Rørvig lately. I can't remember exactly where I saw the place, but it was in this area here, the zone I outlined in red." She nodded at the map.

Schäfer chewed on his lower lip as he thought. Then he held up the picture of the barn door. His voice was controlled, but he gazed penetratingly into Heloise's eyes.

"Where did you get this picture from?"

"Yeah, where do you think?" She stood up and stepped over to the window, her back to Schäfer.

"I thought I could trust you." His voice was thick with disappointment.

"You *can* trust me!" Heloise turned around and flung up her hands. "I'm coming clean with you right now, right? And as you can see, this isn't in the newspaper. I haven't told anyone else. The most important thing right now is to find the boy, isn't it? And I'm telling you: The barn you're looking for is somewhere up in Rørvig. You're welcome!"

"Why is it constantly necessary to remind you that you're a journalist?" Schäfer asked tiredly. "You're not a detective."

"I'm an investigative journalist. Apart from the gun, there's not a lot of difference between our jobs."

They were interrupted by Schäfer's phone ringing.

"We are not done discussing this," he said and then answered his phone.

"What's up?" he asked, stepping out into the living room to make sure Heloise couldn't hear what was being said on the other end of the line.

Nils Petter Bertelsen's voice was sharp in a way that made Schäfer sit up and pay attention. "We got the results back from Pathology on the handprint on the radiator in the apartment on Sølvgade."

"And?"

"It belongs to a Salah Ahmed."

"Who's he?"

"Danish citizen, born in Iraq, thirty-eight years old," Bertelsen said. "He came to Denmark in 1993. He works as a cab driver and lives in Hvidovre with his wife and new-born son."

"What have we got on him?"

"Not much. He was charged with firearm possession last year in connection with the gang conflict. He was stopped during a raid on Blågårdsgade when he was drop-ping off a fare who happened to be a member of the Loyal to Familia gang. The police searched his taxi and found a knife. He was dragged down to the station, registered, and questioned, but the charge was dropped again immediately afterward."

"Is that all we have on him?"

"Yes."

"Okay, let's pick him up and see what he has to say," Schäfer said. "I'm going to send you something right now that you should ask Bro or one of the others to check out. A neighborhood of summer cabins up north. We received a tip that the barn we're looking for might be up there."

Heloise stood in the doorway to the living room, watch-ing Schäfer as he hung up.

"What's up?" she asked.

Schäfer gave her a measured look and didn't answer the question. He walked over to the kitchen table and took a picture of the map of the neighborhood of summer vacation homes. He sent it to Bertelsen and stuck his phone back in his pocket.

"If Duvall comes back, call me right away. Got it?" He pointed an angry finger at Heloise's beat-up face. "Don't let him in!"

She nodded just once.

Schäfer closed the door firmly behind him. Then he left.

CHAPTER

40

Schäfer pulled over to the curb and nodded at the silver-gray Audi that was parked in front of the apartment building in Hvidovre.

"Isn't that the model of Audi he owns?"

Nils Petter Bertelsen double-checked the license plate in the system.

"Yeah, that's right. The vehicle is registered to one Salah Mahmoud Abu Al-Fadl Ahmed." Bertelsen pronounced the name in an accent and raised his eyebrows at Schäfer.

Schäfer nodded. "I guess that means he's home."

He leaned forward in the seat to look out the windshield, peering up at the top of the apartment block, a hideous, fifteen-story-tall monstrosity in the middle of Rebæk Søpark. The building was occupied by a stew of various tormented souls, petty criminal bums, addicts, immigrants, and young college students who couldn't afford to live in downtown Copenhagen. This was far from the first time Schäfer had come to this address to haul a suspect in for questioning. And it wouldn't be the last.

"What floor does he live on?" he asked.

"Twelfth floor. Apartment 124."

"All right, let's go pick him up."

Schäfer and Bertelsen left their car in front of the main entrance and walked into the building. The elevator smelled like a mixture of curry and urine, and Schäfer's shoe soles stuck to the floor where a puddle of some indeterminate red liquid had coated the linoleum.

When the elevator doors opened on the twelfth floor, an ash-colored mountain of a person squashed his way into the elevator car. The man was dragging an oxygen supply with him and had a CPAP mask on over his nose and mouth. His arms were so padded with fat that it looked like he was stretching them out to the sides even though they hung limply from his shoulder sockets.

"Excuse me," Schäfer said. He sucked in his gut and squeezed his way past the man, managing to avoid touching either him or the elevator wall.

He peered down the long, dark hallway that extended out on either side of the elevator.

"This looks like an apartment building in some slum in Rio de Janeiro," Bertelsen said. "You know, one of those ones that the tradesmen abandoned before they were done and now people are living on the thirty-third floor of a building without any outside walls." He looked around. "It's weird that some people would choose to live here."

"A lot of them don't have a choice," Schäfer said. "But, yeah, there's an overrepresentation of real humdingers out here. Last year Augustin and I questioned a suspect who lived a couple of floors down. We had a case where a female postal worker from Rødovre had disappeared on her third day of work, and witnesses thought they had seen her talking to this guy down at McDonald's." Schäfer nodded in the direction of the fast-food restaurant they had seen on their way into the building. "So of course we came by to have a little chat with the guy, feel him out a little bit, you know. And you know what we found in his bathtub?"

"The missing postal worker?"

"Nope. Twelve decapitated chickens."

Bertelsen furrowed his brow. "What?"

"Twelve chickens that he had bought at various locations all around the greater Copenhagen area so as not to arouse suspicion—not that I have any idea who would have seen that as a concern—and that he had then ripped the heads off with his bare hands. One by one." Schäfer made a gesture as if he were opening the tops of a row of invisible beer bottles.

Bertelsen raised his eyebrows. "Why in God's name did he do that?"

Schäfer shrugged. "To see what it felt like, I guess. Apparently he was into that kind of thing."

"*Chickens?*"

"Yup. It's called avisodomy. Do you know what that is?"

Bertelsen shook his head with a look that suggested that he wasn't sure he wanted to know.

"No, I didn't either," Schäfer said. "But I found out. It's a bird fetish. I don't know which is worse—that there are people who get turned on by birds or that there are so many of them that that shit actually has a name."

"You're kidding me, right?" Bertelsen scrunched up his eyes and eyed Schäfer skeptically.

"Nope."

"A bird fetish?"

"Yup."

"So the man had . . ." Bertelsen wiggled his eyebrows and nodded suggestively. "With chickens?"

"Yup."

"Ew!" His face contorted in disgust. "But what about the postal worker? Did you ever find her?"

An image of the woman's naked, discolored body flashed through Schäfer's mind. Her long, blonde hair wrapped tightly around her neck. Her blueish white lips contracted in fear. The zip ties digging into her slender wrists . . .

"Yes," he nodded. "We found her in a dumpster back behind Big Bowl in Valby, raped and strangled."

"And the killer?" Bertelsen asked.

Schäfer shook his head and set off walking down the hallway.

"Still on the loose."

* * *

They found apartment 124 at the end of the long hallway and stopped in front of the door. A pyramid of shoes of various sizes sat in front of it, the toes all worn out. A pair of black rain boots in a men's size stood in the middle as if someone had just taken them off.

Schäfer put his ear to the door and listened. He heard a quiet conversation going on somewhere in there but couldn't make out what they were saying or even what language they were speaking. He tried to hear where in the apartment the voices were coming from. He knew what the floor plan looked like from earlier raids. All of the apartments in the complex were identical, all of them studio apartments with a sleeping loft and a balcony facing either Copenhagen or, on the other side, Brøndbyøster. He knew that to the left of the front door there was a small, rectangular bathroom, and that the apartment's only room—a combination living room, kitchenette, and bedroom—was straight in from the door.

He pulled his service weapon from his shoulder holster, pointed to the peephole, and signaled to Bertelsen that he should stand to the right of the door, out of sight. Then

Schäfer changed his mind and covered the peephole with the palm of his hand.

He knocked on the door with his pistol grip.

There was movement inside the apartment. A baby started crying. Schäfer heard a woman's voice somewhere inside. She spoke in Arabic, her voice loud and annoyed, as if she were scolding someone.

He knocked on the door again.

He heard someone approach the door from inside. There was a pronounced scraping sound from in there as if someone were pulling a key or other sharp object across the inside of the door.

It was quiet for a moment. Then the woman's voice could be heard again.

"Who is it?"

"I need to talk to Salah," Schäfer said. "Is he home?"

"Who's asking? First I need to know who's asking." She spoke Danish with a thick accent. Her words fell in hard bursts, the vowels sharp.

"I need to talk to Salah. It's important," Schäfer said.

The woman was quiet for a moment. He heard her whisper something. Another voice—a male one—whispered back. They continued back and forth like that for several seconds without anything happening.

Schäfer tried an old trick: "Tell him I have the money I owe him."

He looked at Bertelsen and shrugged. The trick was not all that original, but it usually worked. People's need to control the situation typically vanished when you dangled some money in front of them.

"Okay," the woman said. "Just toss it in the mail slot."

Schäfer smiled to himself. "No, that's all right," he said. "I'll just come back another day. Tell Salah I say hi and tell him I've been . . ."

"No, okay. Wait!"

The instant the door was opened ajar, Schäfer rammed it hard with his shoulder. He stepped into the entryway with his Heckler & Koch raised in front of him. A slim woman in a hijab immediately started screaming, and Schäfer grabbed her shoulder with his free hand.

"Police," he said, guiding her farther into the apartment.

Bertelsen flew past them into the room. "Hands up!" he yelled to the man in there. "Down on the floor. Hands behind your head. Behind your *head*, I told you."

"How many people are in the apartment?" Schäfer asked, looking back and forth between the woman and the bathroom door, which was ajar behind her.

She didn't answer his question. Instead, she eyed him defiantly with heavily made-up eyes and issued what sounded like a fatwa against him.

Schäfer didn't understand a word of what she said, but the gist of her message was clear.

He gave the door to the bathroom a kick so it swung open and hit the wall behind it with a bang.

"What the hell are you doing?" the woman yelled. "You're ruining my door! You're going to pay for that."

Schäfer ignored her. He gazed at the bare white tiles, the shower's caulk-stained glass door. He ransacked the room with his eyes. There was no one in there.

He looked at the woman again and nodded toward the living room.

"Go have a seat."

"I want to see a warrant." She tilted her head back and pointed her chin at him. "You can't just walk in here without a warrant."

Schäfer smiled. "You've been watching too many movies. This is Denmark. So please do as I'm asking. Have a seat in the living room."

The woman reluctantly turned around. She stepped over the man, who lay on the living room carpet with his hands behind his head and walked over to a cradle in the corner. She picked up the crying baby and shushed it.

Schäfer looked around.

There was way too much furniture in the small studio apartment. There was a jumble of knickknacks and decorations packed onto every horizontal surface. Most of the things looked like heirlooms or flea market finds, a blend of patinaed items and worn-out junk. One wall in the small apartment was covered with photo wallpaper showing a beach with palm trees. It was presumably meant to make the apartment look bigger—or Denmark feel less Danish.

Schäfer nodded to Bertelsen, who grabbed the man's hands and raised him into a sitting position.

Schäfer regarded the face in front of him and furrowed his brow. The man, who was kneeling as if in prayer, had round cheeks and bushy eyebrows that grew together, forming a unibrow.

Schäfer looked at Bertelsen again. "That doesn't look like the guy in the archive photo, does it?"

Bertelsen turned toward the man. "Salah Ahmed?"

The man's only answer was to spit, hitting one of Bertelsen's trouser legs.

Bertelsen grabbed him by the collar with both hands and lifted him in one quick, angry motion.

"*Stop!*" the woman exclaimed, trying to come between them. "That's my little brother. He hasn't done anything. We haven't done anything. Get out of here!"

"Where's Salah?" Schäfer asked.

"I don't know. At work, probably? I don't know!"

"His car is parked out front . . ."

"I have no idea where he is, I'm telling you."

"And who are you? His girlfriend? His wife?"

"I'm his wife."

The baby started crying again, and the woman rocked it mechanically up and down in her arms.

"Is the baby yours?" Schäfer asked.

She held the baby closer to her chest and confirmed this with a calm nod.

Schäfer noticed a framed picture hanging on the wall behind her. A picture of a smiling extended family, twelve or fourteen people. Women, men, and children. Siblings, grandparents, cousins. On the right side of the photo he recognized Salah Ahmed from the archive photo.

"Okay," he said and nodded toward an armchair in the corner of the room. There were holes in the upholstery and the foam rubber was sticking out, yellow with dirt. "If you could please have a seat. We have a couple of questions about your husband."

* * *

Schäfer and Bertelsen questioned Salah Ahmed's wife and brother-in-law but did not find out how his fingerprints had wound up on Thomas Strand's radiator. Neither of them seemed to know anything about the case, and Schäfer didn't have the impression that this was due to any unwillingness to cooperate. She wasn't lying, the wife. There had been a genuine blank look in her eyes—an almost defensive incomprehension—when he had shown her the picture of Strand. Schäfer was convinced that she hadn't heard of the man before. The brother-in-law had been harder to read but had also not offered them anything useful.

Schäfer and Bertelsen left the apartment and walked back to the elevator.

"Let's try to have the car brought in and looked at," Schäfer said. "Get it checked for evidence."

A figure came around the corner at the opposite end of the dark hallway. The person was wearing a hoodie with the hood on and pulled well down over the forehead. The build was masculine, broad shoulders and narrow hips, he was walking with a casual posture, a bit leaned back. He was carrying a McDonald's bag in one hand and swinging it lazily back and forth as he walked.

Schäfer stuck his right hand into his jacket and grabbed hold of his gun.

When the man noticed them, he immediately broke the rhythm of his gait. He slowed down but kept coming toward them.

Schäfer heard a cell phone ring. The sound came from the man, and Schäfer figured it must be his wife trying to warn him.

"Salah Ahmed?" Schäfer called.

The man instantly tossed aside the fast-food bag, turned, and ran back down the hallway.

Schäfer and Bertelsen sprinted after him. They rounded the corner by the elevator and pushed open the door to the stairwell. It was pitch black inside. Bertelsen hit the light switch, but the lights didn't respond. There were no windows to let in the daylight.

They could hear the man's footsteps rattling down the stairs like a drumroll against dried cement.

"You take the elevator," Schäfer said. "I'll take the stairs."

Even going down, thirteen flights were enough to leave Schäfer winded. Salah Ahmed was younger and obviously in better shape. Schäfer swore under his breath as he involuntarily slowed down. He felt his way along in the darkness with one hand on the railing and the other on his gun. He had reached the fourth floor when he noticed a light somewhere below him. He heard a door closing. Then everything around him went dark again.

"Damn it," he muttered and forced himself to kick it up a notch.

At the ground floor he cautiously opened the door the man had run out. It led out behind the building and Schäfer could see a bike shed off to his left. To the right there was a snow-covered lawn with a jungle gym, a swing set, and a playhouse. There weren't any people out there, no kids playing. One swing swayed gently back and forth in the wind, its rusty chains squeaking. The only other sound was the hum of traffic from Avedøre Havnevej, which ran in front of the building.

Schäfer followed the freshly made footprints in the snow. They led around the building to the parking lot. As soon as he turned the corner, the footprints mingled with hundreds of other shoeprints into one big porridgey mess from people who had walked to or from the parking lot.

Schäfer's eyes scanned the area.

He sensed a shadow behind a parked delivery van and started toward the vehicle. He was only a few feet away when Salah Ahmed jumped out of his hiding place and ran.

"*Stop*," Schäfer yelled. "Police!"

He fired a warning shot, but the sound did not slow the man's sprint.

The man was halfway to the gray Audi when Bertelsen materialized out of the blue and performed a brutal rugby tackle to Ahmed's chest.

The man's legs looked like they kept moving down the street as his torso was stopped by the blow. He did half a backflip and landed on the asphalt with a pained moan.

Bertelsen put a knee on his back and handcuffed him.

Schäfer caught up to them and leaned over forward with his hands on his thighs, huffing and puffing.

The man on the ground cursed and swore.

"The time is 1:08," Bertelsen said, pulling him up into a standing position. "And you're under arrest."

CHAPTER

41

Lisa Augustin sat cross-legged on the floor in the office, drumming her fingers together. She glanced alternately between the bulletin board on the wall and the printouts of the pictures she had spread out on the linoleum in front of her.

The phone on the desk had been ringing all day with people who thought they had information about the case. But so far they hadn't drawn the winning number.

As it rang yet again, she got to her feet in one quick motion. The front desk had put through an outside call, and she heard a high-pitched female voice with a central Jutland accent on the other end of the line.

"Yes, hello. My name is Anja Christensen. I'm calling because I saw on the front page of *Ekstra Bladet* that you're searching for a suspect in the case of that missing boy."

"That's right," Augustin said, putting it on speakerphone. She set the phone down and started flipping through the papers on the desk in front of her. "What can I do for you?"

"That guy in the picture, the one on the S train," the girl said. "I'm pretty sure his name is Finn Weinrich. I work with him."

Augustin bit the cap off a felt-tip pen and wrote the name down.

"Okay, but you can't see his face in the picture, so what makes you think the guy in the picture is this Finn Weinrich?"

"Something about the way he's standing. And the clothes," the girl said. "But actually it's the case itself that convinces me that it must be Finn. He could easily have kidnapped the boy."

"Why do you think that?"

"Because he's really into kids, like, in a creepy way."

"In what sense?"

"Every time they come into the store, he's, like, practically all over them. A lot of customers complain about it because they find it unsettling."

"Where do you work?"

"At Føtex Food, on the corner of Esplanaden and Bredgade.

"The one that's just across the street from the entrance to Churchill Park by the Citadel?"

"Yes."

"And this guy Finn works there, too?"

"Yes," the girl said. "I work at the bakery counter and checkout, and he's in fruits and vegetables. He's working through KLAPjob."

"Clap-job?"

"Yeah, it's one of those organizations that helps people with intellectual disabilities find work."

"What's wrong with him?"

"I don't know. He's just not, like, normal. There's something not quite right."

"Do you know if he was at work on Monday?"

"No, but I can check the schedule right now," the girl said.

Augustin could hear typing.

"Okay, let me see . . . Monday, Monday . . . We had a shift together, I can see. Oh, right. Now I remember. I worked from seven to five. Finn also started at seven and got off at six. So he had a long shift that day."

Then it couldn't be him, Augustin thought. Lukas disappeared at around eight.

"But I know he gets breaks several times a day."

"Breaks?"

"Yes, we have a long lunch break and a bunch of other short smoking breaks and that kind of thing over the course of the day."

"Can you remember if Finn Weinrich had a break in the morning on Monday?"

"Yeah, there's breaks all day long. And he was gone for quite a while, because I remember that some kids came into the store asking for him, but he was gone."

"Which kids were those?"

"Just some from the neighborhood. People sometimes come in and ask for him because he gives them free apples. He gets chewed out for it by the boss all the time, but he still does it again the second we're looking the other way."

Bingo, Augustin thought.

"Do you know where he lives, this Finn?"

"No, but I know he lives with his mom on a run-down farm somewhere outside of town. I want to say Rødovre, someplace like that."

"There are no farms in Rødovre," Augustin said.

She was born and grew up there, and the closest she had ever been to anything that even resembled a farm in the neighborhood was one time in the nineties, when there had been a county fair in the empty lot next to Damhuskroen's Irish Pub. That was the first and only time she had ever seen a cow being milked, and ever since then she'd never touched the stuff.

The girl chuckled on the other end of the line. "Well, okay, but then I don't know. I'm from Vejle and I've only lived in Copenhagen for five months, so . . ."

"That's fine," Augustin said. "How old is he, do you know?"

"I would guess about thirty, thirty-five, somewhere around there."

"Do you know if he's working today?"

"He isn't," the girl said. "His next shift on the schedule isn't until the day after tomorrow."

Augustin thanked the girl for calling and hung up. She immediately opened the civil registration database and searched for Finn Weinrich. A civil registration number and an address popped up. It was in the Copenhagen suburb of Glostrup, right next to the highway and not far from an equestrian center with a riding school Augustin knew. She had been right, the girl. It was an old farm property, and it was registered to a Kirstine Weinrich, age sixty-seven. The only other resident at the address was Finn Weinrich, age thirty-one.

Augustin's eyes slid down the page.

Kirstine Weinrich, she thought. Kirstine. Kiki.

She got up and quickly made her way to the IT department. She poked her head into the dark office, looking for Schäfer in the crowd, but couldn't see anything other than neon-blue screens. She turned on the light and the fluorescent tubes in the ceiling started waking up in tired, blinding flashes. Several computer engineers squinted at the door in annoyance.

Augustin spotted Michael Voss's bald head in the distance.

"Does anyone know where Schäfer is?"

"He drove off with Bertelsen about an hour ago. I don't know if they're back yet," Voss said.

Augustin nodded in thanks and turned back toward the exit.

"Remember to turn off the light before you—"

The door shut behind Augustin before Voss had a chance to finish his sentence.

She tried to catch Schäfer on his cell phone, but he didn't pick up. She searched for him all over police headquarters and ran into Bertelsen's partner in the kitchenette. He was wearing his coat and pouring himself a cup of coffee in a paper cup.

"Hi, Bro!" She knocked on the door frame to get his attention. "Do you know where Schäfer and Bertelsen went?"

"They're out picking up a suspect in Hvidovre."

August's forehead creased. "A suspect? Why didn't Schäfer say anything to me?"

Lars Bro gave her a teasing smile. "Maybe he was trying to ditch you? But you can ride with me if you want. I'm on my way to Rørvig to check out a tip."

Augustin raised an eyebrow and snorted. "I'll pass."

She returned to her office and grabbed her jacket from the back of her chair. She put her gun in her shoulder holster, typed Finn Weinrich's address into her cell phone, and left police headquarters.

CHAPTER

42

SCHÄFER ENTERED THE interrogation room and closed the door behind him. He looked at the man who was seated on the other side of the desk. He was tall and athletic, with long, sinewy muscles, clearly in good shape. His head was shaved smooth and shone glossily, his sunken cheeks covered in dark stubble.

Salah Ahmed looked directly at Schäfer.

There was something about the look in his eyes that Schäfer had difficulty interpreting. Every guilty person who had ever sat in that chair had looked either defiant or eager to please, but what he saw now was different from anything he had ever seen before.

Was that pride? Honor?

Schäfer stepped over to the table and pulled out a chair, informing the man once again of his rights. Then he pulled a photo out of the case file and pushed it across the table. It was the picture of Thomas Strand at Camp Bastion, the same one that he had shown the Bjerre family.

"I assume that introductions aren't necessary," he said.

Salah Ahmed looked down at the photo. He mumbled something or other in Arabic. Then he looked up again.

"You don't speak Danish?" Schäfer asked.

"I speak Danish just fine," he replied with a heavy Copenhagen dialect. There was only the vaguest hint of foreignness in his intonation.

"Good, that will make it a little easier for us to have a conversation."

Schäfer took out the next picture and set it in front of the man. It had been taken by the police photographer in the Pathology Department and showed the entrance hole in Strand's lower face. The hole was magnified ten times and looked like the impact crater from a meteor.

"What can you tell me about this guy?"

"He looks dead," Salah Ahmed said, meeting Schäfer's eyes.

"Good observation." Schäfer nodded, looking at the man for a moment. Then he leaned forward in his seat. "We know you're behind this, Salah." His tone was pleasant, almost brotherly. "So do yourself a favor and cooperate. You'll be in a better situation then when the evidence is turned over to the prosecution and they decide to file charges against you. Because believe me, they will!"

Salah Ahmed said nothing.

Schäfer leaned back in his seat and clasped his hands in front of his stomach. Waiting. Patient.

He still didn't have anything on Ahmed other than his fingerprint on the radiator in a dead man's apartment. If Schäfer didn't come up with anything else, he would go free after the twenty-four hours Schäfer was allowed to detain him before he either had to be questioned before a judge or released.

Schäfer needed to get a confession out of the man. He needed to get him to talk.

"You're Iraqi?" he asked.

"I'm a Danish citizen, like you."

"But you were born in Iraq?"

"Yes."

"What do you think of Denmark?"

Salah Ahmed snorted. "Denmark or Danes?"

"Is there a difference?"

He half smiled and nodded. "There's a difference."

"All right," Schäfer said. "Then what do you think about Danes? Or to be more specific: What do you think about this Dane?" He nodded at the picture of Thomas Strand.

"I'd like to talk to a lawyer." Salah Ahmed leaned back in his chair with a look that revealed that he had said all he intended to say about the matter. "I know my rights. I want a lawyer."

"That's all very well." Schäfer's gaze cooled. "But unlike what you've seen on *CSI* or *DNA* or whatever other Hollywood shows, that's not how the cookie crumbles here in Denmark. You're welcome to a lawyer once *I'm* done with you, not a second before. And if you don't—"

The door behind them opened and Schäfer looked over at it in irritation. Bertelsen stood in the doorway and signaled that he should come out into the hall.

Schäfer got up and left the room. He turned to Bertelsen as soon as the door was closed, a bit peeved at having been interrupted so early in his questioning.

"What is it?"

"We ran the Ahmed family through the system."

"And?"

"He has a cousin."

"Most people do," Schäfer said.

"The cousin's name is Kareem Hussein Al-Fadl Ahmed. He works for the military."

A buzz spread through Schäfer's chest. He nodded to get Bertelsen to continue.

"He's a trauma psychologist at Svanemøllen Barracks. He works with the soldiers."

"And Thomas Strand?"

Bertelsen nodded. "Strand was his client."

Schäfer nodded, pleased. "Good job, Nils Petter."

He turned to return to his questioning session.

"There's more," Bertelsen said.

Schäfer looked back at him.

"Ahmed's immediate family came to Denmark in 1993. His parents and grandparents, his older sister, and his younger sister. But in the paperwork it says there was also a younger brother, but he didn't come to Denmark."

"Did he stay in Iraq?"

"It doesn't say anything about that. It just says that there were eight people in the family, but only seven of them came to Denmark in 1993."

"Okay," Schäfer said.

He opened the door again and his eyes met Salah Ahmed's across the room.

"All right, here's the situation," he said and walked over to the table. "Kareem is sitting in the next room and he's ready to talk." He sat down heavily in his chair and then waved his hand apologetically. "So I don't need your help after all, but I will of course make sure that you get a lawyer as you requested, and I wish you good luck going forward."

Schäfer pulled his phone out of his pocket and started scrolling down his list of contacts.

"I assume you don't already have a lawyer and you're not in a financial position to pay for one of the good ones, so it'll be an appointed one. They're almost as good, or . . ." He shook his head. "Well, they're better than nothing anyway."

"He deserved it," Salah Ahmed mumbled.

Schäfer looked up from his phone. "I'm sorry, did you say something?"

"That bastard." He nodded at the pictures of Strand lying on the autopsy table. "He deserved it."

"Oh, so *now* you want to cooperate? Is that what I'm hearing?"

The man didn't say anything.

"It's now or never," Schäfer said. "If you confess, the punishment will no doubt be less severe than if you—"

"I couldn't care less about the punishment."

He had to care at least a little bit, Schäfer thought, since he had started talking. He gave a subtle nod to the one-way window in the door to the room, the sign that he wanted to request the papers for Ahmed to sign.

"I couldn't care less about the punishment," Salah Ahmed repeated. "Just like you couldn't care less about someone like me."

Schäfer looked him in the eyes. "Excuse me?"

"You asked what I think about you Danes," he said. "I think you don't care. If it doesn't involve you—your families, your kids—then you don't care. You send an asshole like this guy . . ." He put his index finger on top of the picture of the bullet hole. "You send him to Iraq, to Afghanistan. But you're not interested in what he does when he's down there. You couldn't care less who he kills."

"Of course we care," Schäfer said, his brow furrowed. "If we didn't care, we'd let you go it on your own."

The man scoffed. "After the Manchester Arena bombing a few years ago, you told each other: 'Children! Now they've started going after children!' Do you remember that?"

Schäfer didn't respond.

"All the TV stations showed pictures of the attack," Salah said. "Picture after picture after picture, right? There was one of a young girl in jeans missing half of one of her pants legs. She left the concert location on crutches, covered in blood stains. Do you remember that? The media showed that picture nonstop. For days. For weeks!"

Schäfer nodded once. He remembered that very well.

"And then you held a memorial concert and lit candles and whatever the hell. I . . ." Salah Ahmed stared into space as if he were picturing the whole thing. He looked back at Schäfer again. "The week after the attack, I was reading the newspaper. And squeezed in between all the other news, in the middle of the paper, there was a tiny little note that said that forty children had been killed in a bombing in Syria. Only four lines. Planes from the American-led coalition had bombed civilians, families of ISIS fighters."

"That's war for you," Schäfer said gloomily.

"Is it?" Salah raised his eyebrows and smiled joylessly. "You couldn't care less about the dead children as long as they're not *your* dead children. My brother was killed by a bomb like that, an American bomb. In the middle of the night. We were asleep at home in Baghdad. Yazid was in the bed next to mine. And then . . ." He snapped his fingers. "Then he was gone, but there were no pictures of that in your newspapers, no memorial services, no public outcry. You couldn't have cared less. He was six years old. Oh well!" He shrugged as his eyes teared up. "He wasn't one of yours."

Schäfer didn't say anything. What could he say?

"I have a kid now," Salah said. "A little boy. And to know that he can grow up in a world where there is one less Thomas Strand . . ." He nodded to himself. "I'm fine with that. So to answer your question: Yes! I avenged Yazid and all the others like him, and I'm fine with that. Your soldier murdered innocent children—ask Kareem! He murdered innocent people for *fun*, and there wasn't a single person here in this country who even raised an eyebrow."

Schäfer regarded him with a neutral expression. "What children did Strand allegedly kill?"

"I had a fare over Christmas one time, picked the customer up in my cab out on Amagerbrogade somewhere. A chatty guy who tells me that he was a soldier at the barracks out in Østerbro, Svanemøllen, you know?"

Schäfer nodded.

"I tell him that my cousin works there and it turns out this guy knows Kareem. He says that I should tell him hello from a Thomas Strand. Nice guy, I think, and drop him off on Sølvgade. I spend New Year's Eve with Kareem and tell him about the conversation, talking pleasantly about this Strand guy, and then Kareem's face suddenly turns red. I can tell that something is wrong, but he says that he can't tell me what it is, that he needs to maintain patient confidentiality. But I keep digging into it until by the end of the night he finally gives in . . ." He leaned forward in his chair indignantly. "Then he tells me that that bastard shot women and children in Afghanistan, that he killed innocent people—children!—for *fun*."

Salah Ahmed's body was tense with indignation, like one big middle finger gesturing. He leaned back in his chair and shook his head.

"I couldn't forget that story, and I knew where the man lived . . . So he got what he deserved."

The door opened and Bertelsen handed the papers and a ballpoint pen to Schäfer.

Schäfer set them both in front of Salah Ahmed and watched as he signed the confession. Then Schäfer nodded a couple of times; bit his cheek a little.

"Well," he said, leaning back in his chair. "What you described about your little brother is tragic, of course, and you'd have to be a callous jerk with a heart of stone not to feel sympathy for your story. But there's just one problem we haven't talked about yet . . ."

Salah looked Schäfer in the eye.

"Lukas Bjerre," Schäfer said.

Salah suddenly froze in his chair.

Schäfer saw his eyes wander, and then the martyr-like expression was back. It only lasted for a split second.

But it was enough.

Lisa Augustin turned left at the end of Jyllingevej, and the scenery immediately changed from a suburban purgatory of burger restaurants and hardware stores to a neighborhood with fields and secluded country estates. She drove down the highway through the snow-white fields and stopped where a long dirt road ran off to the right.

Augustin turned off her GPS and peered down the road. She could see a building at the end. She pulled a pair of binoculars out of her glove compartment and focused them on the property.

A barn door stood open at the end of the unpaved road. A black pickup truck with mud splattered up the sides was parked just inside the door, and to the left of the barn there was an L-shaped farmhouse. The white paint was flaking off its walls and it looked as if it had been there for many years. Some of the roofing tiles were missing and the roof sagged in the middle, as if it were one sneeze away from collapse. Under the gray sky, framed by the bare, frozen fields, the property looked like something out of Chernobyl.

In disrepair. And abandoned.

It was hard to imagine anyone actually living there, Augustin thought.

Something in the barn caught her eye—some movement in there—and she aimed the binoculars at it. A person came into view behind the pickup. The person had their back to Augustin and she couldn't tell if it was a man or a woman.

Then the person turned around and walked out of the barn.

It was a man wearing a light blue pilot's suit. His knees were dirty, and he was carrying a black trash bag over one shoulder. He crossed the courtyard, walking quickly as he glanced from side to side.

Augustin recognized his face from the search she had done.

"Well, hello there, Finn Weinrich," she mumbled. She picked up her phone and called the switchboard. "Hi, this is Augustin. I've identified a suspect at an address in Glostrup and need assistance."

She gave them the address and contemplated for a moment whether she ought to wait or go in right away.

You never knew which minutes were most critical in a situation like this. Maybe Lukas was still alive in there. Maybe Finn Weinrich was getting rid of important evidence while she sat here with her hands in her lap.

Augustin got out of the car and looked around for another way to enter the property. She walked down the main road a way. A column of orange-brown Scots pines extended the whole way up to the property like a wall of dead branches.

She took a long step over the drainage ditch and made her way toward the barn, hidden by the pines, the cold cutting into her face.

She reached the building and hid behind it for a moment, listening. She could hear the metallic sound of a spade or shovel hitting the soil somewhere around the other side. She pulled her service weapon and held it out in front of her, arm straight, while she moved toward the sound.

The courtyard was empty when she reached it.

Augustin peered toward the barn, searching for the round windows and closed mouth from Lukas's Instagram photo, but the building didn't have the right shape or color, and there also weren't any windows in the door. She tried again to locate the digging clang of metal against the frost-hard ground, but it had stopped now.

She was about to make her way over to the main house when she heard something move behind the pickup inside the barn.

She took hold of her gun with both hands and walked into the barn. She couldn't see what was on the other side of the pickup and moved cautiously and silently back along the side of the vehicle.

Augustin heard movement again and held her breath.

She quickly stepped out front behind the car and aimed her weapon at the noise.

A rat jumped out of a tipped-over trash can and darted across the cold cement floor.

Augustin exhaled hard. "Fuck," she whispered and lowered her gun.

She just barely sensed a figure appear behind her. Then she felt the shovel hit her hard, slamming into her cheekbone.

44

"LUKAS BJERRE," SCHÄFER repeated. "What did you do to him?"

Salah Ahmed shook his head, tilting his mouth down. "I don't know anyone by that name."

Schäfer raised a surprised eyebrow. "That's weird."

"What's weird?"

"Well . . ." He made a show of shrugging his shoulders. "Your whole spiel about how Thomas Strand deserved to die because he murdered innocent children. It's weird because that narrative will no doubt be used again when people find out that you did the same thing, that you're like him."

Salah Ahmed's eyes narrowed into two thin lines. "I am nothing like him."

"But your argument was that every child's life is sacrosanct?"

"It is," he said and nodded stubbornly. "Thomas Strand murdered innocent children in Afghanistan. And he was proud of it."

"But now you've killed a Danish child, so . . ." Schäfer shook his head, mystified, and looked as if he were trying to solve a Rubik's cube using ESP. "How are you any different?"

"I'd like to talk to that lawyer now," Salah Ahmed said.

Schäfer dropped the comedy. "I know you were the one who kidnapped the boy."

Salah Ahmed glanced briefly at Schäfer and then away. Then he crossed his arms and said, "I have no idea what you're talking about."

"Where is he? Is he here?" Schäfer took the picture of the barn door out of the file and tossed it in front of him. "Where is this place?"

"I would like to speak with that lawyer now."

"And I would like to lie down on a sun lounger with a cold beer in my hand, but that's life. So unfair," Schäfer said. "Tell me, what have you done with Lukas. Is he dead?"

Salah Ahmed didn't respond.

"I can tell you that your Audi is being transported to the National Forensic Service as we speak, where it will be poked and probed from top to bottom by experts who won't give up until they've found evidence," Schäfer said. "Once they find it—and believe me, they will—you will rue the day you touched a hair on that child's head."

Salah started looking uncomfortable, sitting there.

"It was media coverage you were looking for, right? Well, you're going to get that now, buddy. I can already see the headline." Schäfer flung out his arms as if he were unrolling a news banner. "*Child-Killer from Bagdad*. Welcome to the front page!"

"You have no idea what the hell you're talking about," Salah Ahmed yelled. "I've never hurt a child!"

"You left the boy's jacket in the moat at the Citadel, and that was a pretty dumb move. Because there was evidence on it. Traces of blood with Strand's DNA. Do you see this here?" Schäfer waved the confession statement in front of

Ahmed's nose. "You just put your autograph on this, so when we hand over the technical evidence to the prosecutor revealing that Strand's murder and Lukas Bjerre's disappearance are linked, then you're going to have a hard time convincing anyone that you're some kind of Zorro."

"I haven't done anything to him."

Schäfer read the man's body language. "But you know what happened to him?"

"It . . ." Salah Ahmed's eyes wavered indecisively. "It wasn't me that did it."

Schäfer held his breath.

"It wasn't me," Salah continued. "I was standing up on the embankment after I had taken care of Strand, and then I saw the boy get thrown in the water. But it wasn't *me* who did it. I would never hurt a child."

Schäfer hesitated, puzzled, and watched Salah. "You saw someone throw Lukas Bjerre into the moat at the Citadel?"

He nodded once. "It wasn't me that threw him down there, okay? It wasn't *me* who did it. I took the wet jacket off the boy and threw it away . . . We put him in the car, turned the heat up full blast, got him dried off and gave him . . ."

"We?" Schäfer asked.

Salah Ahmed's mouth opened and closed a couple of times.

Then he said, "I put him in the car."

Schäfer speculated who else had been involved in the killing of Thomas Strand. Someone had gotten Salah Ahmed the nine millimeter. Someone had picked him up afterward. Schäfer thought about the brother-in-law, whom he had had a hard time reading, and about the family portrait hanging on the wall in the apartment in Rebæk Søpark. He decided to hold off on pushing for more information on that.

"Why didn't you take him to a hospital?" he asked instead. "Or call the police?"

"Because he said that he wouldn't be safe with you."

Schäfer looked puzzled. "Of course he would be safe with us." He leaned slowly forward in his chair. "Salah . . . what did you do with him?"

Salah Ahmed didn't respond.

He looked as if he were weighing his next move. Then he nodded to the pen and the notepad on the table in front of Schäfer.

"Pass me those," he said.

45

L ISA AUGUSTIN LAY on the cold cement floor of the barn doubled over in pain. Her lower jaw felt like it was dislocated, and at least one of her upper molars was loose. She rolled over onto her side and spat out blood. Then she looked around the barn and spotted Finn Weinrich.

He was squatting a few feet away from her with his hands to his cheeks, skinny and scared. He was rocking oddly back and forth as he stared at her.

Augustin reached her hand up to her shoulder holster, but before she got there she spotted her gun. It was lying on the floor in front of her.

"I'm sorry," Finn Weinrich chanted and then hit himself in the face. "I'm sorry. I'm sorry. I'm sorry."

Augustin heard car tires crunch in the gravel out in the courtyard and doors slamming. She grabbed her gun and aimed it at the man.

"Lie down on your stomach," she ordered. "Hands up over your head."

"Behind the house," Finn Weinrich mumbled. "I dug a hole. Dug it. I'm sorry. I didn't want . . ."

"Lie down on your stomach, I said. *Flat* on your belly. *Now!*"

Three officers appeared behind the pickup. "Augustin?" one of them called out.

"I'm in here," she said.

One of the police officers, a boulder of a man, walked right over and grabbed hold of Finn Weinrich. He carefully folded him over, as if it were origami, and dragged him out of the barn. One of the other officers squatted down next to Augustin and put a cautious hand over her service weapon.

"It's okay," he said and lowered her gun. "He's gone now."

Augustin nodded. "I think he buried the boy. He said there was something back behind the house somewhere."

She got to her feet unsteadily. Blood poured out of her mouth onto the light gray cement floor.

"We just need to call for an ambulance for you first," the officer said, reaching out to keep her from moving.

Augustin pushed his hand away and walked out into the courtyard, swaying. She looked over at one of the police cars where Finn Weinrich was standing, his torso on the hood, and his hands cuffed behind him.

She walked over there and snapped at the officer to get him to stand Weinrich up.

"Where's Lukas?" she asked. "Where did you bury him?"

The man shook his head, disoriented. Then he spotted something over Augustin's shoulder that made him break out into a frightened, whining wail.

She turned and saw a rusty red Citroën BX coughing its way down the unpaved road. The car stopped when it reached the courtyard in front of the farmhouse, and a large woman stepped out of it.

"What in the world is going on here?" she asked angrily.

"Kirstine Weinrich?" Augustin asked.

"What do you want?" she thundered. She looked at Finn and shook her head. "What have you done *now*, you little nitwit?"

"Police," Augustin said and started to approach her. "Stay where you are."

The woman ignored the request and sped up. Her eyes darted over to Finn.

"What did you do, Finn? Did you steal something?"

"Freeze," Augustin repeated.

The woman continued toward her son.

Augustin grabbed the woman's right arm and she immediately swung at her with her left arm.

Augustin ducked and kicked the woman's feet out from under her, so she hit the ground with a shriek of dismay.

"Mick," Augustin said to one of the other officers. "Get her under control while I talk to the suspect."

Her colleague took over. Augustin went back over to Finn and nodded to him.

"Come on," she said. "You're going to show me what you buried out back."

* * *

Finn Weinrich led Augustin and one of the other officers among the trees behind the main house and pointed to a small pile of dirt that he had tried to conceal with a few dead branches.

"It's down there," he said and pointed.

"It?" Augustin asked.

He nodded.

Augustin exchanged a quick glance with her colleague, who stood behind Finn.

"What did you bury here, Finn?"

"The backpack," he said. His nose was running in the biting winter cold. "The boy's backpack."

"And where is the boy buried?"

Finn Weinrich stared at her in confusion and slowly shook his head. "I don't know . . . I don't know . . ."

Augustin cautiously struck the top of the pile with her foot and an orange shoulder strap came into view. She put on a latex glove and pulled the whole backpack out of the dirt with a firm tug.

She held it up and looked at it. It was the orange Ninjago backpack they had been looking for. The dirty stormtrooper reflector dangled from the zipper pull.

She turned to Finn. He looked confused, scared.

"Finn, where did you get this backpack?"

"I found it."

"You *found* it?"

"I'm sorry. I shouldn't have taken it."

"Where did you find it?"

"At the Citadel."

"You found this backpack at the Citadel," Augustin repeated. "Were you the one who threw the schoolbooks into the bushes there?"

"I'm sorry."

"It's okay, Finn. Did you find the backpack and empty the stuff out of it?"

He nodded.

"Why did you take it with you?"

"Because it . . . it was just lying there, and . . ."

"And you thought it was . . . what, nice?"

"It is nice." He nodded again. "Can I keep it?"

Augustin shook her head. "No, unfortunately you can't. We need to take it with us. It belongs to a little boy named Lukas. Do you know him?"

"I've seen him in the store. And in the newspaper."

"You've seen Lukas Bjerre at Føtex Food?"

"He likes red apples the best." Finn smiled. "There aren't many people who do."

Augustin exhaled heavily and looked around. She touched her cheekbone, which ached. Then she turned to her colleague and said, "We need to seal up this bag and get it over to NKC. We also need to get a team out here and search this whole place just to be sure." She turned to Finn. "Do you and your mom live out here alone?"

The look in his eyes stiffened. Then he nodded.

Augustin spoke to her colleague again. "Okay, bring them in to the police station so we can question them formally, but take them in in two separate vehicles. I don't want that woman near her son."

Augustin made eye contact with Finn.

He gave her a grateful smile.

CHAPTER

46

"Excuse me."

On her way back out of the coatroom at the medical clinic Heloise nodded politely to a short young man. He had actually been the one who had just bumped into her with his elbow as he wrapped his Moncler scarf around his neck.

The man didn't say anything.

He started buttoning up his coat and glanced at Heloise's battered face in the mirror next to the row of coat hooks.

She stopped and made of point of staring at him. "I said, *excuse me.*"

The man turned his head and gave her a questioning look. "Uh . . . okay."

"Okay? Did you just say *okay*?"

"Yes, okay. It's all right!"

Heloise scrunched up her eyes. "Are you kidding me?"

The man looked at her as if she were insane. He glanced quickly over his shoulder to see if she was really talking to him. "I'm sorry?"

"Exactly, you effing doofus. Remember that next time!"

"Just what is going on in here?" a voice asked from behind, its intonation biting.

Heloise turned toward the sound.

The gray-haired medical secretary with stern, penciled-in eyebrows stood in the doorway to the coatroom eyeing them.

"What's going on in here?" she asked again. "Is everything all right, Jonas?"

The man with the scarf nodded and stepped past Heloise.

The secretary gave him a friendly smile. "Call after nine AM on Monday. The results should be back by then."

The man thanked her and left the clinic. Then the secretary turned to Heloise and eyed her coolly.

"I don't know who you are or what you're doing here, but here in this clinic we speak kindly to one another. And besides, we're closing now, so if you could please—"

"It's me, Heloise Kaldan . . . I'm one of Dr. Bjerre's patients."

The woman's expression changed, and her pink lips parted in astonishment.

"Oh my Lord, I hardly recognized you." She took a step closer to Heloise and put on the eyeglasses that had been hanging around her neck on a long pearl necklace. She studied Heloise's face with a concerned expression. "What happened?"

Heloise made a noise that sounded like a combination of a sneeze and a laugh. "Would you believe me if I said I'd walked into a door?"

The woman looked into Heloise's eyes. Then she removed her glasses again. "Who did this to you?"

"I just want to know if you can fix it and if you have time to do it now," Heloise said.

The woman pointed to Heloise's split eyebrow. "We can put a single stitch there, so the wound doesn't keep reopening."

"Great. Thanks!"

"But Jens isn't here, so it'll be Pelle Laursen who does it. He's in with his last patient right now, but if you'll have a seat and wait . . ." She nodded toward the waiting room. "You can help yourself to a cup of coffee or tea if you'd like."

Heloise walked into the waiting room. She threw a pod into the machine and looked out the window while it brewed. There were tourists in the Marble Church tower. Little Playmobil-like people standing up above the dome, pointing out at the city, strangers sitting on her bench.

She took her coffee cup and sat down in the same arm-chair she had sat in the other day. She leaned her head back so it was resting against the backrest and sighed heavily.

How the hell had it all gone so wrong?

Her left eye had stopped throbbing. The skin around it now just felt stiff and leathery.

She took out her phone and looked at it. There were no unanswered calls or texts. Not a peep out of Martin since he had left her apartment, nor did she expect to hear from him, either.

Was Schäfer right? Should she report him for assault?

She was mad at him, but she was also mad at herself. She should have ended it a long time ago.

Heloise touched her eyebrow, where the gash was. The wound immediately started bleeding again. She swore under her breath and looked around the room for something to wipe the blood off with.

She stiffened.

For a long moment she didn't breathe.

There on the wall—in the middle of the neatly arranged pattern of lithographs and art photography—hung a small, framed photograph of an old barn door.

She recognized the pattern in the wood.

Those two round windows . . . The metal bolt . . . The lines that sketched the outline of a creepy face.

It hadn't been somewhere in the woods in Rørvig where she had seen it. It had been here, here in the waiting room. Lukas Bjerre had taken the picture in his father's clinic.

Heloise jumped when the phone at the front desk started ringing. Heloise quickly looked over her shoulder as her pulse accelerated in her chest. Then she looked back at the picture again, questions screaming in her head.

What had she overlooked? What was she misinterpreting?

She thought about the soldier Gerda had told her about and the red light he had interpreted as a laser beam from a sniper's rifle.

He sees something he recognizes and follows through, based on his automatic reflex. The problem is just that when you do that, two plus two doesn't always equal four.

The soldier had seen a pattern he recognized and interpreted it incorrectly, Heloise thought. There hadn't been any laser aimed at him. It had been an assumption, a *wrong* assumption.

Two plus two does not always equal four.

A thought began to form.

Jens had dropped his son off at school Monday morning. She knew that, but . . .

What was it exactly that Gerda had said? *Who* had she seen on the schoolyard?

Heloise's eyes widened and adrenaline surged through her body.

She stood up and walked back out to the coatroom. She pulled her leather jacket down from its hanger, causing the empty clothes hangers to clang against each other, and hurried out into the stairwell.

She ran down the stairs, taking them three at a time, and as soon as she was out of the building she dialed Gerda's number on her cell phone.

"Hi, Heloise!" Gerda said. Her voice sounded happy.

"Gerda, listen up. This is important." Heloise spoke quickly. Her voice was serious and she could sense that she had Gerda's full attention now.

"What's wrong?"

"That morning in the schoolyard." Heloise glanced quickly over her shoulder as she walked down Amaliegade. "Last Monday. Are you positive that you saw Lukas being dropped off at school?"

"Yes," Gerda said. "Why, what's wrong?"

"What exactly did you see?"

"I . . . I said hello to Jens in the schoolyard after I said goodbye to Lulu, and . . ."

"Yeah, I know. You said that. But did you see Lukas?"

Gerda was quiet for a long moment.

"Did you see Lukas?" Heloise repeated. "Or did you just see his father in the schoolyard and *assume* that Lukas had been dropped off?"

Gerda hesitated.

"Well, I saw Jens wave to Lukas," she said. "I came out into the schoolyard and was on my way to the crosswalk . . . and then I saw Jens wave to Lukas as he walked into the school."

"Did you see the boy or not?"

"Well, now I'm not sure, Heloise. Jens did wave, though. Who else would he have been waving at? What are you saying?"

"It's like your client, Gerda. He saw a red light in the dark and assumed it was a gun being aimed at him. You saw Jens wave in the schoolyard and assumed that he had dropped off his son."

There was silence on the other end of the line.

"It's *him*," Heloise said. "I think he murdered his own son."

S CHÄFER FELT HIS phone vibrate in his inside pocket. He pulled over to the side and took it out to see if it was Augustin calling again. She had called from Glostrup a half hour earlier to say that the Apple Man, whose actual name was Finn Weinrich, was on his way in to police headquarters for questioning. Her assessment was that he was a child-like young man with an intellectual disability who had randomly happened upon Lukas Bjerre's schoolbag at the Citadel, not a cold-blooded murderer.

Schäfer glanced at his phone. It said KALDAN.

He rejected the call and made a mental note to remember to call her back later.

He put his phone away and drove on down the road, looking around for the right address. When he found it, he pulled over to the side and looked at the house. It was a red wooden house with white mullioned windows and a big, white porch that ran all the way around the whole house. It looked like an old Swedish farmhouse, like the setting for a film version of Astrid Lindgren's *Emil of Lönneberga*. Not the kind of building you typically found on the outskirts of Køge.

Schäfer double-checked the address, which Salah Ahmed had written down on the notepad. This was it. He was in the right place.

He could see in the national registry that the property belonged to a veterinarian named Camilla Lyng. There was a powder-blue Volvo station wagon parked in the snow. The rear hatch was open, and Schäfer could see that the trunk was full. A suitcase was wedged in between some rolled-up comforters and a cooler. A backpack, a pair of hiking boots. A blue IKEA bag full of things.

He looked over at the house again as a figure appeared. A woman carrying a red nylon sports bag came out of the house and quickly walked over to the car.

Schäfer stared at her in astonishment.

She seemed a bit older—maybe two or three years—but other than that the woman in front of him was nearly identical to Anne Sofie Bjerre. Her dirty blond hair was gathered into a loose ponytail that rhythmically lashed her oilskin coat as she walked. Her face was tense, her shoulders pulled up against her ears.

Schäfer got out of his car and approached the woman.

She stopped abruptly in her tracks when she noticed him and cast a quick glance back toward the house.

Then her eyes met Schäfer's.

"Can I help you with something?" she asked with a harried expression.

She looked like someone who had put all her money on black and was now watching the little white ball as it danced and hopped unpredictably around the roulette wheel.

He took a few steps closer to her. "Camilla Lyng?"

She grabbed the sports bag and clutched it in front of her. "Who's asking?"

"The police."

The woman's expression imploded, like a failed soufflé. Her chips were being collected, Schäfer thought. The house always wins.

He kept an eye on her hands and on the bag she held in front of her. He nodded at the Volvo.

"Are you going somewhere?"

The woman didn't respond.

"Are you alone?" he asked and glanced over at the house, where a thin column of smoke rose from the chimney. "Is there anyone else in the house?"

"I'm alone." She started walking toward the trunk. "And now you'll have to excuse me. I was just leaving."

"Where are you going?"

"I have an appointment."

"That's kind of a lot of luggage for an appointment." Schäfer nodded at the trunk.

"I need to go," she said and squeezed the sports bag in between the other items. She slammed the back hatch closed.

"You're not going anywhere until we've talked," Schäfer said.

The woman ignored his command and opened the car door.

"Stop!" He sped up and reached out for her arm.

There was a screech from the old hinges as the front door opened behind them.

Schäfer pulled his gun in one quick, fluid motion and aimed it at the sound.

A glass bottle shattered as it hit the floor of the porch and red soda poured down the white stairs.

Lukas Bjerre stood on the top step.

THE FIRE WAS still burning and crackling in the fireplace, creating a pleasant ambiance. The home's living room was furnished like a hunting lodge with taxidermized foxes and birds of prey on every horizontal surface. There were big, chunky pieces of leather furniture in shades of terra-cotta atop a herringbone-patterned tile floor. Camilla Lyng sat down heavily on the sofa across from Schäfer.

Her expression was both relieved and troubled.

Lukas sat beside her. He stared up at her face, as if he was afraid she would vanish into thin air if he took his eyes off her.

"I'd really like to speak to your aunt alone for a moment," Schäfer said, nodding soothingly to him. "Do you think that would be all right?"

The boy pretended not to see Schäfer. He looked at the woman anxiously and grabbed onto her. "Don't go, Kiki."

"I'm not going anywhere," she said, squeezing his hand. "I'm right here. Take Jack outside for a bit. He could use some fresh air."

The black Lab lying in a wicker basket in the corner of the room raised his ears when he heard his name. The dog looked blind, Schäfer thought. His eyes looked like two glass orbs, milky white and marbled.

Lukas reluctantly got up off the sofa without breaking his eye contact with the woman.

"It's okay," she said. "I'm just going to talk to the policeman here, and then I'll come out and get you when I'm done."

The boy walked over to the dog. He petted it on the back and it ambled out of the room with him.

Schäfer watched the woman. As soon as Lukas was out of the room, it was as if the air seeped out of her. She sat there, deflated, staring out the window.

"Kiki?" he asked. "Short for Camilla?"

"No, that's not why."

"Then why?"

She shook her head. "It's just something he calls me."

Schäfer raised his eyebrows to encourage her to elaborate.

She shrugged, looking tired. "I was in New Zealand several years ago for work and I bought Lukas a children's book when I was there, about the Maori, the indigenous people who live there. There were a bunch of Maori words in the book including *whaea kēkē*, which means auntie. I explained to Lukas that I was his *whaea kēkē*, but he couldn't pronounce that, so he said *Kiki* instead." She smiled sadly. "For some reason it stuck."

Schäfer heard the front door open and saw Lukas through the window. He was standing out on the porch, peeking into the living room at them. Schäfer looked over at Camilla again.

"I know that Lukas was dropped off here on Monday."

She nodded.

"Why didn't you contact the police as soon as you realized that he had been reported missing?"

Camilla looked at him for a long time before she responded. "Because I knew that you would just hand him back over to Jens and Fie. And the whole thing would start all over again."

Schäfer's brow furrowed. "What whole thing?"

"Jens," she said. "He beats him. Routinely. Last Monday morning he went a step further. They had an argument on the way to school, and . . ." She closed her eyes and shook her head. "I couldn't send Lukas back after what happened."

Schäfer still looked puzzled. "Are you saying it was Jens who dropped Lukas into the moat? That he tried to kill his own son?"

She nodded. "If they hadn't rescued him . . . He would be dead, no doubt about it."

"They?"

"Yes, the men who dropped him off at my place."

Schäfer noted her choice of words. "How long would you say this has been going on? How long has Lukas's father been beating him?" He looked out at the boy, who immediately stopped staring and turned his back to the window.

Camilla pulled a tired hand over her face. "It started when Jens began working abroad. You know Doctors Without Borders?"

Schäfer nodded.

"Those trips with that organization completely changed him. It didn't happen overnight, but he gradually became more and more aggressive. He started taking drugs, prescribed morphine to himself 'for use in his medical practice.'" She shrugged. "It got really bad when he came home from Syria. He saw something down there . . . When he came home it was as if his personality was completely changed." She took a deep breath and thought back. "It started when Lukas began first grade. That was when Jens started hurting him."

"Why didn't you report it?"

"Oh, you'd better believe I reported it!" She looked at him with lightning in her eyes. "Why do you think they cut me out of their lives?"

Schäfer looked puzzled. "You *reported* it? Are you sure?"

"Of course I reported it!"

"There's nothing in our records about that. There aren't any old reports or cases involving the family in our system."

Camilla shook her head, speechless. "I don't know why I'm surprised. You guys aren't on top of anything!"

Schäfer raised his chin and looked down his nose at her, but he didn't say anything. If her report hadn't made it into their internal reports, it wouldn't be the first time some caseworker or social worker had screwed up. Mistakes happened all the time, also within the police. He knew that. Neglected and abused children fell by the wayside. It happened far too often.

"Did anyone else know?" he asked. "If the boy was being beaten, there must have been signs. Someone must have wondered."

She shook her head. "Jens is a doctor. He always has an explanation, an alibi. He received training from Doctors Without Borders before his foreign deployments. Plus, Lukas has done his best to conceal it. He told me that he told his teachers all his scrapes and bruises came from the fencing and the fights from his role-playing games."

Schäfer nodded heavily. He had had many cases involving kids who stubbornly defended the parents who abused them, little kids who automatically forgave a father with blood on his knuckles.

Camilla stood up from the sofa and walked over to a bar cart with a glass top and brass frame that was in the corner. She pulled a pointy glass stopper out of a carafe, poured herself a whiskey, and took a sip. Then she sat back down across from Schäfer again.

"You mentioned that Jens received training from Doctors Without Borders," he said. "Training in what?"

"All of the doctors they send abroad receive crisis management training. They learn what to do if they get kidnapped or if they end up in a dangerous situation down there. Jens told me about it before he left for Sudan. That was his first trip."

"What did he say?"

"That they taught them how to navigate unexpected situations, how to come up with believable lies in just a few seconds, an alibi, camouflage. An optical illusion. They were supposed to be able to bluff their way out of situations where their lives were at stake, and Jens was good at it. He could fool anyone."

"And what about Lukas's mother? What was her role in all this?"

Camilla snorted. "Fie never said anything when Jens hit Lukas. She never *did* anything. She always just sat there, staring uncomfortably into space to avoid making eye contact with me whenever it happened. And she numbed herself with booze. She's an alcoholic," Camilla said and raised her whiskey glass. "The only thing Fie worries about is if there's still vodka in the bottle."

Schäfer looked out the window and saw the boy wandering around outside. The black Lab followed him good-naturedly, wagging his tail in delight every time the boy knelt in the snow and put his arms around the dog's neck.

"But *you* reported it?"

She nodded. "At one point I had had enough. I reported Jens to Social Services. But they screened the family and concluded that he was a nice, conscientious doctor and that therefore I must have misinterpreted what I'd seen." Camilla folded her hands together in her lap. "I haven't seen him or Fie since."

Schäfer thought about Anne Sofie's reaction when he had asked about the name on the piece of paper he'd found in the notebook. She'd had an odd look on her face for a second.

"Your sister said they didn't know anyone named Kiki."

Camilla's eyebrows shot up. "She's lying. She and Jens both know that Lukas calls me that. But I can't imagine that they were interested in leading you to me."

"Do you think your sister knows that your brother-in-law dumped Lukas in the water on Monday?"

Camilla shrugged. "Not necessarily. Jens could easily have kept that hidden from Fie. I'd imagine that he runs around at home playing the victim as part of his cover."

It struck Schäfer that Jens didn't know that his son was still alive. His astonishment when Schäfer had told him that they had found Thomas Strand's blood on Lukas's jacket had been genuine.

Schäfer looked at Camilla. "You've been meeting secretly, you and Lukas, during the school day. Is that correct?"

She nodded. "The last year has been especially bad for Lukas. Fie's drinking has really started to get out of hand. She doesn't dare talk back to Jens, so she just disappears into the laundry room whenever he's in a bad mood."

"The laundry room?"

"Yes. Their building has a communal laundry room down in the basement. She hides her vodka down there. Jens has told her she can't drink anymore, so they don't keep any alcohol in their apartment, but Lukas has seen her hide bottles in the laundry room." Camilla ran her fingers through her hair and looked out the window at the boy. "What happens now?"

"What do you mean?"

"What's going to happen to Lukas? Even if Jens ends up in jail, Lukas doesn't want to go back to Fie. I know that. It might sound strange, but . . . even though Jens is the one who hit him, he feels like his mother is the one who let him down the most. He doesn't want to live with her anymore."

Schäfer nodded. That didn't sound the least bit strange to his ears. If he had had an aunt like Camilla Lyng when he was little, he would have preferred to live with her too. But unfortunately that kind of thing wasn't so straightforward.

"It's too early to know what will happen with his custody. That's not my area," he said. "But unfortunately the truth is that Lukas will most likely be sent back to his mother."

Camilla closed her eyes. "But Fie is profoundly unfit. She couldn't protect her own child. And she's a drunk."

Schäfer cast a fleeting glance at the whiskey glass in Camilla's hand and nodded. "Yes, but that's not necessarily enough for her to lose custody."

"Why not?"

"Because they'll consider the bigger picture, and when they do that they'll probably decide that Lukas is not in imminent danger as long as his father is out of the picture. It's possible that the authorities will think being placed outside the home for a short time will benefit Lukas, so your sister can get her life in order. But as long as she's going to work, maintains a relatively orderly home, and promises to stop drinking, then there's not that much that can be done." Schäfer's gaze fell on the Volvo in the driveway. "Where were you and Lukas going when I arrived?"

"We were just getting out of here, away from the pictures in the newspaper," she said, leaning defeatedly back on the sofa. "I have a friend in Germany, so I thought we could stay with her for a while . . ."

Schäfer stood up and gestured for Camilla to do the same.

"Now what?" she asked.

"We're going to Copenhagen, all three of us. Lukas has a long series of interviews and doctor's exams ahead of him and he's going to need you more than ever."

* * *

"Buckle your seat belt," Schäfer said and looked back over his shoulder.

Lukas and his aunt sat in the back seat, both of their faces an ashy gray, but bravely agreeing with what needed to happen.

Schäfer started the engine with one hand and pulled his cell phone out of his jacket pocket with the other. He could see that Heloise had called eight times. She had also sent him a whole army of texts.

He opened the first and read it.

The barn door is at the medical clinic. Call me!

A THIN FOG HAD settled like a ghost over all of Copenhagen in just a few hours. There was no wind at all. The temperature was up to forty-three degrees, and the slightly damp air felt almost warm after the recent freezing cold.

Heloise stood, shifting her weight from foot to foot, by the back door to police headquarters on Otto Mønsteds Gade, the entrance Schäfer always used.

She peered into the fog at cars as they drove by and checked her cell phone every thirty seconds. It was 4:11 PM, and she had been trying to reach Schäfer since she had left the medical clinic, but he hadn't picked up and no one seemed to know where he was.

When at long last his black Opel pulled up in front of the building, Heloise made eye contact with him through the dirty windshield and threw up her arms in frustration.

"I've called you a hundred times." She held her hand up to hear ear like a phone handset and gestured grumpily through the window.

Schäfer lowered his window and tried to shoo her away. "I don't have time now, Heloise."

"But haven't you gotten my messages?" she asked. "It's at the clinic, that picture from the case file is hanging in the waiting room at the clini—"

He held up a hand to stop her. "I don't have time right now. Go home and I'll call you later."

Heloise furrowed her brow. She realized there were two passengers in the back seat and cast a quick glance at them. Then she gaped at Schäfer.

Schäfer clenched his teeth and grasped the wheel so his knuckles turned white. Then he nodded.

"All right," he grumbled. "Go around to the main entrance and ask them to escort you up to the second floor. Have a seat outside my office and wait until I come for you. You will not call anyone, and you will not write a single word. Got it? You will just sit, as quiet as a mouse and not say a peep!"

Heloise nodded hastily.

Schäfer shook his head and closed his window.

* * *

"Right this way."

Schäfer held the door open for Lukas and tried to catch his eye.

The boy's eyes swept anxiously from side to side, scanning the room they entered. This room was reserved for questioning minors who had suffered any sort of violence or abuse, and unlike the other interrogation rooms at police headquarters, it was furnished in cheerful, confidence-inspiring pastels. There was a salmon-colored sofa in the middle of the room and a bowl of candy on the coffee table. There was a plastic basket of toys, children's books, and stuffed animals on the floor. Things that Lukas—judging from the look on his face—had outgrown.

"If you'd take a seat here, then one of my colleagues will be in to see you in a moment," Schäfer said. "She's nice and you can trust her, so it's very important that you tell her your story as honestly and in as much detail as possible." He nodded confidentially to the boy. "The more we learn about what happened, the better we can help you. Do you understand?"

For the first time, Lukas looked Schäfer in the eye.

"I don't want to go home," he said. His voice was reserved and sharp. It did not invite debate. "No matter what she says, I'm not going home."

Schäfer was not prepared for the coldness in the boy's eyes. The steely resistance in his gaze. It wasn't a look you got from ten-year-olds, he thought. The eyes before him reminded him more of the ones he used to gaze into when he sat in the interrogation rooms one floor farther up in the building. Up where the furnishings were sparse and the colors drab.

"No matter what *who* says?" Schäfer asked.

"My mom. If you try to force me to live there again, you'll regret it."

Schäfer squinted one eye and zoomed in on the boy with the other as a deep silence settled over the room. The boy continued to stand there, back straight, chin up. His words hung in the air between them like an unambiguous threat.

Schäfer frowned and nodded.

"All right," he said. "As I said before, tell my colleague what you have to say. Then we'll see what happens next, okay?"

Schäfer didn't wait for a response. He walked out the door, leaving the boy alone in the room.

Michala Friis stood waiting in the hallway when Schäfer came out, and he shook her hand.

"Thank you for coming so quickly."

"Of course," she said and nodded. "So, what have we got?"

"Well, everything points to the father abusing the boy. We're talking persistent physical abuse and then attempted murder on Monday. The aunt thinks Jens is suffering from PTSD, that he went through things in war zones that have damaged his mental health and activated this violent behavior in him."

Friis listened attentively as Schäfer spoke.

"We're going to go pick the parents up now, and in the meantime I need you to talk to the boy and figure out the general situation here. He seems very angry. Cold! Get him to tell his side of the story." Schäfer shrugged. "Just do what you do best."

"Roger that," she said and walked over to the interrogation room.

Schäfer took a few steps in the opposite direction. Then he turned back to Friis again.

"Admit it!" he said.

She glanced back at him and raised one eyebrow. "What?"

"That you belong here with us. It means something to you, working here. It's a feeling you don't get from working other places."

Friis smiled. "Perhaps."

Schäfer sucked in his cheeks and nodded contentedly. "Mm-hmm, what did I tell you?"

Friis chuckled. Then she wiped the smile from her lips and opened the door into the interrogation room.

* * *

Schäfer spotted Heloise as he made his way down the hall toward his office. She was sitting on a stainless-steel bench that was bolted to the floor, staring at the portable computer that sat on her lap, her fingers tapping away furiously at the keys.

"Kaldan," Schäfer called out.

Heloise looked up with a start. She had a bandage on the one eyebrow.

"What happened?" she asked eagerly. "I saw Lukas. Where did you find him? What does he say? Who was that woman sitting next to him in the car?"

"Close that computer and come with me. In here," Schäfer said, unlocking the door to his office. He pointed to a chair at the back of the room. "Have a seat!"

Heloise did as she was told.

Schäfer paced back and forth a little, studying her as if she were a bomb he needed to deactivate. "You can't write anything yet."

"What happened?" Heloise asked, curious.

"I need a couple of hours. Then you'll probably get your story."

"Was it the father? Did he do it?"

Schäfer didn't respond, and Heloise sat up straighter in her chair.

"I was right! Jens Bjerre is behind the whole thing, isn't he?"

Schäfer held up his hand. "Not a peep, Kaldan! I'm telling you—I need a couple of hours. You'll get your story."

Lisa Augustin poked her head into the office and looked at Schäfer. "Hey, I understand the boy's here?" She smiled, relieved. "Phew! Man, I didn't think we'd find him alive."

With a nod, Schäfer made her aware that they weren't alone.

Augustin looked over her shoulder and noticed Heloise. "Oh. Hey."

"You make some pair, the two of you," Schäfer said, shaking his head. "Look at you!"

The women looked at each other, taking in each other's facial injuries.

Schäfer started walking toward the door and signaled to Augustin that she should follow him.

"Heloise," he said and pointed in the direction of the exit with his thumb. "I'll call you tonight so you can get the quotes you're fishing for, but you need to skedaddle now. Lickety-split!"

Heloise wrinkled her forehead. "But you said I should wait for you up here?"

"Yes, but I don't have time to take care of you right now. It's just important that what you've seen here today does not end up online. Not yet anyway. Do you understand what I'm telling you?"

Heloise eyed him hesitantly. "Are you going to go pick up the parents now?"

Schäfer didn't respond.

"Can I come?"

Schäfer looked at her in disbelief. "What the . . . No! You can't *come!*"

"If you let me come along, then I'll wait to break the story until you say so."

Schäfer shot her a warning look. "You're going to wait to break the story, *period*! And you're *not* coming with me."

Heloise stared into his eyes for a few seconds. Then she nodded. "Okay, but I'll wait here until you come back."

Schäfer pointed to the metal bench in the hallway.

"You sit right there."

* * *

They drove off in two police groups maneuvering through the fog and the evening rush hour traffic, past the Black Diamond library building and down to Kongens Nytorv.

Bro and Bertelsen continued down Bredgade heading toward the clinic on Amaliegade, while Schäfer and Augustin turned right at Charlottenborg.

The car tires sounded liked a drumroll as they drove over the cobblestones, and they braked with a squeal in front of the residential property on Heibergsgade. The tourists at Nyhavn turned at the sound, craning their necks and holding out their cell phones.

"Do you think he's armed?" Augustin asked as she unbuckled.

"Maybe," Schäfer said and hopped out of the car. "I haven't been able to figure him out at all, so we're taking precautions."

They rang the buzzer for one of the building's other residents and quickly made their way up the narrow staircase instead of using the elevator. When they reached the top floor, the door to the apartment was open and Augustin and Schäfer exchanged a quick glance.

They drew their service weapons and stepped into the front hall. A cold wind raced down the hallways toward the open front door.

Schäfer held up one hand and they both stood still, listening. There was no noise coming from inside the apartment.

They split up and searched the rooms one by one. Schäfer reached a half-open door at the end of the apartment's long hallways and gave it a silent push with his foot.

The door opened slowly, creaking, and Schäfer peered into the room.

Jens sat at a desk at the far end of the room. The door to the balcony behind him was wide open. It was completely quiet. He sat staring blankly into thin air and didn't react when Schäfer stepped into the room.

"Jens," Schäfer said. He held his gun up in front of him, his arm out straight. "Stand up."

Jens slowly turned his head toward Schäfer.

"Is . . . is there any news?" His voice sounded strangely slurred, like a whisper underwater.

"Stand up," Schäfer repeated. "Come on! Stand up!" He glanced at the desk. It was covered with open jars and boxes of pills. There was a syringe and a rubber tube next to a glass full of a clear liquid.

Jens stood up with difficulty. His eyes focused for a moment on something infinitely far away, as if he were looking right through Schäfer.

Then suddenly he zoomed in on the gun in Schäfer's hand and nodded slowly.

"Ah, I see," he said and put his hands down flat on the desk. "You've found him . . ."

"Step away from the desk," Schäfer said. "Turn around and put your hands behind your head!"

Jens turned around.

"I never meant to hurt him," he said slowly.

Jens gathered his hands behind his head and took a couple of slow steps toward the balcony. His silhouette was highlighted in the open doorway by the streetlight.

"Freeze," Schäfer said. He aimed the gun at Jens. "Stop!"

Jens took another step.

"*Stop!*" Schäfer launched into motion, lunging through the room to reach him.

Jens still had his hands clasped behind his head as he leaned over the railing and then vanished.

"*What the hell!*" Schäfer yelled as he reached the balcony. He grabbed the railing and looked down at the ground below.

Jens had landed on a bike rack five stories down. His lower body was draped over the frame of a white women's bicycle, a pool of blood slowly spreading around his head like a halo.

"Fuck!" Schäfer yelled and kicked the balcony door.

Augustin appeared in the doorway to the room. She ran across to the balcony and peered down toward the ground. Then she nodded slowly and looked around the office.

"What about the mother? Where is she?"

"I don't know, but we need to find her now!" Schäfer turned toward the pills on the office desk and picked up a box at random.

"What is it?" Augustin asked.

"Morphine." He browsed through the medications, reading their labels. "Sleeping pills, narcotics, all sorts of different shit."

"Well, he chose the easy way out, then."

Schäfer looked down at the ground again and shook his head.

"That down there does not look like an easy way out."

50

"DEAD?" ANNE SOFIE Bjerre repeated, shaking her head, stunned.

Schäfer studied her attentively.

They had been waiting for her out in front of the apartment on Heibergsgade when she showed up with clinking shopping bags from Irma, the grocery store. And now she sat opposite him in an interrogation room at police headquarters. Her eyes were big. There was an almost blissful expression in them. The expression had appeared the second Schäfer had notified her that Lukas was alive, and the news of her husband's suicide did not seem to dampen her euphoria at all. To the contrary, the emotion seems to have wrapped itself around her whole body like a cheap satin sheet.

"And you're saying it was Jens who . . . That he tried to kill Lukas?" She shook her head, speechless. "I never would have believed that would even occur to him."

"And yet I suppose it doesn't come as a complete surprise," Schäfer remarked dryly. "You knew Jens beat him. And you did nothing."

Anne Sofie regarded him in silence. Then she cautiously asked, "Where is Lukas now?"

"He's here," Schäfer said. "Here in police headquarters."

Her eyes lit up. "Can I see him?"

Schäfer gave her a blank look. "He doesn't want to see you."

Anne Sofie's expression stiffened. Then she slowly nodded.

"It will take time," she said. "He'll learn to trust me again."

"The drinking needs to stop!"

She nodded in agreement. "Yes, of course!"

"*Completely*," Schäfer emphasized. "If you keep drinking, I can't guarantee you that Social Services won't take Lukas away. Do you understand?"

"I've touched alcohol for the last time. I promise you that."

"I'm not the one you need to make promises to. Lukas is."

"Yes, of course. Never again!" Anne Sofie held up her hand, as if she were ready to swear an oath. She was silent for a second, and then she smiled hopefully. "When can I see him?"

"You'll need to talk to Social Services about that," Schäfer said. "That's not my department. But my impression is that you'll have a week or two to get the apartment ready and whatever else you need to get a handle on as a result of your husband's death."

She nodded and folded her hands on the table in front of her. "And where will Lukas be until then?"

"With your sister."

Her gaze drifted away from Schäfer. She had a daydreamy look in her eyes.

"When he comes home, everything will be different." She nodded. "Everything will be fine again then. I know it."

Schäfer raised one unimpressed eyebrow. He stood and mentally sized her up.

"Yes, you'll get one more chance now, Anne Sofie. If you ask me, you don't deserve it, but . . . you get one more shot. So you give it everything you've got, you hear?"

Schäfer left the room and headed straight for his office, his stride rapid and angry, and then he stopped when he spotted Heloise Kaldan on the bench outside his office.

Schäfer shook his head and tiredly rubbed his eyes. "You're still here?"

Heloise looked up at him and shrugged. "Yeah, what did you expect?"

"What the hell have you been doing for all these hours?"

"The same as you: my job! I finished writing most of my article and now all I need is for you to fill in a few blanks. Plus a couple of quotes would be good." Heloise got up. "What did the father say to the accusations?"

Schäfer took a deep breath and looked at his watch.

"If you get the head start you're asking for, then you'll get out of here and leave me be?"

Heloise smiled and drew an X over her heart with her index finger.

"All right." Schäfer nodded. "But we'll just need to go grab a bucket of coffee first. This might end up being a long night."

CHAPTER

51

T HE SOUND ECHOED like a gunshot through the large
interior of the church as Editor-in-Chief Mikkelsen
tapped on the microphone with his chubby hand. People
jumped in their seats and looked up at the altar.

Mikkelsen cleared his throat and in a melancholy voice
welcomed the many who had gathered.

"Dear friends, esteemed colleagues, and—most of all—
the lovely Clevin family."

Heloise glanced over at Kaj Clevin's family, who occupied the four front rows in the Marble Church nearest the
large white casket. The casket containing Kaj's dead body
was adorned with an almost flamboyant sympathy spray
featuring English roses, baby's breath, and lilies, and there
were bouquets with silk ribbons and elegiac words of farewell all the way down the aisle.

Heloise's eyes continued to roam the church as
Mikkelsen rattled off a string of platitudes about life and
death, that great uncharted adventure. The Marble Church
was filled with people who had turned out to send old
Clevin off on his final journey. Most of the newspaper's

employees were there, as were a handful of aging jet-setters, businesspeople, and the other papers' food critics.

"Look," Heloise whispered to Mogens Bøttger. "The Restaurant Kings."

She pointed with her thumb to the pew four rows behind theirs, where the city's leading restaurant owners sat side by side wearing dark suits and sufficiently reverent facial expressions.

None of them had ever received a fair review from Clevin, and the more money they had raked into their tills, the more vicious Clevin's reviews of their establishments had become. And yet, Heloise thought, they had shown up to pay their final respects to the man.

Mogens chuckled. "Believe me," he whispered. "They're only here to make sure the bozo is dead."

Heloise had to press her lips together to suppress a smile.

*   *   *

The funeral service was painfully long. Halfway through, faces throughout the church began to be illuminated by the bluish white glow of cell phones, and by the time the show was finally over and the coffin driven away, people poured out into the rain as if they were part of an emergency evacuation.

"Are you coming, Hollywood?" Mogens asked, nodding at Heloise's big sunglasses. "My sources say there's oysters au gratin and hors d'oeuvres on the menu at AOC, so we'd better hurry over there before Mikkelsen vacuums up the whole buffet."

Heloise stood up, glanced at the exit, and then froze.

Martin was standing just inside the door. His arms hung limply at his sides. His wet hair was plastered to his forehead, and the fabric on the shoulders of his camel hair jacket was drenched from the rain.

He looked pleadingly at Heloise.

"I just need to take care of something first, Bøttger," she said without taking her eyes off Martin. "You go on ahead."

Heloise walked up to the altar and waited as the last of the guests left the church.

Martin walked down the length of the church toward her. His face was crumpled and tormented. He stopped a few feet away from her and waited to speak until they had heard the church door close behind the last of the guests.

"I knew you would be here," he explained. "I had to see you."

"What do you want?" Heloise asked. Her voice was cool, but not hostile.

Martin looked around a little. Then he looked at her again and his voice began to shake. "I feel awful, Helo."

"I know." She nodded.

"What can I do?" he asked. "What can I . . ."

"There's nothing more to be done. It's over." She smiled sadly. "It's actually been over since it began, and I should have told you that." She pushed her sunglasses up onto the top of her head, revealing her injuries.

Martin cringed at the sight.

He took a step closer to her and Heloise instinctively stepped away.

He shook his head in despair. "I can't stand knowing that you hate me."

"I don't hate you."

"You don't?"

Heloise shook her head and smiled briefly, in forgiveness.

It was quiet between them for a long time. They had said what was left to say.

"You should go," Heloise said.

Martin hesitated, trying to put off the unavoidable.

"Martin . . ." She nodded toward the exit. "You need to go now."

Heloise lingered in the Marble Church after he had left. She sat down in one of the pews in the front row and leaned her head back. Her eyes slid over the paintings of the apostles on the inside of the dome above her as she inhaled the scents of old wood, disintegrating tapestries, and divinity. The scent of her childhood.

She closed her eyes, allowing the tranquility to fill her, and the experiences of the last week to sink into her soul.

She had spent the previous night at Gerda's place.

Gerda had confided in her that she had ended her affair with Kareem, her coworker at the barracks. She had discovered that Kareem was somehow involved in the murder of her former patient. Kareem's cousin had been charged in the case along with another family member, and Gerda didn't know yet what *his* role in the case was. Had he shared confidential information with his family that they had then acted on without his knowledge or consent? Or had he been involved in planning the murder?

Gerda didn't know, but the police were investigating, and she didn't want anything more to do with it or with him. She also didn't know what was going to happen between her and Christian—including whether she was going to tell him about the affair.

For her part, Heloise had told her about her pregnancy, miscarriage, and breaking up with Martin.

Gerda had listened, nodded, and cursed Martin. Then with a look of resolve on her face, she had stood up and fetched a document from her desk drawer.

"Here!" she had said and passed it to Heloise. "Christian and I had agreed that we would ask you together, but I just can't think of a better time to do it than now, so . . ."

"What is it?"

"It's a guardianship plan. Christian had our lawyer draw it up several months ago, but he's hardly been home since, so . . . well, now I'm asking."

Heloise had looked puzzled and skimmed the pages. Then she had looked up at Gerda with her eyes wide.

"Christian's parents are dead, as you know," Gerda had said. "I only have my mother, for however many years I get to keep her. And neither of us has any siblings. So if we—God forbid—should get hit by a bus, we want you to raise Lulu, to be her official guardian. We want her to live with you."

"But . . ." Heloise had shaken her head, speechless. "Didn't you hear any of what I just told you? I can't take care of a child, Gerda. I'm . . . I'm damaged goods."

"Oh, for crying out loud, you're not! That's my whole point. Do you think I would leave my daughter to you if you were so damaged? You've taken some punches in life, yes. But, contrary to what you think now, that's not what defines you as a person. You've been lying at the bottom of a silent lake for a few years, but you're on your way back up to the surface again, Heloise. I can *feel* it. Plus, you're one of the best people I know, and I can't imagine anyone better suited to taking care of Lulu if disaster should strike."

Heloise had remained silent.

"Okay, let me ask in another way," Gerda had said. "If Christian and I dropped dead and we hadn't asked you to sign this document, what would you do when Social Services came to take Lulu away?"

"I would fight tooth and nail for her."

Gerda had given her a smile that said: I rest my case.

"I know that right now you think your life would be easier if you walled yourself off, that everything would be easier if you never truly needed to care about anyone else. But, sweetie . . ." Gerda had passed Heloise a pen. "You already do care."

* * *

Heloise opened her eyes and smiled at the apostles on the church ceiling. She decided right there on the spot to draw a line in the sand. From now on she would remember all the good things and put the bad ones behind her. Gerda was right: What had happened did not define her. The life ahead of her was still an open book.

Heloise jumped when a text arrived. She pulled her phone out of her leather jacket and read the message. It was from Mogens, who wrote:

> *What's taking you so long? You're missing all the fun. Mikkelsen is already so drunk he's started hitting on the waitstaff, and his wife looks REALLY pissed. Come NOW, Kaldan!*

Heloise smiled and put her phone back in her pocket. She got up and walked over to the custodian's office at the very back of the church.

She knocked on the door and poked her head into the office.

"Hi, Bobo. Am I interrupting anything?"

The old man looked up from his armchair and smiled.

"Heloise? No, I always have time for you. Is there anything I can help you with?"

"Do you think I could entice you into unlocking the door to the stairs?"

Bobo got up out of his chair with a groan of effort and pulled his ring of keys out of his coat pocket.

"Are you going up the tower?" he asked.

Heloise smiled.

"Yes."

52

"I HAVE NO IDEA how I could have overlooked that."

Lisa Augustin removed the pictures from the bulletin board in their office at police headquarters. The Lukas Bjerre case was officially closed, and they were taking down the investigation file and packing it away piece by piece.

Schäfer gave her a look that said, *Come on!*

"What?" she asked, raising her chin.

"You know very well what happened," he said. "You forgot to ask the right questions because you were so dazzled by that trauma psychologist. You got sloppy, and it cost us. Period!"

"But she *said* she saw the father drop the boy off," Augustin protested.

"Yes, and you should have asked what exactly her statement covered. You know eyewitness accounts can be unreliable. You should have checked and double-checked! Instead, you wrote in the case report that we had a witness who had seen the boy in the schoolyard. Not the father, the *boy*! Do you realize how many resources we could have saved if Jens Bjerre's alibi had been doubted from the start?"

Augustin didn't respond.

She looked down and started gathering up the documents on the desk. She opened the cardboard box on the floor and put the papers into it.

"Three strikes and you're out, Augustin," Schäfer warned her. "This was Strike One." He scratched his beard stubble in annoyance and calmed down. Then he nodded. "Although I made a mistake, too."

Augustin looked over without raising her head.

"I should have asked for all the witness statements to be corroborated. I was the investigative lead. In the end, it was *my* responsibility. So let's say that we're one-to-one, and then we'll tighten up our act a little more next time. Agreed?"

"Agreed." Augustin nodded.

Schäfer turned to the bulletin board and took down the map of Zealand with one firm tug. He crumpled it up and threw it in a high arc into the wastepaper basket. Then he proceeded to the rest of the investigative materials: pictures from Lukas Bjerre's Instagram account, DNA results from Rud Johannsen, statements from teachers and instructional assistants, pictures of the down jacket under the ice at the Citadel.

He plucked it all down from the wall and carefully packed it away in the cardboard box.

"What about all the pictures?" Augustin nodded to the photo albums sitting on the shelf behind Schäfer's desk chair. "What do we do with those?"

"Those go back to the family, to the mother. Could you carry them down to the mail room and have them sent off?"

Augustin nodded. "Is Lukas still at his aunt's house?"

"Until the end of the month," Schäfer said. "Then he's going back home."

Augustin did not look like she approved.

Schäfer shrugged. "Yeah, it sucks, but that's how it is. It's not our job to fix dysfunctional families. We're not social workers. We've done everything in our power, and now the boy moves along in the system."

"The system that's already failed him once," Augustin pointed out dryly and gathered up the photo albums from the shelf. "Is there anything else we need to send so I don't need to make two trips down there?"

Schäfer shook his head, and Augustin left the room with the photo albums in her arms.

He ran a hand over the back of his head and looked around for anything else that needed to be archived. He walked over to the bookshelf and started gathering up the various documents they had received from Michael Voss. The photos of Finn Weinrich from the surveillance videos from Østerport Station were on top of the pile.

Weinrich had been questioned by both Augustin and Schäfer, and apart from a pathological fixation on young children likely due to his own developmental disability and childlike outlook, there wasn't anything to suggest there had been anything suspicious about his interactions with Lukas. The man had been cleared in the case and sent home. Schäfer had watched the mother leave with her adult son, as if he was a dog on a leash. Yet another child left with an unfit parent.

Schäfer gathered up the documents in front of him and carried the stack over to the cardboard box. He quickly flipped through the papers as if it was a bundle of freshly printed banknotes and set them in the box.

Then he closed the cardboard box, put on his jacket, and left the office.

* * *

Schäfer took a pack of Kings out of his pocket and pulled one cigarette out of it. He stuck the cigarette in his mouth without lighting it and nodded warmly to the colleagues he passed as he strolled down the hall, heading for Otto Møn-steds Gade.

He had made it to the stairs and had just put his hand on the door handle when something made him stop. A tin-gle in his scalp at the back of his neck.

Schäfer stood still as he tried to decipher the feeling.

What was it that didn't add up?

He turned around and quickly returned to his office.

He walked straight over to the cardboard box and opened it. He peered into the box, questions whizzing around in his head.

What was it that had triggered that prickling sensation in his scalp?

He pulled the thick stack of papers back up out of the box and set it on his desk. It was the summary of the boy's internet history, websites he had visited, role-playing apps, Netflix streaming history, Google searches. Augustin had been through the whole stack the night they received it and reported that nothing odd had stuck out.

Schäfer's fingers worked quickly, his eyes scanning the boy's searches.

Warcraft . . . war lords . . .

Then he stopped.

He pulled the page out of the stack and held it up in front of him, his hands shaking. It was a word that Lukas had searched for on the internet six days earlier. Just a single word, typed into the search bar in Google.

Warfarin.

Schäfers eyes raced up and down the page. Why the hell had the boy done a search for a rat poison?

He could see that the search had resulted in a bunch of different web hits, and Lukas had clicked on an article from a regional newspaper in northern Jutland with the headline: *Bank Director Uses Rat Poison to Kill Wife*.

Schäfer opened his computer and found the article. It was a couple of years old and was about a murder case in Sennels, a little village outside of Thisted.

Schäfer read quickly, his eyes jumping from subheading to subheading.

The branch manager of the local Jyske Bank had been charged with putting rat poison in his wife's vodka. His wife had died of massive internal hemorrhaging after having consumed the beverage.

Schäfer looked up, staring into space.

How had Lukas gotten warfarin on his jacket? And why hadn't Schäfer seen the Google search until now?

He clenched his teeth and cursed Augustin.

Strike Two.

53

T HERE WAS A loud *rip* as Anne Sofie Bjerre pulled the duct tape off the roll. She looked over at the open closet, where Jens's side had now been emptied. The hangers on the metal closet bar were empty, the shoe rack was dusted and bare.

She pulled the top of the last garbage bag closed and wrapped the tape around it. Then she carried the bag out into the stairwell, to the others, pressed the elevator button, and went back into the apartment to put on her shoes.

She looked at herself in the mirror in the front hall and smiled.

One more chance.

Those were the words the policeman had used. She had one more chance.

She knew she had made a mistake. She knew that all too well. All the times Jens had lashed out, all those times Lukas had cried and been afraid, pleaded for her help . . .

She should have stopped it. She should have protected her son.

She hugged his little body tight in her mind and promised that everything would be different now. No more Jens. No more drinking. No more lies and secrets. They would be a family now, she and Lukas. Because—after all—she loved her son. She loved him more than anything.

Everything will be different now.

She walked back out onto the landing and pulled the elevator grille open.

Anne Sofie dragged the bags of clothes out to the dumpsters behind the building. With every bag she threw away she felt lighter, purified and free.

She closed the last dumpster lid with a bang and brushed the dust off her hands. Then she headed back into the building.

She almost bumped into Old Eva inside. Her downstairs neighbor was laboriously limping her way up the stairs from the laundry room in the basement carrying a plastic shopping bag under one arm and a crutch under the other. She shook her head in annoyance when she saw Anne Sofie.

"They're still here, those vermin. We're going to have to call him again."

"Call who?" Anne Sofie asked with a smile.

"The rat guy. The exterminator," the old woman said. "They're still here, those critters. I nearly stepped on one of them down in the laundry room."

Old Eva kept talking and Anne Sofie nodded absentmindedly.

She had stopped listening. Her thoughts had immediately begun revolving around the bottle in the basement.

She pushed the elevator button. The hoist mechanism creaked as the elevator began its descent to the ground floor, slow and humming. There was a *ding* when it arrived, and Anne Sofie pulled the door open.

She stood there for a moment without getting in.

Then she turned on her heel and walked over to the stairs down to the basement.

*　*　*

She turned the light on in the basement room and quickly walked over to the sink next to the dryer. She opened the cabinet underneath and squatted down.

The laundry soap and fabric softener were in front on the shelf. The harsher chemicals were lined up in a row behind that. Drain cleaner. Bleach.

She pushed those things aside, looking for the vodka at the back of the cupboard. The bottle was wrapped in a blue checkered dish towel and wedged in behind the drain trap.

Anne Sofie took the bottle out of the cupboard and stood up. Her movements were quick and decisive. She unscrewed the cap from the bottle and held it over the sink drain.

This all has to go, she thought.

They were going to start over again, she and Lukas. Everything would be different from now on. She had told him that. She had *promised* that.

She eyed the bottle hesitantly.

It was half full, the vodka inside cold and as clear as water.

Tomorrow, she then nodded to herself. She would become a good mother tomorrow. She would make every effort, and everything would be different.

Tomorrow . . .

She closed her eyes and brought the bottle to her lips.